This is the third and final book of
The Deep Woods Adventure

The beginning of our story may be found in
book one, entitled
OUT OF THE NEST

The continuation of the search is contained in
book two, entitled
INTO THE HIGH BRANCHES

TO FIND A WAY HOME

by P. M. Malone

Illustrated by Terry Lewison

*Raspberry Hill, Ltd.

This is a work of fiction. All characters and events portrayed in this book are fictious. Any resemblance to real individuals, places, or events is coincidental.

A Raspberry Hill, Ltd. publication
P.O. Box 791
Willmar, MN 56201

ISBN: 0-9631957-2-7
Library of Congress Catalog Card Number: 93-085304

1st printing: August, 1993
Printed in the United States of America

For Ruth Koscielak, her son, John, Crystal Oftedahl,
Jan Briones, Suzanne Wilson, Pam and Chantel Peyton,
Dee Stinson, Mike Nistler, Pete Scheffler, Patricia Olson,
Tom Chervney, Sue Shelton, Sandi Swartz, JoAnn Wright,
Bud Hanson, Jim and Marilynn Tiede . . .

parents, students, teachers, friends, media personalities. . .
readers and givers all,

without their enthusiasm and encouragement at the outset, you
would not be holding the third book in your paws.

Special thanks to:

Sweet Mary Kelly . . . for introducing author and illustrator.

Glorious Sandy of the flaming red hair . . . for invaluable help with
our watercolors.

Wonderful Irish Colleen . . . for gentle lessons in grammar,
punctuation, and vocabulary.

My partner in our radiology practice, Spencer, who provided me
time to tell my story.

Most especially my amazing wife Wanda . . . lover, mother, designer,
gourmet chef, best friend, and editor extraordinaire!

TO FIND A WAY HOME

LIST OF CHAPTERS

A Far, Far Wickerworld

INTRODUCTION
TO FIND A WAY HOME

Do you remember the morning we left the nest in the big oak tree? It seems so long ago. We had just met Ephran. That curious little gray squirrel led us through the snow-covered woods, across Great Hill, to the frozen Pond. And from there we followed him on a series of adventures that have taken some strange and unexpected turns.

Who, for instance, would have dreamed that Ephran would find himself in a little park, smack in the middle of a Many Colored One Warren? Actually, on that snowy morning we first met, Ephran would not have believed such places existed.

But then, Ephran has learned a lot. I think he's taught the creatures who were willing to watch and listen a few things too. Not all of the learning came easy, for him or for the others. That seems the way of things though, doesn't it? As Jafthuh, Ephran's father, once said, "Most of the nuts laying around on the ground are spoiled. It's the ones you have to climb after that are best."

Well, at this point, one would think that Ephran's curiosity must be pretty well satisfied. And Frafan's quest for his brother was successful. So is the story over?

Not really. After a long and difficult journey there is only one good place to relax, to mull over what's been gained, to find peace, and to get on with the important things in life. That place is home.

For Ephran, Kaahli, and Frafan home is very far away. How in the Great Green Woods will our friends ever find their way back to The Pond? After all, they came to be where they are in the back of a van. Who knows how far they were carried? Or from which direction? And, somehow, they're going to have to pass directly through that frightening town, an alien place full of strange machines and noises and...

Wait a moment! I almost forgot. Our friends have a fellow traveler. Wytail, the big park squirrel, has asked to come along to the deep woods. He should be able to guide them through the town.

Oh dear, I'm not at all sure I trust Wytail. I suppose I shouldn't feel that way, but he was such a terrible bully. And I have a notion that he may still harbor bad feelings. After all, getting revenge on Ephran for embarrassing him in front of all the other squirrels must be in his mind.

Well, it won't do a lot of good to sit and worry. The warm season hasn't arrived yet and I think it best to put on a warm jacket, pull a snug cap down around our ears, and set out along our woodland trail. It promises to be an exciting and suspenseful trip home. That, I hope, should not surprise any of us.

FOLKS YOU'LL MEET ON
THE DEEP WOODS ADVENTURE:
Those found in earth, water, trees or sky

* * * * *

Aden (Aye - den): An older gray squirrel. Kaahli and Laslum's father.

Blackie: A female farm cat, black and white in color.

Brightleaf: A rabbit from Bubbling Brook Warren.

Cloudchaser: A large drake mallard duck.

Darkbush & Fairchance: Rabbits who nest in Great Woods Warren.

Deela & Elgan: A pair of grouse.

Ephran (Ee - fran): A young and curious gray squirrel who lives with his family in the north woods.

Farnsworth: A bashful raccoon.

Fastrip & Sorghum: Especially tiny and clever cottontails. Warden of Great Woods Warren and his mate.

Fetzgar (Fets - gur): A muskrat who has many houses on The Pond.

Flutterby, Payslee, & Peppercorn: The three pigeon sisters who live in the barn on The Farm of Cages.

Frafan (Fray - fan): Ephran's small but smart "second" brother. (From Odalee's next litter)

Fred: A yellow hound dog.

Highopper, Longrass, and Sweetbud: Young cottontails, offspring of Truestar and Mayberry.

Jafthuh (Jaff - the): Ephran's father, mate to Odalee

Janey: A happy wren who nests at The Pond.

Janna: Ephran's "second" sister.

Kaahli (Kay - lee): A beautiful female gray squirrel.

Kartag, Mulken, and Darkeye: Forestwatchers (Crows)

Klestra: (Cless - trah) A feisty red squirrel. Ephran's best friend.

Laslum (Lahs - lum): A male gray squirrel. Kaahli's brother.

Maltrick (Mall - trick): A wily red fox.

Marshflower: A female mallard. Mate to Cloudchaser.

Mat & Willie: (Mathilda & Wilhelmina) Rat sisters from Trash Hole.

Mayberry: A male cottontail rabbit. Governor of Great Woods Warren.

Mianta (Mee - an - tah): Ephran's "first" sister; a littermate.

Milkweed: Redthorn's mate, sister to Truestar.

Odalee (Oh - dah - lee): Ephran's mother.

Phetra (Fet - rah): Ephran's "first" brother a male littermate.

Queesor: A small male gray squirrel who lives in the park.

Redthorn: A hostile male rabbit. Milkweed's mate.

Rennigan (Ren - a - gun): A bachelor buck fox squirrel.

Roselimb: A female gray squirrel. Mate to Phetra.

Ruckaru: A rooster pheasant with very precise speech.

Scaffer: A troublemaking gray squirrel from the park.

Smagtu (Smag - too): A shy skunk.

Steadfast: A very old gray squirrel who lives in the park.

Tinga & Ilta: Two of Ephran's "second" sisters.

Truestar: A female cottontail. Mate to Mayberry.

Winthrop: A large white owl.

Wytail: A big strong gray squirrel. Bully of the park.

One by one, two by two,
   Sometimes many, sometimes few.
Called to gather by silent voice
   Not by wisdom, nor by choice.

Chant of the Delyhabra

CHAPTER I
A WHOLE NEW WAY OF
LOOKING AT THINGS

lestra, the red squirrel, woke with a start. His first thought was that it was too early...far too early in the day to consider leaving his cozy nest. He lay for a while, as the lonely sound of the wind sighed through thin and leafless bushes. What, he wondered, had caused his eyes to pop open? He listened carefully, but there were no unusual sounds. And the air smelled fresh and untainted.

Could a dream have awakened him? It most certainly could have. As a matter of fact, he was sure he'd been dreaming. There had been many dreams this cold season. This dream, though, the one that woke him up, left no memory.

Most of Klestra's dreams were about his good friend, Ephran, the gray squirrel. Ephran's lovely mate, Kaahli, was often in them too. Many of those dreams had been the dark and frightening kind, the kind no one would care to remember.

Ephran and Kaahli had disappeared the day a pair of Many Colored Ones invaded The Pond with their terrible thundersticks. A search along Rocky Creek with Ephran's second brother and sister, Frafan and Janna, had led to the red barn on The Farm of Cages. Frafan, Ephran's younger brother, did something there, in that big barn, Klestra would never forget as long as he ran the branches: Frafan had jumped right smack into the gaping black craw of a most fearsome groaning and smoking monster! Fred, the yellow hound, (another of Ephran's unusual friends) had called the monster a "van"! Whatever a van was, its big jaws had clanged shut with a terrible finality and it had rumbled off on round black legs. Frafan had been carried away inside.

So now Frafan was gone too. Missing, just like his brother. Apparently he'd been convinced that his seemingly senseless action was the only way to follow Ephran and Kaahli's trail, which had grown cold with time. And no wonder it had grown cold. No way to follow a trail through the sky. According to Rennigan, Ephran's fox squirrel friend, that's how either Ephran or Kaahli (maybe both) left The Pond — through the sky on the back of a duck. Klestra had tried, over and over, to picture that unlikely scene. He could not decide if it was believable. And, if it really did happen, what connection it had with what he and Frafan and Janna had learned in the barn at The Farm of Cages.

"Janna!" Klestra said, realizing he should look in on Ephran's younger sister, "I'd better get over and see how Janna is doing today. I wonder if she's up and about yet."

He crawled through the tight tunnel he'd gnawed in the little

1

tree, and scrambled out the hole. Peering across The Pond, toward Ephran and Kaahli's tree on the far side, he saw no sign of movement. Janna must be asleep inside the big, leafy nest. No use waking her just because he wasn't able to sleep. He would let her rest for a while yet. Later he would go over and have lunch with her, as he did every day.

He felt sorry for the little female gray. The cold season had grown very long for her. For him and her both, actually. If he was worried, and if he fretted about Ephran and Frafan, how much more upset must she be? Both missing squirrels were her brothers, after all. Adding to her discomfort had to be where she'd become stranded. The Pond, much as Klestra loved it, was not Janna's home.

Her family's tree was far away, near a place called Corncrib Farm. Each time he visited her, Klestra could see that Janna was growing more and more restless. But what could he do? It would be folly to travel now, across a wide expanse of unknown woods, with the cold season at full strength. There would be no food and scant shelter. No, they would have to wait...wait until the warm season brought fresh seeds and buds to the trees and bushes.

He had tried to keep her company, to keep her entertained. He had tried to teach her things...little secrets of the sort he'd taught Ephran. But she, unlike Ephran or Frafan, did not seem to be quite so enthralled by red squirrel tricks.

Ever since he and Janna had returned from The Farm of Cages, Klestra had decided that, eventually, he would try to take Janna home...to the nest he'd heard so much about, and to her parents, Jafthuh and Odalee, who sounded so clever and loving. He wished he could remember his own parents.

It would be a sad journey though. He could not think about what he felt — that getting Frafan and Janna to travel to The Pond in the first place had been a mistake. And Frafan had made another mistake, most likely a terrible blunder, by jumping into the van.

The heaviest of the snow had melted, leaving long brown grass and once-tall and proud reeds broken and bent to the ground. What had been last warm season's home for countless frogs, birds, snakes and insects, was curled and flattened, like weary dancers laid down to rest.

Klestra looked up. Why did it seem the sky was always covered with clouds now? He ran down the tree and to a nearby elm stump. Digging through old leaves and twigs, he opened what had, at one time, been one of his best-stocked food caches. However, he'd raided it a number of times, often to take treats to Janna — goodies to cheer her up. Other hungry creatures had discovered the hiding spot too. The better part of his food had been eaten.

Scratching around, Klestra came across a large pinecone. Why, he wondered, had he tucked this old thing away? He scratched his head.

The pinecone was too big and too tough to be appetizing. He would be lucky if any of it was tender enough to chew. He must have been very hungry when he stashed it. Sad to say, it was about the only thing left. He turned the cone over and over in his paws. He chewed off two of the more promising seeds. They were so big he was barely able to carry them in his mouth.

The little red squirrel scrambled back into his tree and found a wide branch. He put the pinecone seeds down next to him and turned to face Ephran and Kaahli's nest. If Janna came out he wanted to be able to see her, to call to her, to assure her he was here. Then he'd run to her. She'd be happy to see him. They'd have a bit to eat while they talked. Kaahli had hidden some very nice morsels around her tree.

He picked up one of the seeds, the widest and thickest of the two. It was so big he had to hold it to his chest in order to nibble on the tenderest end.

Klestra's mind was occupied with many things...food, Ephran, Janna, Corncrib Farm. The branch he'd chosen was not one he would have used had he not been distracted. The limb was too exposed. There were no branches above to shield him from seeking eyes in the sky. Worst of all, he'd not even taken the precaution of looking around before sitting down to eat.

Suddenly, without a sound, and just as he was about to discard the largest of the tough seeds and try the smaller one, Klestra found himself swept off his branch and into the cold air. He had not heard or smelled anything amiss. There had been no cry, squeal, or screech in the morning stillness.

Besides being where a squirrel wasn't supposed to be — sailing through thin air — there was another very wrong feeling. Pain in his chest. Fierce pain. Immediate and horrible pain. He could barely breathe. His first instinct was to scream. To fight and scratch. But something told him to wait — to be still.

He glanced down and was able to see what had snatched him from the tree.

"A stick! A stiff and solid young branch!" he thought. "How? Had it fallen from a nearby tree and swept him from his perch? How had it gripped him so suddenly and so tightly?"

From the branch grew a terrible long thorn. The thorn was stuck into the firm pinecone seed he'd been nibbling on, squeezing it firmly against his chest. It had penetrated nearly all the way through the seed, causing a long, irregular crack in the seed's smooth surface. If it had gone any farther, it would have slid past his ribs...and put its fatal point into his heart.

When the shock lessened, he realized what looked like a stick was not a stick at all. It was a leg. And the thorn was not a thorn...

3

With a bone-rattling chill like he'd not had before, Klestra understood he was in the clutches of a red-tailed hawk, a hawk so large it was able to carry a full-grown red squirrel through the air with but one claw, a hawk whose talon was a whisker away from taking his breath away forever.

With an instinct he did not know he possessed, Klestra went limp. Somehow he knew that the hawk must be made to think that its first strike was fatal, that the victim it clutched so tightly breathed no more. Luckily, the thorn he now knew was the hawk's talon was without feeling of its own. The hard spike could not send messages back to the hawk's brain, could not tell the hawk how far it had penetrated. If the hawk had any inkling Klestra was wide awake, watching and thinking, it would have adjusted its grip and made sure the red squirrel would never watch or think again.

Though the pain in his chest was agony, Klestra found he could lessen it by taking tiny breaths. That would be best anyway. Deep breaths might alert the hawk.

Fortunately, Klestra was being carried along with his paws down. The hunter could not see his face. And this position gave Klestra an astounding view and appreciation of the territory he'd been exploring since he was born. He marveled at the way the earth moved under him. So this was flying! Ephran's fondest dream. Why his gray squirrel friend dreamed of such a horribly frightening experience was more a puzzle than ever. Klestra found that it made his fur stand on end. Maybe, he told himself, one could get more interested in flying, even enjoy it perhaps, if not in the grasp of a hawk.

After snatching Klestra, the bird had banked sharply, gained altitude, and set its course up Rocky Creek. Klestra concentrated on Rocky Creek and put out of his mind how hard it was to breathe. The stream looked very different from up here. Ice had formed along its banks. Puddles of open water looked grey and cold. Worse than frigid water or ice were the rocks. They seemed to stare back at him, a firm and unforgiving glare.

He tried to think. It surprised him that he could think at all. Maybe shallow and rapid breathing was good for thinking, for forming plans. Somehow he doubted it. More likely quick thinking came from that same instinct, the instinct that was doing its best to keep him breathing.

Prospects for ever climbing back into his nest were slim. He knew that. But he would not give up. Ephran would not forgive him if he did.

As sudden as a hummingbird's appearance, an idea came to him. Perhaps there was a way to separate himself from unwanted wings. He looked for a soft place on the earth below, as soft as possible anyway.

"Klestra went limp."

Clustered spruce trees, a short distance from the shore of the creek, caught his eye.

As though he was giving directions, the hawk turned a bit, just enough to take them over the edge of Rocky Creek and toward the spruce. This would be the place to try his idea. Prickly or not, those thick and springy branches would be his only chance. Besides, he couldn't wait too long. He didn't have all day to find the ideal landing spot. When the hawk arrived at its nest — or wherever it ate breakfast — the time for thinking would be over.

For a moment, Klestra supposed there should be other factors taken into consideration when dropping from this height. But how could he, one of fur and not feathers, know to think of the wind carrying him as he fell? How could he know to take into account the speed and direction he was traveling when he bid the hawk farewell? All he knew is that he wanted to land in the spruce and not on the hard earth or even harder rocks. And it seemed appropriate to start his fall when dear and springy branches were directly beneath him.

So, when the spruce appeared under him, he arched his body, twisted his head, and bit the hawk's leg — as hard as he could. Immediately the pain in his chest was replaced by a sensation nearly as fearsome... maybe more fearsome. He was falling, falling from a very great height...with nary a branch to grasp!

As he tumbled, he tried to concentrate on the spruce below. But they kept disappearing. Slowly and gracefully he fell, end over end. Everything was confusing. Wow! He was getting very dizzy! He found himself looking back up at the hawk. The skyhunter had already adjusted its flight to recapture what had been lost. It would try to catch him in mid-air.

This was a race, pure and simple. And of course, his reaching the earth was hardly a promise of safety. More likely it was a promise of instant and permanent darkness.

To Klestra's dismay, even as they grew rapidly closer, the spruce trees swept away behind him. Ah, yes, forward speed and high breezes should have been considered. Dark earth raced up to meet him. Then, thank Bright Stars and Pinecones, something appeared he hadn't seen before...a thicket of bushes.

He struck the bushes with his backside, eyes glued to the hawk. Branches snapped and broke, bent and bowed, as Klestra shot through them like icy skystones on a thundery day. Despite the slowing effect of the branches, Klestra struck the earth hard enough so what little air remained was jolted from his body.

"Oooff!" he grunted.

The hawk spread its folded wings and landed beside the bush. Angry hunter and breathless victim eyed one another. Beak open, the skyhunter forced its way through the stems, to within a pawslength of the fur on Klestra's neck.

Klestra's chest burned like fire. He needed every bit of air the forest could provide...and he couldn't get it in fast enough. Every bone in his body felt broken. All was ended. He could not move...did not feel like moving. He would not see The Pond again. He told himself there was little chance he would have seen Ephran or Kaahli or Frafan again anyway. The search had been a crazy gamble. But what would happen to Janna? Poor little lost Janna. He closed his eyes and waited.

The hawk screeched. Why didn't the skyhunter get it over with? Klestra opened an eye. The hawk was struggling to work its way into the bush. But now, instead of being its strength, the big body and wings were a hindrance. The harder the bird tried to force its way in among the stems, the harder the bush pushed back. If a bush was willing to help, why not cooperate? Besides, Janna needed him. With all the effort he could muster, Klestra rolled over, away from the hawk and its seeking claw.

Well, he had survived the long fall. An amazing feat by itself. It would be a nice story to tell, someday, to someone. If he got the chance. Crows would like it, if no one else. But he could not catch his breath, his back hurt so badly he was unsure he would be able to run even if he could breathe, and the hawk was far from deciding this particular squirrel dinner was a lost cause.

Then Klestra saw his salvation. A hole. Not a tree hole. An earth hole. Among the roots of the bushes. He made his legs move, though they didn't want to. His head slid into the hole. He pushed at the hard dirt with his hindlegs, just as the stem of the bush broke under the hawk's weight, and just as that terrible talon reached out again. Then his body was in the hole, tail and all. He rolled into a tunnel.

"Out! Out! Get out! My place...my place!"

Klestra's body jerked. A little light came from behind him, from the opening he'd more or less tumbled through. The hawk was digging furiously up there. But Klestra was deep in the earth. There was no chance any bird could get to him now.

Klestra looked down to see the white face of a chipmunk below him in the tunnel.

"Out, I said...."

"Oh, shush!" he said to the chipmunk. "You sound like me, trying to chase Ephran out of his own tree. Whether you like it or not I'm in your hole. And whether you like it or not, I'm staying."

CHAPTER II

CROWS IN BRANCHES,
TRACKS IN MUD

Mianta felt the fur on the back of her neck stiffen. The sound of claws scraping on wood came to her ears. Someone or something was forcing its way through the hole into her den! And only a few days after she and Laslum had settled down for the cold season.

"Laslum!" she croaked into her mate's ear.

Laslum's legs moved, and his eyes opened a slit, but before either of them could prepare to fight, she realized the intruders were not hunters. Two squirrels popped through the hole: Phetra, her brother, and his mate, Roselimb. Harsh words rushed to her tongue. Why had they come to waken her and Laslum during this time of bitterly cold air? Why weren't they asleep in their own nest? She would scold them like they hadn't been scolded since they were young, like the worst tongue-lashing of which Odalee might be capable. But one glance at their faces: weary, drawn, and incredibly sad...melted her anger like snow on a warm paw.

"Roselimb...Phetra," she managed. "What in the world brings you here?"

Roselimb's dark eyes were vacant. Phetra's expression made Mianta shiver. "A story almost too terrible to tell," he said.

Roselimb and Phetra took turns speaking. When one's voice cracked with emotion the other would pick up the story. They told of the snowstorm. Mianta and Laslum remembered it. It was a storm so vicious it had forced the squirrel family into their nests early. It was a storm that caused Jafthuh and Odalee to worry about their young ones even more than they had before. It was that storm, they told in halting words, that swallowed Janna. It was the reason Frafan was left alone in the bitterly cold woods, far from Corncrib Farm.

"In the midst of the blowing snow, I would not allow my brother to search for my sister," choked Phetra. "Then, when it was too late, I left him by himself, without help or hope."

With her paws Mianta wiped away the tears from his face, before they could freeze. His unhappiness flowed into her heart. His misery almost overwhelmed her.

"Phetra," she murmured softly to him, "don't feel so badly. What could you have done?"

He closed his eyes and hung his head. "It's not what I could have done. It's what I didn't do. I should not have left him alone out there."

For a long while words spilled from the shivering gray squirrels.

The more they talked, the steadier became their voices. The warmth of the nest and the sympathy of loved ones comforted them. The tears slowly dried.

Decisions had to be made. The first one was difficult. Should this disastrous news be brought to the nest of Jafthuh and Odalee?

"It would break their hearts," said Laslum.

They decided there was no reason to upset the old squirrel couple. The other thing they agreed upon was that, at this point in time, there was nothing any of them could do for Janna and Frafan. Even though Roselimb thought she could find the linden tree that offered protection from the snowstorm, there would be no satisfaction in the discovery. Whatever had happened in that part of the woods was over and done with...some time ago.

Mianta dug a large butternut from leaves in a corner of the nest. Her guests ate it gratefully. When they prepared to leave for their own nest their eyes were dry, but without fire. It seemed a great effort for them to put one paw in front of the other. It appeared that neither of them had enough energy to jump from one branch to the next.

Seeing their weariness of leg and spirit, Mianta said, "Why don't you stay with us? There is no reason to go back to your den. It would be a comfort to have you here. We've stored more food than we can possibly eat. There is a den in this tree just below us. Laslum used it before we were mated. I've kept it fresh and clean."

Phetra and Roselimb agreed to Mianta's idea more quickly than they would have under other circumstances. Everyone wanted to be close to loved ones now.

And so it was that most of the cold season was spent together. Snatches of fitful sleep, and occasional nibbles on stored nuts, were interspersed with brief conversation.

During one of those times, when Mianta and Laslum were both awake, Laslum said to her, "Your father did not want you traveling during the cold season because you would be having young this coming warm season. Jafthuh's prediction will not come true, will it?"

She looked at him sadly. "I'm afraid not, Laslum. It seems the dread in my heart will not allow it. I cannot imagine having a new family until I know what's become of those I already dearly love."

As the cold season wore on, the sun took longer and longer to set over the Many Colored Ones' den on Corncrib Farm. The day father and mother would wake up, and the terrible news must be shared, drew closer and closer.

One bright and brisk morning Laslum decided to sun himself on the broad limbs of a large oak. The tree was much taller than the one they nested in, and its branches closer to the sky. Mianta felt the brisk air with her nose and said, "Bright sun or no, it's still too cold to enjoy the high branches." She curled back into their nest.

While he was laying there, trying to absorb some warmth from puny sunlight, three crows flew into the branches of a nearby ash tree. There had been crows somewhere about, off and on, throughout the cold time, but this was the closest they'd come. Laslum opened an eye. These birds were strangers. He closed his eye again, and tried to ignore them.

One of the crows looked over at Laslum and said, "Eeyah! This treeklimer lays 'till. Him breathe?"

"Whook airs?" asked another.

"Tink him one dem crazies? One dem golook fer silver skyhunter?"

"Nah," answered the first crow, "Farm s'Cages longfar disp lace."

"Yah," replied the second, "Dose treeklimers donefer. Silver skyhuntert ake air dem."

Laslum raised his head. "What are you saying? Are you talking about gray squirrels near a farm with cages? When...?"

"Wo, Wo, Wo! Look dis! Up pa natum, furry 'un!"

"Please," said Laslum, getting to his paws. "Don't make fun — for once. Listen to me. Tell me about the squirrels you saw near the Farm of Cages. Did you hear any names? When did you see these squirrels?"

One of the crows turned toward his companions and nodded in Laslum's direction. "And dey call crow snosey! Dis 'un got smeller bigas smushroom."

"Yah," said another of them to Laslum, "'smind y'own bizness."

"Please...," Laslum said again, but the crows ignored him, lifted into the air, and flew off.

This short conversation with the crows, unenlightening as it may have been, gave Laslum hope. Until their visit, he had been convinced Frafan and Janna were almost certainly victims of the terrible snowstorm. He wanted to feel more hopeful, but could not. The wind, bitter cold, and lack of food might have taken their breath. If not that, their youth and inexperience... along with any one of a number of forest hunters. Then, after hearing the crows' words, his own optimism had been reborn. The sighting of gray squirrels near The Farm of Cages would not be a major event under most circumstances. However, this was a strange time of season for treeclimbing travelers. And the mention of a "silver skyhunter" certainly sounded like the sort of mystery that might be associated with Ephran or Frafan.

In any case, eavesdropping on the crows resulted in him leading a group of doubters — Mianta, Phetra, and Roselimb — on a search for The Spring, and the nest of Aden, Laslum's father. Laslum did not know

11

the way to The Farm of Cages. If they found Aden, the old gray squirrel could almost certainly lead them back to that terrible farm where he'd been imprisoned. But would he agree to do so? The Farm of Cages promised both danger and bad memories. Might Frafan and Janna — and Ephran and Kaahli as well — now be in cages there? What if they were? Could some sort of rescue be managed, as Ephran and Kaahli had done? Mianta, close behind Laslum, stopped to catch her breath. She pulled her tail close around her body as a swirl of cold air passed over. Keeping warm was a constant struggle. It was even harder to find enough to eat. She shivered and looked over at Laslum, the fur on the side of his head laid flat by the wind. He felt her gazing at him, turned to her, and gave her a quick smile. He then ran toward her branch.

"Are we near The Spring?" she asked.

"I think so. It's difficult to be certain. Everything looks so different with no leaves on the trees."

"When we find your father do you think he can lead us to the place you were caged?"

"He's an experienced forest traveler and knows that part of the woods. I'm sure he can find the Farm of Cages."

The travelers came to a swale, a cleavage in the earth sloping gently away from them. Dirt-speckled snow, the last remnants of blinding storms and gentle flurries, lay in the lowest part of the little valley. Last warm season's brown leaves were clumped in damp, soggy piles, ready to take their places in the earth...to help new leaves grow.

The slope was clogged with bushes, trunks and branches intertwined in either hugs or battle. They were leafless, but that made no difference: they were so dense it was not possible to see what lay on the other side.

"Those ash trees over there," Laslum pointed, "are close enough for jumping and continue beyond these bushes. Let's see what lies on the other side."

As they climbed into the highest limbs of the ash trees, one of the prettiest pieces of forest Roselimb thought she'd ever seen came into view. Considering that the forest wore her least attractive face during this season, the view was beautiful anyway. She could imagine how wondrous it would be when the warm season arrived, when leaves became thick and green.

Trees were straight, tall, and almost perfectly spaced. Sheltered beneath the trees' wide arms were bushes of all sorts, in stately clumps and clusters, not a scraggly one in the lot. From where she sat, she could not pick out a broken branch. Soon, she knew, the bushes would burst forth with buds and blossoms. The gently rolling earth looked clean and well-kept, as though something or someone made sure untidy twigs and rotted limbs were picked up and hidden away. The sky seemed huge. A tinkling sound came to her ears, the sound of running water. Countless tiny streamlets flowed clear and pure, from the earth itself. It was a hill of water. They had indeed reached the origin of Spring Creek!

"Congratulations, Laslum!" said Phetra. "You have led us right to Spring Creek. Where do you think we might look for Aden's nest?"

"Any thick tree around here, I guess," said Laslum. "Let's split up and see if we can find it."

The squirrels spread out around the hill of water. Up and down, around and around...every tree of any size was carefully searched for a used den hole. After a short while, Laslum's muffled voice came to the others: "Over here, everyone! I believe I've found my father's nest." He wiggled out of a hole in another ash tree, the entrance worn smooth by many comings and goings.

"Wonderful! Where is wise Aden?" asked Mianta as she scrambled to the hole. "I'm very anxious to see him."

"He's not here," Laslum said.

"Not in his nest?" repeated Roselimb.

"No," Laslum shook his head and sighed. "I've looked around the woods a bit too. No sign of him. He hasn't been gone long, though. His scent is clear. One could almost imagine the leaves in the nest are still warm. There's plenty of food inside, so I doubt he went in search of a meal."

"Well...where would he have gone? If he had plenty of food? Exploring, maybe?" Phetra wondered.

Laslum motioned with his head. "Look over here. While I was looking for his nest I noticed something on the other side of the hill...where Spring Creek is born as many tiny waterways."

Laslum led them to a tree, a larger one, that looked down on Spring Creek. The view was breathtaking. Oak, ash, and cottonwood formed two lines, like tall and dignified sentinels, one on either side of the creekbed.

"What did you want to show us, Laslum?" asked Phetra.

"This," he said, pointing to the earth.

"It's muddy," observed Phetra, puzzlement on his face.

"Yes, it's muddy. Look closely."

"Pawprints!" said Roselimb.

Laslum nodded. "Aden had a visitor. A visitor who must have brought news. News that caused him to leave his comfortable and food-filled den."

"Who? What kind of visitor?" asked Phetra.

"Oh, Phetra, don't you recognize those kind of pawprints?" said Mianta.

Phetra, still puzzled, curled his nose.

"Well, I know what sort of animal makes tracks like that," said Roselimb. "Aden was visited by a dog."

CHAPTER III
FLIGHT OF THE LOST ONE

ings set, Cloudchaser sailed beneath heavy clouds toward what appeared to be a small patch of open water. It lay dark and grey at the edge of a great lake covered with ice and snow. The big drake mallard breathed deeply and let his eyes close for a moment. He must not let the need for sleep cause him to make a mistake.

He shook his head, blinked twice, and searched brown reeds near the water for movement...for unusual shapes, animal-like shapes, outlines of things that might spell danger. The season for Many Colored Ones to hunt would have to be over. At least this far into cold country it should be over. For some of those Hunters he was unsure if rules made any difference. And he knew the only season understood by foxes and hawks was determined by a growling belly.

Satisfied there were no hunters nearby, he lowered his orange legs and settled into the bitterly cold water.

Brown and bowed reeds, standing in sparkling ice, surrounded him. All was quiet. No blackbirds twittered. No frogs chirped. There was no sign of other ducks. Obviously, he was far behind those of his kind, those well on their way to warmer places. This lake, for instance, was one of deep water. Ice formed on it late in the season. Though he'd flown over many times he'd seen ice here only once, and that was as he and his mate, Marshflower, flew back for the warm season, not at the beginning of the cold time.

To fly was taking so much more strength than he thought it would. The spot in his chest, beneath thick feathers, where the thunderstick pebble had bitten so deeply, ached constantly now. The exertion of flying with squirrels on his back, done in the panic and need of the moment, was far greater than he'd realized at the time. It had taken all his reserves. Muscles that had barely healed had been stretched and torn all over again.

The air, too, was colder than he cared to fly in. And the wind was gustier. More food was needed, at a time when food was hard to come by. The thought of food caused him to dip his head beneath the surface. The water was shallow here, and he silently thanked warm sunshine from days past for a few small pale green plants still growing on the rich, brown bottom.

The drake chewed slowly, savoring what flavor remained in the leaves. The plant had not seen sunlight for a long while and its sweetness was almost a memory. It tasted nothing like the deep green and shining white tubers he used to pull from the bottom of The Pond. Ah, The Pond.

He'd flown that way again, of course. After healing and resting at the Farm of Cages, he'd gone back. To tell someone, hopefully Klestra, all he knew. To bring hope to the deep woods. Ephran and Kaahli yet breathed! But The Pond had been deserted. Just as it had been after he'd rescued his two treeclimbing friends from The Many Colored Ones and their thundersticks.

All he'd seen that cloudy day, flying above Rocky Creek, was a flock of swans, wings set toward warmer air. He'd been distracted by the big birds, birds whose flight to warmer water should be far later than his own. Because of them and their haunting cries, he failed to notice three squirrels, two gray and one red, in the trees beneath. And they, eyes and ears likewise directed to the swans, did not see him.

Cloudchaser sighed deeply and tried to push fear from his mind. But it was insistent. Would he ever find Marshflower and the young ones? Could he win the race with the cold season, which had settled firmly over all the land and water he'd crossed? Would he give in to weariness, and rest his eyes for too long a time? Would he wake to find himself frozen in place, unable to move, looking into the eyes of a fox, prancing gingerly over the ice toward him?

Marshflower, wherever she was, had no idea he still breathed. Unless that thing Ephran called "luck" stayed with him, maybe she never would. But if she met Ephran and Kaahli, next warm season, they would tell her he had survived the thundersticks that terrible day on The Pond. Then she would set out on her own search. And, unless he won today's — yes, and tomorrow's — battle for breath, she would not find him. She'd never see him, or what might be left of him, down here in the reeds and the water and the mud. He would, after all, come to the fate everyone was certain he'd met in Lomarsh.

Cloudchaser struggled to keep his eyes open, knowing weariness would claim him sooner or later. Then he noticed a muskrat den, all but hidden in the reeds. He swam to it, hoping it might be a good place to sleep, like the nest in The Pond atop Fetzgar's old den. Open water surrounded the den. But, if the air became any colder, ice would form fast and thick. Then he'd be no safer atop the den than if he slept on the open earth.

He would have to take the chance. With one more look around, he crawled onto the pile of reeds. He pulled as much dry vegetation around himself as he could reach and fluffed up his feathers. Oh my...It felt good to rest! In the far reaches of his mind he could pretend Fetzgar was swimming around, cussing and snorting about some fancied problem. He could imagine Ephran and Kaahli stretched out beside him...Marshflower laying close by, watching the young ones playing in the water... blackbirds screeching back and forth...

The clouds had rolled away and the sun dropped over the edge of the earth, sending long dark red-orange beams through bare tree branches. Stars dotted the darkening sky, winking at him from so very high. Far higher than he could dream of flying.

Dreaming. Ephran was a dreamer. And for such a long time the brave treeclimber's dreams had been of flying. When he finally got his chance, it had been an offer made in sheer desperation. There had been no other way to escape The Many Colored Hunters. Cloudchaser smiled to himself. The gamble had worked. Had Ephran been able to enjoy the flight? He had certainly seemed to, considering how badly hurt he was.

He showed the same old enthusiasm, right up to the time when he closed his eyes, high in the sky on a duck's back! When he finally woke up, in the big barn, something had changed though. Something had left his eyes, his mind, his voice. Something had drained from him besides the dark red juice.

Cloudchaser wished he could have waited to see Ephran recovered. Really recovered. More than just the use of his legs. But, if he was ever going to, he had to leave. If he was to ever find Marshflower, it was now or never. And at this late time, more likely never than now. Besides, Ephran was in good paws. Kaahli was at his side. Cloudchaser had made sure of that too. But he would go back, if there was any chance. He would see Ephran and Kaahli again. Some day. Sometime. Somehow.

He fell asleep with memories, tucking his head beneath his wing.

The night was still and cold. The lack of any air movement may have been Cloudchaser's salvation. For he slept the sleep of those who are nearly at the end of things. He would not have sensed the approach of any kind of hunter. As it happened, his scent stayed close about him, as did the warmth generated by his own body.

He woke suddenly, heart pounding. The sun was already up, the water around him frozen solid. But he, atop the muskrat den, was high and dry. He pushed the brown reeds away, stood up, and flapped his wings. He thought they felt a little stronger. He looked around once again. Nothing. No birds, no hunters, no animals. No open water.

Hunger made his stomach rumble. He could not fly far without putting something in his belly. He poked his beak into the den beneath him, pushing aside old vegetation. There were roots and bulbs down there, mixed with rotted snails, the remains of small fish,...and pieces of frogs. It smelled as bad as it looked. Much of it had a greenish tinge. He'd never eaten this sort of thing before, and his mind rebelled. But where else would he find something — if even this big lake was covered with ice? If The Many Colored Ones had picked clean their fields of yellow corn?

He ate as quickly as he could, trying to ignore the taste and texture, trying to keep his mind on other things. He thought of the wind, high aloft. It would be at his back today. It would make things easier.

He would be able to fly a long way.

When the desperately empty feeling was gone, he spread his wings and lifted away from the frozen lake. It felt good to fly again. Higher and higher he went, far above the trees and just beneath small fluffy clouds, racing along with him. He passed over clusters of dens, dens of Many Colored Ones, smoke curling from their fires. He saw many of those objects They traveled in, shiny enclosures that ran so fast on their black paths — faster than he could fly. Other times, when there had been no hurry, he had followed those paths, curling around hills and through valleys as far as he could see.

The sky was mostly his. Once in a great while a huge silver bird, put above the clouds by Many Colored Ones, would appear. Cloudchaser would judge where it was headed and fly far from its path.

The air grew warmer, but whether that was due to the sun climbing higher or that he was getting closer to the place of everwarm air he could not tell. One thing for certain: his wings were getting very tired. And his stomach did not feel right. Was it hunger again? What a bother! How much more distance he could cover if he didn't have to worry about eating!

A sharp cramp in his belly made Cloudchaser quack loudly. It felt almost like the thunderstick pebble had, only this time there was no sound. He was too far from the earth to be struck by thunderstick pebbles anyway.

He moaned softly, set his wings, and dropped toward the earth. What in the name of Bright Blue Brooks was the matter? The hurt was not in his wing. Nor in his old wound. It did not feel at all like aching muscles. And he was thirsty, thirstier than he'd ever been, like he could drink all of the water in The Pond. Green and brown earth raced up toward him. He lowered his legs. There was little choice about where he would land; he was nearly helpless. He adjusted his wings slightly to avoid crashing into a group of small willow trees at the edge of a woods.

Cloudchaser landed in a tangle of tall grass. Unable to control his descent, he struck the earth so firmly and swiftly he could not stay on his feet. He tumbled unto his side and slid a short distance in the grass.

Amidst a flurry of feathers, two brown birds, somewhat smaller than himself, burst from the weeds near where he landed. His belly hurt so much that Cloudchaser could not even bring himself to stand and watch them.

He lay on his side and groaned in pain. His breath came in short bursts. His feet twitched. So this is where it was to end, he thought. Not in his beloved water, but in deep grass at the edge of a woods. He would be a fox's dinner after all. But why? What had happened to his stomach?

"Cloudchaser landed in a tangle of tall grass."

"Well, it's a duck, for mercy sakes!"

Cloudchaser swiveled his head, as best he could. "Who is it?" he asked.

"Talks too," said another voice.

"Had it though. On the way out."

The voices belonged to the birds. He could see them now, standing partly hidden in the grass. Brown birds. The ones he'd frightened as he landed so ungracefully. Grouse. A pair of grouse, male and female.

"I need help," Cloudchaser groaned.

"Don't we all," said the male grouse. Then to its partner, "You wondered what fell from the sky, almost on top of us. Now you've seen. An injured duck. Let's go. He'll attract a fox."

"Wait!" said Cloudchaser.

"Wait? Sure. Wait. Wait for trouble. So long, mallard."

"I won't hold you up. You owe me nothing. I only wondered...is there water nearby?" asked Cloudchaser, fighting to get every word out, wanting desperately to dip his head beneath water — and drink deeply and forever.

"No time for questions. Come on, Deela. Once a hunter gets its stomach filled with him it won't be so hungry for us."

The female grouse looked into Cloudchaser's eyes. "He's right," Cloudchaser managed to say. "The fox...will thank you for leaving me here."

She took a step toward Cloudchaser, head bobbing up and down. He supposed she was searching for thunderstick wounds.

"Ohhh...come on, Deela!" cried her mate.

Ignoring him, the female said to Cloudchaser, "No water nearby." She poked her beak into his wing feathers and asked, "What ails you, duck?"

"Deela!" her mate fairly shouted.

"Quiet, Elgan!" she said firmly. And to Cloudchaser, "I ask again: What ails you? I see no dark red juice on your feathers."

"Don't know," said Cloudchaser, "I saw no thundersticks today..." Then it came to him. "Food! No open water. No corn. I ate what I could find buried in a muskrat den..."

"Ah!" The grouse nodded her head. "Muskrat den. Poor place for a bird to find a meal."

Another cramp racked Cloudchaser's belly, and his eyes closed.

"Don't you know what to do about tainted food?" she asked.

Cloudchaser forced his eyes open and shook his head.

"You don't know? I shouldn't be surprised. I don't imagine that birds who fly back and forth in the sky and spend no time in the woods, could be expected to know what might help for spoiled food," she said.

The drake took a deep breath. "Please..."

"Elgan is right. Your flesh will keep the fox from disturbing us for at least a few more days. You will serve your purpose. What are you to us? Why do you ask a grouse for help?"

"There is no one else to ask," groaned Cloudchaser.

"I know that. What I mean is why you would expect me to help."

"I expect nothing. I could only hope you might be among the few who had reasoned things..." Cloudchaser grimaced and moaned again.

"'Reasoned things?' Reasoned what things?"

Cloudchaser opened his eyes and looked directly into hers. "Reasoned that the fox would be delighted to have one of the feathered ones work against another."

Deela looked at Cloudchaser for a long while. Her mate started to say something but she interrupted him.

"Elgan, go and bring some cloander seed."

"Deela!"

"Go! Now! Quickly! The mallard has little time left to listen to your grumbling."

CHAPTER IV
OLD LESSONS UNLEARNED

This cold season was especially dreary and chilling. Maybe, thought Odalee, the longest and dreariest she'd ever experienced. But then, she'd never before spent so much of a cold season with her eyes wide open. Though full of worries and uneasiness, being awake had not been a total waste. The mother of the Corncrib Farm squirrel family had learned a few things...things Frafan and Ephran would have found fascinating.

For instance, she had no idea bluejays were so plentiful in this part of the woods, especially during the cold season. She was surprised at how active and noisy they were, even when the air was frigid. She had come to know, on sight, a red fox who, every second or third day, used a pathway right beneath their tree. She found herself laying with chin on paws, admiring her two beautiful daughters, Ilta and Tinga, who slept soundly beside her and her mate in the big oak den.

And she had lovingly listened to Jafthuh, the male she'd mated on a sunny day that seemed so very long ago, as he snored contentedly. In the den's dim light she counted every one of the whiskers on his snout. She hadn't noticed before that those whiskers were turning silver!

She saw Blackie occasionally, laying on the wooden deck outside the den of The Many Colored Ones. So desperate was she to talk to someone — anyone — that, more than once, she almost ran over to strike up a conversation with the old black and white farm cat. Though the cat was Frafan's friend, she could not quite overcome the feeling that chatting with a hunter would be an unacceptable thing to do. So, though she found the whole idea intriguing, she never got around to actually doing it.

She came to realize that crows were probably her best hope of learning the fate of Frafan and Janna — as well as that of Ephran and Kaahli. The sound of the black forestwatchers would send her scurrying from where she curled in warm leaves. But the birds never came near the big oak. Whether this was by design or chance she could not tell. Only once did any of them even fly close.

That one time the crow had looked down at her and said some silly, garbled thing that sounded like, "Sofer, sogoot." She had no idea what it meant. Or if it meant anything at all.

Jafthuh, Tinga and Ilta did wake up occasionally. But, when they did, they did not feel like talking. All they wanted to do was to nibble on a stale nut or two and tuck their faces back in their paws.

Finally, as the cold season prepared to depart the deep woods, impatience and loneliness got the best of her. Odalee set out for the nest of one who was always ready to talk: Mianta.

"Jafthuh!"

Odalee's sharp command woke the old male gray from a sound sleep.

"Hmmph!" he snorted. "What is it?"

"Mianta and Laslum are gone," she announced.

He was awake immediately.

"Gone? Where gone?" He rubbed his eyes.

"I have no idea."

"Exploring...to see Phetra and Roselimb...," he offered, fumbling around in his half-awake mind.

"This time of season? Without saying a word to us?"

Jafthuh stood slowly and shook his head.

"Golden Gooseberries, Mother, have you been off snooping into your offspring's nest?"

Odalee smoothed the fur on her foreleg. "I am Mianta's mother," she said. "I went to visit."

"Visit, eh?" He eyed his mate. "Mother, I thought we promised one another that, once our young were grown and mated, we would not spend time worrying about them. I thought we agreed we had to breathe our air and they had to breathe theirs."

Odalee pursed her lips and looked directly into his face. "Did we mean it? Especially when half of them have disappeared under disturbing circumstances?"

"Well, I'll be..." And he stomped his paw on the floor of the big nest, feigning disgust. He looked at her again. And scratched his chin. Then he wrinkled his nose. "Yeah," he said. "Know what you mean. Letting them alone is easier to say than do."

"Jafthuh," she said imploringly, "first it was those crows with news of Ephran's and Kaahli's disappearance. Then Janna and Frafan traipsing off to The Pond. Now Mianta and Laslum gone. And no word of any of them."

"What would you have us do, female?"

"Go to the nest of Phetra," Odalee said firmly.

Jafthuh's face widened in surprise. "And what do you expect to find there?"

"Phetra and his mate, Roselimb. I hope."

"Maybe. Maybe they are asleep in their nest. Then again, they might have gone to Great Hill with Frafan and Janna," Jafthuh said. "Remember, I did suggest they stop and get advice from Phetra, since he'd already made the trip from here to Great Hill. Despite my warnings about too many treeclimbers running together, I'm not at all certain that Phetra...and almost certainly Roselimb...would be able to resist going along."

"Yes, Roselimb has itchier paws than Phetra," said Odalee, a new worry crossing her brow. "But the warm season will be here soon. I can feel it. Even if they did leave with Frafan and Janna, they might have returned to their nest by now."

"Then they would have brought us news, if there is any news. In either case," said Jafthuh, "I don't see how going to the nest of Phetra is going to help you rest easier. If they are gone, you will just have something else to fret about. If they are there it is unlikely they will know anything we don't."

"At least I'll know I have some family left. And where they are."

"I told the young ones that I don't approve of travel this time of season," Jafthuh reminded her. "It can still get very rough out there in the woods."

"I know."

"That doesn't make any difference to you either, does it?"

"No. I am far past the point of worrying about possible dangers. I must know what is happening to my family. Besides, you're too sly to let anything happen to any of us."

"Ah, you clever and flattering female! You are just as wonderful a liar as you were the day I found you. You know it is your wisdom, not mine, that has seen us through so many seasons."

He took her in his front paws and hugged her close. She hugged him in return and murmured, "You are my comfort."

"Poor comfort I am. Crows brought us news once. And Mianta and I repaid them with insults. I wonder if they might have come back if I'd been more understanding...and less narrow-minded..."

Jafthuh cut his words short and lay stock-still. Odalee did likewise.

"Did you hear that?" he whispered.

"Yes," she said quietly.

Again they heard it. A gentle scratching sound at the base of their tree. Then, a tiny "Meow!"

Odalee looked at her mate. "A cat!" she said, and scurried out the hole.

Jafthuh, just behind his mate, looked down to see the old farm cat, standing among the roots of the big oak, looking up at him. Odalee peered down.

"Hello, folks," said the cat. "Sorry to disturb you."

"We were awake, Blackie," said Odalee.

"You know my name."

"Of course we know your name," answered Odalee. "And I suspect you know ours as well."

"Yes, I do."

Jafthuh cleared his throat. "What do you want...uh...cat?"

"Blackie!" hissed Odalee, "her name is Blackie."

"Information is what I seek," said Blackie. "I needn't tell you that many days have passed since Frafan and Janna left. My curiosity as to what might have happened to them overcomes my better judgment."

"How would we know what's happened to them?" Jafthuh demanded.

Blackie ignored Jafthuh's rudeness. "I know the crows brought you the message that caused Frafan and Janna to leave in the first place. I thought perhaps..."

"No," said Jafthuh. "Crows are untrustworthy. The message you speak of is the only one we've received. And that message has been a disaster for this family. I suspect it was a lie from the outset."

Odalee turned to her mate. "Why do you say that now, Jafthuh? You believed it at the time. You felt as we did, that the crows carried their unwanted message with great sadness."

"I didn't want to believe it then and I don't want to believe it now," said Jafthuh.

"I suppose it makes no difference if the message was true or not. They are all gone anyway," said Blackie. "Frafan believed the crows."

"Frafan was...is...young. He's had little experience with the woods and its creatures," said Jafthuh.

"Frafan is very wise for his age," the cat said.

"I'm glad you think so," said Jafthuh. Then, under his breath to Odalee, "I can't believe we're sitting here talking to a cat!" And he closed his mouth.

"In any case," said Blackie, "when you see Frafan, I'd like you to give him a message."

Odalee and Jafthuh were silent.

"We are friends, you know," said the cat.

"There is no question of that," Odalee said in a quiet voice. "And I appreciate that you say 'when' we see Frafan, rather than 'if' we see him. But why not give him the message yourself?"

"There are reasons," Blackie said slowly. "I can no longer climb. My sight grows dim. My legs are always stiff. Sleeping seems to be the only thing I do well...and often. But I want him to know that I thought of him. That I missed his presence — and our talks by the lilac hedge."

"He would like that," said Odalee. "He enjoyed those conversations very much. And he regarded your friendship very highly."

"Yes, well...," sighed Blackie. "Tell him, if you please, when you next see him, that his persistent teacher hopes her lessons helped in his journey. And remind him that some enemies are better friends than friends."

Jafthuh's brow wrinkled.

Odalee said, "I'm not sure I understand your words, but I will tell him."

"And, to both of you," said Blackie, "I want you to know that I have a very strong feeling that Frafan is breathing and well. Somewhere. And that he will be successful in his quest. Actually, I have the impression that he may already be on his way home." The cat smiled up at them. Then she said, almost like an apology, "You have to understand that I've learned to trust my feelings."

"That's very encouraging, I'm sure," Odalee managed, looking more and more puzzled.

"Farewell," said the cat. And she turned and very slowly walked back toward the den of The Many Colored Ones.

Jafthuh watched her for a long time, until she disappeared through the wooden flap in the big den. Then he said, almost in a whisper, "What kind of hunter is that? A hunter who leaves puzzling messages of encouragement for a treeclimber?" He turned to Odalee. "Let's wake up Tinga and Ilta. We will leave as soon as they are ready," he said.

Odalee looked at her mate with wide eyes. "Am I hearing you right? Now you want to go to the nest of Phetra and Roselimb?"

"I've decided it's a reasonable idea," he said gruffly, but with a grin. "I won't get any peace around here anyway."

Though he and Odalee were ready to travel, Ilta and Tinga were not. Long hibernation, with little to eat, left the two young females groggy and hungry.

"It seems we will have to let them wake up and stretch their legs for a few days," said Odalee to Jafthuh.

By the end of the second day the young ones seemed ready and anxious. At last they would have their grand adventure. As the morning sun of the third day peeped through the trees, golden rays fell upon four gray squirrels, high among the oak branches, busily stuffing themselves with fresh buds and last warm season's acorns and walnuts.

"Eat well," said Jafthuh. "I have no idea what trees or bushes grow along the trail we will follow...or when or where we will find our next meal."

"Oh, father," said Ilta, "I have no doubt you will find a safe path, and plenty of buds and nuts along the way as well."

The old male smiled proudly, and did not deny her trust.

"Look. Over there," Tinga interrupted. She pointed toward the den of The Many Colored Ones.

The two inhabitants of that den, bundled in heavy pelts, had come out of their big nest together, and walked slowly toward the woods. Jafthuh had watched them, at a distance, ever since the squirrel family had moved into the big oak tree. He had decided that the larger was a

27

male and the smaller a female. He had also concluded They were old for their kind. They walked haltingly, bodies bent slightly forward.

The male went ahead. In one forepaw he carried a long stick, wide, shiny, and curved at one end. The female had something else, something wrapped in a big white covering. She bore her load carefully and tenderly, close to her heart. They walked a little way and stopped where trees met short grass.

The treeclimbers watched in silence as the male placed the wide curved end of his strange stick firmly in the earth. The dirt, barely thawed, was hard to move. Jafthuh had a fairly clear idea of what the male was trying to accomplish. It was digging a hole. He and Ephran had watched Many Colored Ones do this sort of thing when They erected a vine to enclose a group of cows.

The mound of earth grew higher and higher as the male dug the hole wider and deeper. Finally he set the stick against a nearby tree and wiped his brow with the back of a forepaw. The female unwrapped what she held and lay it gently on the earth.

Odalee leaned forward. Jafthuh knew what the bundle contained without having to look. Blackie lay very still on the white sheet.

The Many Colored Ones stood for a time, heads bowed. Each put a forepaw on the black fur and stroked it, very lightly, one last time. Finally, the female bent and lifted Blackie in her paws. She wrapped her very tightly, as though to protect the gentle old cat from the cold soil. She lowered her burden into the dark earth. The male picked up the wide stick once more and pushed dirt back into the hole. Ilta and Tinga's eyes grew bigger and bigger.

"All of you..." Odalee whispered, "help me remember Blackie's message for Frafan."

* * * * *

So Jafthuh found himself in the branches, a good deal earlier in the season than he cared to. He looked over at Odalee, followed closely by Ilta and Tinga, balanced on the branch of a small oak.

"Starting our warm season ahead of time again, aren't we?" he said to her.

"I remember some of these same trees from early last season. We were coming from the other direction then. I was heavy and uncomfortable with young ones inside me."

"Lighter belly this time, eh, Mother?"

She nodded at him. "Much lighter, Father."

They ran along, from tree to tree, moving away from Blue Lake. He said, "Here is the place the fire ate."

Odalee said, "I can still smell it. Do you know where Phetra's nest is from here?"

"She lowered her burden into the dark earth."

Suddenly, bare and blackened forest appeared ahead.

"Not exactly," said Jafthuh. "From his description I had a pretty good idea where the old one was, the one they had before the fire. He said they were going to try to build as near as possible to where the first nest had been."

From the branches of a sturdy tree, Ilta shouted, "Here is Phetra's nest!"

She did not enter, but waited for her mother. Odalee jumped to the tree and ducked through the hole. When she reappeared her face showed disappointment and a bit of confusion. She said, "As I feared, they are not here. But their scent is. Strangely, it is much weaker..." She glanced at Jafthuh.

"Weaker than what?" he asked, eyes narrow.

"Weaker than it was in the den of Mianta and Laslum," admitted Odalee.

Tinga said, "Are you saying that Phetra has been at the nest of Mianta after he left here?"

"I'm sure of it," said Odalee.

"Why didn't you tell us this earlier?" Jafthuh demanded.

"It made no sense before. I thought perhaps I was confusing Mianta's and Phetra's scent. But now that I smell Phetra's, without his sister's, I know I was not mistaken."

"Why would Phetra leave here and go to Mianta's nest?" asked Ilta.

"Good question," said Jafthuh. "I'm afraid the obvious answer will not make sleep come easier. And he must have brought Roselimb with him." He looked at Odalee.

"Yes, her scent was there too. Phetra and Roselimb must have had news. They must have brought it to Mianta and Laslum," Odalee said.

"And whatever that news was, they did not choose to share it with us," said Jafthuh.

"Why wouldn't they come to our nest?" asked Tinga.

"Maybe because they did not want to worry or excite us," said Ilta.

"You have struck the right nutshell, daughter," agreed Odalee. "But, disturbing news or not, they have all run off somewhere. The news must not be final. What they have learned has brought hope and possibility. It has sent their paws scurrying somewhere."

They sat in the branches for a time, near the entrance to Phetra's den. Finally, the old male stirred.

"Well, I don't know how the rest of you feel," said Jafthuh. "But it seems to me that possible destinations are limited. I can think of only one place they might have gone. I think we must follow them...to The Pond."

CHAPTER V
NEWS AND NEW MASTERS

he floppy-eared dog licked the face of the small Many Colored One seated next to him. The little One giggled happily and, with his forepaw, wiped off the sloppy kiss.

Fred lay down on the floor. Who, he thought, would have dreamt that this yellow hound would find himself here, back in the old blue van, bouncing along the gravel path with those same folks, folks from The Farm of Cages?

Though the van was the same, this trip was considerably different from that first trip. For one thing, this time everybody rode up front. Fred liked it much better up here, where there were plenty of windows and light, and lots of scenery to watch. Another thing, the season now was almost the reverse of what it had been before. The time of snow was over, instead of just beginning. Frafan and Farnsworth weren't here, of course, and there were no cages in back, rattling and sliding on the shiny floor. The van was traveling in the opposite direction it had that other time too. At least Fred thought it was most likely the opposite direction. Couldn't be sure.

That first trip, when he'd been enclosed in a cage, the van had set out from the Farm of Cages and traveled to Master's den. This time it had left Master's den and, if it was like any other creature in this big confusing world, it had to be going home: to the Farm of Cages.

Brittle Bones, this had been one wacky old day! Confusion and sadness and happiness, one after the other. First had come sharp rapping on the wooden door to Master's den. Nothing gentle about it. Bam! Bam! Racket had been so confounded loud that it woke him up from what had been a very nice little snooze. He'd been dreaming he was swimming in one absolutely huge dish of gooey dog food. And, much as he sucked in, the goo in the dish never went down. Stomach never got full either. Opening his eyes to the banging, he'd watched as Master opened the door. Standing in the doorway had been two of Them, almost like Master; Many Colored Ones, as big or bigger than Master.

Nothing so unusual about visitors at the door. Happened every now and then. Only These acted different. Looked different too, in their brown pelts with green patches on the forelegs. Serious. No loud talking. No noises that Fred had come to know as laughing.

Thought maybe he ought to be friendly so he tried to lick their front paws. They weren't nasty or anything. Pretty much ignored him. Talked real stern at Master, much as Master did to Fred when Fred got a little rambunctious. When Master turned, They followed. Master shuffled his hindpaws. Fred knew Master wasn't happy about these visitors. And He sure wasn't happy about leading Them to his very cold, very big white box.

Fred knew what was in that box. He tried not to think about it. It was where Master kept his food, some of it anyway. Mostly the birds and animals he'd hunted. The last thing he'd opened it for had been two pheasants, so nervously and quickly cleaned they still had feathers on. They had been put in the box just the day before. Master had been hunting, once again long after hunting season was supposed to be over and done. Fred did not go along. Fred had made it clear to Master that hunting was no longer of any interest to him.

As the Others talked, Fred had sensed fear in the room. First he thought the visitors were afraid of Master, as were most Others. Certainly the animals and birds of the meadow and forest were afraid of Him. But, surprise of surprises, the scent of fear came from Master!

After They had looked in the white box, the strangers had taken all of Master's thundersticks. They pointed to the wall where the talking bone hung. Actually, Fred knew it wasn't a bone. But it looked like one: narrow in the middle, wide at both ends. Master picked up the bone and talked into it. The coiled vine attached to the black bone jiggled. Was Master trembling? Master talked at the bone for a while, his voice far different from the confident one Fred usually heard.

They all sat then. Nobody made any noise. Strangers eyed Fred now and again, making him nervous. Master, head down, looked at the floor. There came another knock at the door.

When it opened this time, Fred recognized who stood there. It was Them, the large and small Ones from the Farm of Cages! Oh, yes! These folks meant petting and playing. And food! Good food. Lots of food.

Squatting down outside his den, Master had scratched Fred behind the ears, just the way Fred had always liked to be scratched. He couldn't be positive, but Fred thought there might have been a drop of water in Master's eye. Then the two brown Ones led Master away.

There was no question in Fred's mind. Master had just said good-bye. And it sure seemed this good-bye was meant to be a real good-bye. A forever kind of good-bye.

The sadness left pretty quick. Fred almost felt guilty about that. But he and Master had parted company a long while ago. What Master had been doing in the deep woods was wrong. It was against the rules. And He knew it. And Fred knew He knew it. After taking a stern cuffing or two for refusing to go, or for running away as soon as the thunderstick had spoken, Master had finally left him home during hunting trips.

Anyway, it was time for a new nest. If this was the case, he could not have picked a better home had he all the choices in the world.

Right now, the Farm of Cages was an ideal place to be. Why, the farm was right at the edge of the deep woods! And Fred had urgent business in the deep woods.

The van finally bounced onto the path leading to the yellow den. The small One got to his hindpaws and, as soon as the van came to a stop, opened the door. Fred followed the small One, jumping from the van to the gravel path. The small One ran across the frozen ground; skipping, leaping, clapping its front paws. Its mouth made loud and happy sounds the whole while. The large One stood by quietly, forepaws on rear hips, a wide and unmistakable smile on its hairy face.

"Oh, Mounds a' Grub and Soft Nests!" thought Fred as he romped with the small One, yelping with glee, "This is where I shoulda been all the time. Smell that air! Lookit that food dish! Not big 'nough to swim in, but plenty big."

The small One eventually tired of running and playing. It gave Fred a big hug and put its paw firmly around Fred's collar. It led the dog to a nearby tree and fastened a stout vine to the collar. It gave Fred one more hug and ran off toward the yellow den, into which the larger One had already disappeared.

"Hey!" Fred barked after the retreating figure. "How about puttin' some food in this here dish?"

He snorted when the little One didn't so much as turn back toward him. "Hmmmph. All that little critter kin do is think of his stomach. What kinda creature's that..."

"Well, well. Look who's back. Fred's the name, isn't it?"

Fred nearly jumped right smack out of his pelt. In the tree he was tied to, on a branch almost directly above his head, perched a pigeon. The bird, completely white, smiled down.

"Hey! Flutterby! That's who y'are, ain't it? Suprized ya remember me."

"Good to see you, Fred. Actually, it really hasn't been that long since you were here. And you remembered my name too. Yes, I am called Flutterby."

"Where's yer sisters, Flutterby? Thought you gals pretty much stuck together."

"Usually we do. They must have taken off while I took a nap. Looking for something to eat, I suppose."

"Smart gals. Rip-snortin' good idea." He eyed the Many Colored One den.

"What are you doing here, Fred? The last I saw of you, you were being loaded into the back of the blue van."

"Yep. Nuther one a them goofy days, that one. Seems I git a lot a'those. Anyway, went fer a little ride."

"I know. You left with Frafan. And the raccoon fellow,

33

"Well, Well, Look who's back."

Farnsworth. We, my sisters and I, tried to follow. What happened to all of you that day?"

"All sorts a stuff. They let Farnsworth go. On the edge a the woods..."

"That part we knew. We stopped to talk to Farnsworth. What about you and Frafan?"

"They took me home, ta Master's den... Say, speakin' a whut went on that day...whut come a that crazy old rooster pheasant? Think he called hisself Ruckaru."

At that moment, two more pigeons fluttered down, into the tree. One was speckled, like it had been splattered with mud and snow. The other was patches of color, as though it couldn't make up its mind what color it wanted to be.

"Hello, Fred!" they said, at the same time.

"Fred, do you remember my sisters, Payslee and Peppercorn?" asked Flutterby.

"'Course. Hello there, ladies. We wuz just talkin' about that strange old pheasant that wuz here not so long ago," said Fred.

"Oh, you mean Ruckaru. He has been gone for some time," said Payslee.

"The Many Colored Ones placed his cage outside of the barn, near the fields, and just opened it," said Flutterby.

"It took the foolish bird a long time to work up the courage to leave the cage and try his wings," said Peppercorn.

"So nobody's in cages no more," said Fred.

"Oh, there always seems to be an occupant or two," said Payslee.

"At the moment we have a small fox and a rabbit resting inside the barn," said Peppercorn.

"Cages right next to one another," smiled Flutterby. "I think they are actually becoming friends...sort of."

Flutterby tilted her head at Fred. "Speaking of friends, you didn't finish telling me about Frafan. Was the little treeclimber still in the van when They let you off?"

"Yep, he were."

"Hmm. He didn't stay in it, you know. When the van returned, it was empty," said Flutterby.

"Empty, huh?" Fred scratched his backside. "Well, that figures. Didn't 'spect he'd take a round trip ride in that van. Little cuss wuz gettin' purty antsy when I left him. Had ta get outa there sooner or later."

"That brings us back to you, Fred," said Flutterby.

"Yes," continued Peppercorn, "what are you doing here?"

"We never thought we'd see you again at the Farm of Cages," said Payslee.

"Tell ya, I get confused often enough that I never know where I'll end up," giggled Fred. "Might's well here as anyplace. Actually, probly better'n most places."

"But you were brought here by Them," said Payslee.

"In the blue van," added Flutterby.

"Do you know why?" asked Peppercorn.

"Think so. Think These are my new Masters."

"What, may I ask...," said Flutterby.

"Ever happened...," said Peppercorn.

"To the old One?" finished Payslee.

"Don't know fer sure. Hard to figure out what They're up to sometimes. But I think He got caught, ya know. Been huntin' at the wrong time fer quite a spell. Think He hada let me go."

"Well then, this is wonderful," said Flutterby with a big smile. "We're going to have a fresh face..."

"And fascinating night-stories...," said Payslee.

"About a whole different world," said Peppercorn.

"Sounds great," said Fred. "My old den, the one in the warren of Many Colored Ones was purty boring. Never saw a pigeon. Couldn't even git the squirrels around there t'talk to me. Speakin' a squirrels, you folks seen or heard anything a' my other friends, Janna and Klester?"

"No, we haven't," said Payslee, with a shake of her head.

"Not since we guided them back to Rocky Creek," said Peppercorn.

"They said they could find their way to The Pond from there," said Flutterby.

"That's where I gotta go then, to The Pond," said Fred.

A surprised look appeared on Peppercorn's face. "To The Pond?" she asked.

"Why do you want to go to The Pond?" asked Payslee.

"Klestra and Janna have no further news, you know. If you think they might be able to help you find that Ephran fellow, I'm afraid you'll be disappointed. They only went back there because they wanted to spend the cold season in familiar nests," said Flutterby.

"Not them got the news," said Fred. "It's me. I think I know where Frafan ended up. Maybe Ephran and Kaahli too. You gals better get busy and loosen this here vine I'm tied with. We gotta get goin'. Those treeclimbin' friends 'a mine are gonna need help gettin' home."

CHAPTER VI
THIN ICE

Mayberry lay with his nose close to Truestar's warm, furry neck. He'd been awake for some time now and his mind would not let him go back to sleep.

It had been a long while since Milkweed had returned to Great Woods Warren with her news from the shores of Rocky Creek. And astounding news it had been: Redthorn was gone, his breath ripped from him by a badger. Frafan and Janna had witnessed this, as did Klestra, Ephran's red squirrel neighbor. And they, along with another of Ephran's unusual friends, a dog named Fred, had set out for the peaceful Spring, to seek out Aden, father of Ephran's mate. The possibility existed that Ephran and Kaahli were at The Spring with Aden.

Then, later in the cold season, an exhausted rabbit from Bubbling Brook Warren had appeared at the entrance to Great Woods Warren with word from a cottontail called Brightleaf. Unfortunately, the message was terribly garbled. Apparently, early in the cold season, two treeclimbers had returned to The Pond. The names of the two squirrels could not be remembered, and the only other part of the message was that Ephran's brother was still searching. Evidently, Frafan was not one of those who returned. Was one of them Janna? Might Frafan's search, wherever it carried him, be for nought? It certainly would be if the two squirrels who had returned to the base of Great Hill were Ephran and Kaahli themselves.

It had been difficult to keep his mind on the daily needs and problems of Great Woods Warren. How he wished there had been more news...that the fates of all his treeclimbing friends were known. But it was not to be, and he knew his duty during the hardest of times lay here, in the warren with his mate, his young, and their families.

But now the cold season was nearly broken. He could feel it, as did the rest of the rabbits in his warren.

Truestar stirred. "Ummm. Good morning, dear one," she said, when she saw him looking at her.

"And to you," Mayberry replied, and licked her nose.

"You've been awake for a time," she said, "judging by those big wide eyes."

"Yes."

"And you've been thinking."

"Yes, again."

"There my guessing will stop. Among all the matters that might concern the Governor of Great Woods Warren, I don't know which might wake him from his slumber."

Mayberry stretched his rear legs. "No mystery to it. The

37

unknown fate of our friends, the treeclimbers, fills me with uneasy thoughts."

"Ah," said Truestar, standing and shaking herself. "You speak of Frafan and Janna."

"Them, of course. But I think of Ephran and Kaahli yet as well. I cannot imagine who might be back at The Pond."

Truestar licked her paws: one, then the other. She watched her mate, who gazed up at the roof of the warren, a faraway look in his eyes. "The Governor's legs grow restless," she said. "You feel the need to search again, don't you? To solve this puzzle?"

His eyes widened. Then he smiled. "I should realize, after many seasons sharing the same nest, that I have no secrets from the one who knows my heart. Yes, Truestar, every time we go out to patrol, to look for fresh or preserved greens, I find myself wanting to run further, to peek down Rocky Creek, to see if they — or someone — might be about. Someone with news..."

"Well, if these matters nudge your heart, it is something that must be done. When will you go?" she asked.

His eyes grew wider yet.

"Go? You think I should go? You wouldn't mind?"

"Ah, my dear, why should I mind? Should I be troubled that I find myself sharing your affection for gray squirrels? I have not forgotten, after all, who tried to warn me, tried to save me against all odds, when a great white owl swooped down on me near the shores of The Pond. Besides, the air grows warm and Redthorn is no longer a threat. I can see to the needs of Great Woods Warren in your absence."

And of course she could. Actually, there were times he was quite certain that she had far more to do with keeping the warren clean, ordered, safe, and peaceful than he did.

And so the decision was made. Plans were laid, the warren was informed, new duties were outlined. By the next morning all was arranged, and most of the rabbits of the warren gathered around its largest entrance to bid their leader farewell. The only cottontails not present were the does who were busy caring for newborn kits.

One of the younger bucks came up to Mayberry and said, "Governor, I am concerned for you. And I am concerned for us as well. My mate has little ones. We all feel better when we know you are close by."

"Is this leaving of the warren neccesary?" asked another older rabbit. "Does it serve a purpose?"

"Oh, Mayberry, I'm worried too. Hunters will be all about you, seeking their first warm season meals," said Fairchance, a female with delicate features.

"Fairchance, your generous spirit is always concerned for

others," replied Mayberry. "To all of you I say there will be no more danger than there always is for shorttails. As to whether the reason I leave be important, I feel it is. Ephran has taught me that our fates: shorttails, longtails...all here in the forest...are tied together like wild grape vines twisting through the branches of a hackberry tree. What we don't know can indeed harm us...like the fox hidden behind a bush. I must know where these treeclimbers have run and who is in Ephran and Kaahli's nest on the shores of The Pond. And what they've learned, which may be of great importance to us all. Besides, I leave you in the best of paws," he said. "Truestar and Sorghum will watch over the warren while we are gone."

Sorghum, a tiny female rabbit who was mate to the Warden of Great Woods Warren, smiled widely. Mayberry continued, "I will travel with my young ones: Sweetbud, Longrass, and Highopper. Fastrip, Warden of our warren, will accompany me as well."

The rabbits shifted, trading uneasy glances.

"Couldn't find the way without me, you know," Fastrip whispered, behind his paw, to a nearby cottontail. His whisper was loud enough for everyone to hear.

"Actually, they have to take something along for owlbait," Sorghum, Fastrip's mate whispered, just as loudly.

"Say there! Are you talking about me?" Fastrip demanded.

"Oh, Brown Grass and Blueberries! Would anyone dare speak so disrespectfully of the mighty and fearless Warden of Great Woods Warren? Would anyone suggest his best use might be to feed a carrion-eater?" Sorghum smiled sweetly at him.

"Of course not!" Fastrip replied, raising his nose in the air, apparently satisfied Sorghum's answer was sincere.

"...Unless that particular warden had a brain the size of a mustard seed and an ego inflated to the size of a thundercloud," she finished.

"You are being disrespectful!" Fastrip cried. "You are! You are! You are! You are being disrespectful of the Governor's right paw!"

"Paws are for stepping on." Sorghum said.

"Why...why...you...," Fastrip sputtered, jumping up and down, grimacing horribly, "...you'll be about as much help to Truestar as a blackbird is to a crow. You will be at her ear, pecking and complaining constantly."

"At least Truestar will have something worthwhile to listen to. I wish I could say the same for Mayberry."

All the rabbits laughed loudly, Mayberry as well.

"I'll get even," Fastrip said to Sorghum, wagging a paw at her, "wait and see."

"Thank you, Fastrip and Sorghum. Your antics make a rough path smoother," Mayberry said.

And they evidently had. Even the cottontails who had been the most nervous about Mayberry leaving the warren now wore smiles, and seemed to have forgotten their concern.

"Where will you go first, Mayberry?" asked Milkweed, who stood next to her sister, Truestar.

"I think we will travel to Rocky Creek," said Mayberry. "And from there our path will almost certainly lead to The Pond. Unless we learn something that directs our paws elsewhere."

"When will you return, my mate?" Truestar asked softly.

Mayberry put his face close to hers. "I will return to you as soon as I find them...or at least as soon as I know what happened. I would not stay far from your side any longer than I have to."

* * * * *

Mayberry led his little group through the trees and bushes. The woods was damp and still. Water in the air had frozen on everything. Branches, leaves, weeds and grass all wore a thick white pelt. Slender tendrils of ice seemed to burst from the tips of every branch, sparkling crowns topped every stem and weed. Even the darkest shadows seemed lit by white brilliance. Mayberry could not remember ever seeing the forest look quite so beautiful.

Water from melted snow had filled the low spots in the earth and had re-frozen in irregular and lacy patterns. Blades of frosted grass poked up at the edges of the ice, like the whiskers of a prickly porcupine.

Without having to be told, the travelers stopped as soon as they were out of sight of the warren. Each turned in a different direction and sat quietly. All ears, except for Mayberry's bent one, were held high. No one made a sound for a long while.

"There are no worrisome sounds in this direction, father," Longrass finally said.

"Not from where I listen either," said Sweetbud.

"Only the tinkling of frozen water as it falls from the branches," said Highopper.

"Even so," said Mayberry, "there may be hunters about, laying silently yet. Keep eyes and ears alert as we go."

The young ones tried to go slowly and carefully, but Sweetbud kept wandering off to gaze into every bush and hillock that was especially gloriously adorned with its icy coat. Meanwhile, Longrass and Highopper could not seem to keep from playing and scuffling in what snow remained.

A sober Fastrip remarked, "You know, Governor, they are not watching for hunters as they should."

"True, my friend," Mayberry answered, with a shake of his head.

"They are young. And bursting with enthusiasm for a new adventure. I remember. You do too. Help me keep watch for them."

Mayberry tried to steer clear of danger by keeping to open paths — where surprises from hidden enemies would be unlikely. They traveled that way for a time, stopping now and then to nibble at a patch of early greenery.

As they neared a thick line of bushes Fastrip said, "I think we near Rocky Creek and..." His words were cut short by the sound of breaking ice and splashing water.

"What was that?" said Longrass.

The woods was quiet again. Then came a snorting sort of sound, and the tinkling of ice once more.

"The sound comes from behind the bushes," said Mayberry. "There is water there. Most certainly still frozen."

"Shall we hide?" asked Longrass.

"I think not," said Mayberry.

He hopped cautiously toward the bushes and stuck his nose through. Then he turned back toward Fastrip and his young ones. "Come," he said. "It is a deer."

The rabbits scrambled through the thick stems. A deer? A deer doing what? How did a deer account for the sound of breaking ice?

A young male whitetailed deer, facing partly away from them, stood nearly in the middle of Rocky Creek. The rabbits watched in silence as the deer's head slowly drooped, then snapped to attention. Suddenly he leaped, an awkward sort of jump, and his front legs came up a bit. Then he fell back. Grayish ice, which had apparently grown softer and softer as the days grew long and the air warm, came nearly up to his shoulders. Tracks on the snow, leading out onto the creek, told the story. The deer had tried to cross the frozen water where he had crossed the whole of the cold season. This time his tried and true path had led to disaster.

The cottontails watched in silence as the deer's actions were repeated over and over. The head drooped lower and lower. And the attempts to free itself became more and more feeble.

Then, without a word to his companions, Mayberry ran out onto the ice, right up to the deer's face.

"Large one," he said, "how long have you been here?"

Closed eyes shot open and the startled deer's body jerked sharply against the entrapping ice. The miserable animal emitted a low groan but said nothing.

Fastrip ran out to sit beside his Governor, and the young cottontails followed. "He is nearly done," the Warden of Great Woods Warren whispered in his Governor's ear.

"Will you speak to me?" Mayberry said to the deer.

The buck looked straight ahead, to the opposite shore, so near and yet so very far away. It did not utter a word.

"Longrass. Highopper. Sweetbud. Get some of those branches. On the bushes there. Those lower ones...those that still bear leaves," Mayberry said.

Longrass cocked his head toward his father. Highopper smiled an empty-headed smile.

"I understand," said Sweetbud. Hopping to the bushes, she grasped a thick branch in her teeth and pulled. The branch, broken nearly all the way through by wind, snow and cold, came away from the bush. Sweetbud dragged it out onto the ice.

"Put it near the deer's mouth," Mayberry ordered.

The female did as she was told.

The deer did not move. It acted as though Sweetbud wasn't there, though she was practically under his nose.

"Eat," said Mayberry. "You are cold and hungry. You must eat."

Finally the deer turned a big brown eye on Mayberry. The sadness there was so deep it caused Fastrip to shudder.

"Eat?" it said, in a high and weak voice. "Why should I eat?"

Mayberry bit his lip. The others stood silently.

"I caused my predicament by my own ignorance," the buck said. "Now I pay. Eating would be further stupidity. A way of prolonging this. I heard your little companion's whisper. He is right. I am done."

Fastrip turned to Mayberry and said, "The ice will not leave soon enough to allow his survival. It will be many days yet before the air is warm enough to melt this."

Mayberry seemed not to hear. "Eat," he said again, a determined look on his face. "Food will give warmth and strength to your body while I think."

"While you think?" the deer snorted. "Why do you have to think next to me? Think somewhere else. Be on your way. Leave me in peace. I don't care to cry out and sink beneath the ice while you sit and watch."

"I have to think of a way to get you out of there," said Mayberry.

The deer's head came up and he turned as far as he could toward Mayberry. Fastrip, and Mayberry's young ones too, looked at the Governor in surprise. There was a long pause before the buck said, "There is no way for a bunch of little cottontails to free me from this icy grip. And why would you feel the need to try? The only thing we have in common is similar tails. But I am a deer, not a rabbit."

Mayberry replied, "You are a creature of this woods, as are we. There is far more that we should mean to one another than realizing our tails are shaped alike."

The deer said nothing for a moment. His eyes locked with

Mayberry's. Then he bent his head and took a mouthful of leaves from the branch Sweetbud had placed nearby.

The rabbits watched for a few moments. Highopper, seeing the leaves were nearly gone said, "I'll get another."

"So will I," said Longrass.

The two young rabbits ran off, back toward the bushes. As they pulled on small twigs with attached leaves, Mayberry's eyes grew bright and his lips parted. His ears came up. He whistled loudly. Longrass and Highopper stopped what they were doing and looked back expectantly. Their father had an idea. They had seen this look before.

"Larger branches," Mayberry said, almost breathlessly, "as large as you can carry. And don't worry about leaves..." He jumped to his paws. "Wait. I'll help. You too, Fastrip. And Sweetbud."

Mayberry led them to a large bush, with stems twice the thickness of his leg.

"This one," he said.

"But, father," said Sweetbud, "the stem of this bush has not been broken by the cold season."

"Then chew it off. You have good sharp teeth. Here's another," he said to Highopper, pointing to a similar thick stem. "Chew it down. And then chew off the smaller twigs on the top."

"Father!..." said Longrass.

"Governor!..." said Fastrip.

"Never mind. Trust me. You'll see why in a moment."

Mayberry picked up a smaller limb, filled with leaves, and scampered back out on the ice by the deer. While the deer ate slowly, Mayberry spoke softly and earnestly into the animal's ear.

Fastrip, Longrass, Highopper and Sweetbud could not hear what Mayberry told the deer. They looked at one another, totally bewildered. Fastrip shrugged and said to them, "Well, let's get to it. We may not understand yet, but you may be sure your father has some trick tucked behind that crooked ear of his."

It was hard work, nibbling little by little through the tough stems. It took time to get the branches down, and then to chew off the small twigs at the tips. And the rabbits had to stop working every now and then, to listen and test the air for the sound and scent of hunters.

All of them, Mayberry included, labored to carry the branches, one at a time, to where the buck stood in the icy water. The big animal had tried to keep his head up, to look behind him and watch this strange activity. But he seemed to lose interest. His eyes kept closing and his head dropping. Once his legs gave out beneath him and his entire body sunk half a taillength into the terribly cold water beneath the ice. When this happened Sweetbud gasped loudly.

"Hurry," Mayberry said in a low voice, "he does not have much longer."

He hopped over to the buck, whose eyes were now closed and whose breath came in shallow spurts.

"Great one!" Mayberry fairly shouted in the deer's ear, "Wake up!"

The deer opened his eyes with difficulty. He peered at the large branches piled next to him.

"There is nothing to eat on these," he said very quietly. "It is too late in any case."

"They are not to eat," said Mayberry. And he pushed one of the branches under the deer's neck, right up to its front quarters. "Help me," he said to Longrass.

The young rabbit saw where his father wanted the branches moved and soon all the cottontails were sliding branches on the ice, shoving them under the deer's nose. With every addition, the pile of branches became longer and thicker.

"What is this all about?" Fastrip said to Mayberry.

"Watch," he said, and he leaned toward the buck again.

"Back up," he said to the deer.

Groggily, the deer peered at Mayberry. "What...?"

"With your struggles you've made a hole in the ice, bigger than your body. There is room to move back. Back up as far as you can."

"Please," said the buck wearily, "please leave me alone. Whatever you're trying to do, it is too late. And I don't understand why you would bother to do anything for a deer anyway. I only wish a hunter would come along to end all this. Without me there will be more green things for you to eat. Anyway, the water hardly feels cold any more."

"Do as I say." Mayberry's voice was hard as the ice.

The deer looked baffled for a moment but the authority carried in the voice of Governor of Great Woods Warren took hold. He slowly moved backward until his tail was against the edge of the ice.

"Now...can you get one of your front legs up...above the ice?"

With considerable effort, the deer lifted a front leg. At first the hoof caught the edge of the ice and slipped back into the water. The big animal fell sideways, against the ice, then quickly righted himself.

"Again," demanded Mayberry.

"I can't do this," said the buck. "I am too tired."

"Do as I say. Again."

Once more the deer lifted his leg, a dripping and shivering hoof rising out of the creek. The leg dropped on the pile of branches.

"Quickly now, pull yourself up," said Mayberry. "Get your other leg out there too. But don't stand up. Keep yourself on the branches. They will spread the weight of your large body."

Both legs eased up onto the branches. Then half the deer's body came out of the water.

"Now," said Mayberry, "Longrass and Highopper, get behind his front leg on that side. Sweetbud and Fastrip, help me push on this side."

Shoving, grunting, slipping, sometimes almost falling into the icy hole themselves, the rabbits flexed strong rear legs against the pile of brush supporting the shuddering deer's flanks and upper legs. Slowly...ever so slowly...the deer emerged from the cold water. Suddenly the rabbits found themselves running, sliding their soaked and shivering burden swiftly across the ice. With a final grunt and shove they pushed him right up to the far shore of Rocky Creek.

"Huddle close," Mayberry told them.

The deer lay, barely breathing, head on the rocky shore where all snow and ice had melted. Longrass and Highopper put their backs to him, Sweetbud and Fastrip huddled beneath his belly, and Mayberry lay his big warm and furry body across the deer's neck. The young buck opened his eyes.

"Who are you?" he asked Mayberry.

"I am your friend."

Things generally work out fer the best
if ya git yer head workin' the same
direction as yer paws.

Rennigan, from his nest at
the edge of The Meadow

CHAPTER VII
RUNNING IN CIRCLES

J anna's eyes did not want to open. She'd been more exhausted than she thought. It was difficult to understand why sleep came so hard. She'd been here, near The Pond, long enough to feel comfortable. So why didn't she? Why did the surroundings frighten her...and why did the nest still seem like a stranger's?

It was, she told herself, because she was in this big nest all alone. She was not used to being alone. Ever since she'd arrived here with Klestra, so many days and nights ago, her sleep had been fitful. How long had she slept this time? Had a noise wakened her? There was nothing now, no sound but that of a little lost breeze in the branches. She pulled her head from under her foreleg. The air was cold on her nose.

She shook the sleep from her head and crept to the den entrance. The sky above The Pond was as gray as her fur. Though the air had slowly warmed the past few days, The Pond was still a sheet of brittle ice. She squinted. She knew the approximate location of Klestra's tree, but could not pick it out.

Her stomach growled. Standing on her hind legs, Janna scratched in the leaves for something to nibble on. An opened walnut lay near the surface, less than half eaten. Who had nibbled, she wondered? Klestra, maybe, during one of those times he rested here in the cozy leaves...one of those times he imagined Ephran and Kaahli might suddenly scamper up the tree and squeeze into the nest.

She scraped a bit of food from the shell. Sweet Sunshine, she was lonesome! At first, conversations with Klestra: chats about the terrible snowstorm, about Great Woods Warren, about Redthorn's ambush, about the time in the big barn with Fred and Ruckaru and Farnsworth — all the activity, the suspense, the hope, had kept her going, had kept her mind so busy that she had simply not had time to think of her parents, Odalee and Jafthuh. Or of her sisters, Mianta, Ilta, and Tinga. She'd not had a chance to worry about where Frafan and Ephran and Kaahli and Phetra and Roselimb might be, or to consider the fact that a great deal of time had passed since she'd seen any of them.

If only she'd had her "Alone Time" as Frafan had! But she knew very well why she and her sisters, Tinga and Ilta, had not been led away from the nest of Jafthuh and Odalee, to fend for themselves in the big forest. She remembered the whispered conversation on a big limb near the nest.

"Well, Frafan is home again. He finished his Alone Time," Tinga had observed.

"Yes," said Ilta, "and the little beggar seems none the worse for it either."

Frafan was perched in a nearby oak, basking in the sun, apparently trying to figure out a better way to open an acorn.

"Easy for him. He's used to going off by himself," said Tinga.

"Besides," Janna recalled herself saying, "he explores so much he probably knows as much about the woods as father does."

Ilta frowned. "Do you suppose he might have known his Alone Time place before he got there?"

Up to that moment it had not occurred to Janna that her curious little brother's Alone Time was almost certainly a farce. Frafan actually knew more about their part of the woods than father did. It was more than likely...it was a certainty... Frafan would be completely comfortable no matter where father took him for his test.

No wonder he didn't object when father said he'd be the first to be left alone in the woods. No wonder he looked sort of embarrassed when everyone fussed over him on his return.

Despite her suspicions, she did not confront him. When she thought more about it she decided her brother had no reason to feel embarrassed. If he knew the answers to his test, it was only because he had studied so earnestly beforepaw.

For her part, she'd felt ready to go, to be on her own for a while, to see if she'd learned what she needed to know from mother, father, Ephran, Kaahli, and Mianta. Even if the experience might be frightening, Janna felt the time had come. But she had not left the big nest. Neither had her sisters. The lack of water from the sky, and its effects on food in the forest, influenced her parents' decision that Alone Time would be delayed. The fact that a family of owls decided to make their nest close to the farm, while Frafan was gone, was perhaps just as important.

Then, while she was still chewing and remembering, trying not to feel so very alone, not to be afraid, it happened anyway. As sudden and unexpected as the icy drop on her ear in Great Woods Warren, fear came — a fear not unlike what she felt at the beginning of the big storm, when she realized that she'd become separated from those she loved and depended on. And indeed, wasn't that exactly the situation right now? Where was everyone? Why was she here by herself, so far from home and comfort? Where was Klestra?

Janna bolted out of the nest as if thrown from a springy green branch. She as much fell from the tree as ran down it. There was no time for branch-jumping. She hadn't run five taillengths before she was chattering in the loudest voice she could manage.

"Klestra! Klestra!" she shouted as she ran toward The Pond.

There was no answer.

He had told her he wandered away from The Pond at times...for lots of reasons...including the fact that he picked up a great deal of information in the woods. And, even though friendly forest eyes and ears were not plentiful just now, there was a chipmunk's cheekful of unanswered questions. One never knew when or where an important clue might surface.

She remembered Klestra asking her, many times, if she'd be frightened all by herself in Ephran and Kaahli's nest. Or all alone by The Pond when he went exploring. She'd said no. What could she say? Did he expect her to embarrass herself by saying she was afraid? Did he expect her to beg him to let her tag along? Besides, she didn't think she would be afraid. How could it happen? How could she revert to that frightened little gray squirrel from Corncrib Farm...after all she'd gone through? And so far, for many days and nights, she'd been able to control the fear.

Janna stopped short of Klestra's den. She was winded. She sat in the low branches of an ironwood tree, trying to catch her breath, straining to see movement, any movement, in the nearby woods. All she saw was a bird, possibly a hawk, flying away from her, high above Rocky Creek. Was it carrying something? No time for idle curiosity. She had to find Klestra.

Air finally filled her chest again. She ran to Klestra's tree and looked inside the tiny hole. The tree was empty. Nothing on the earth but a big old pinecone. He was gone. Who knew where? Or for how long?

What if something happened to him? What if he never came back? What if he was unable to come back? And why hadn't Rennigan decided to stick around for a while? But she remembered what Ephran had said of his old fox squirrel friend: He was a wanderer, paws itchier than Klestra's. Before he left, Rennigan had told her and Klestra that he would be off, to learn what he could about Ephran and Kaahli. Maybe she should do the same thing. Obviously, everyone had deserted her, had taken off to learn things and have adventures.

Besides, what if the Many Colored hunters returned to The Pond? Where could she hide? Klestra's nest was too small for her. And the hunters must know about Ephran and Kaahli's den.

There was only one choice. She would go home. She should have gone long ago. Ephran and Frafan weren't the only ones who could find their way around the woods. She could do it too. She had learned a bit about her surroundings here. She had traveled along Rocky Creek twice, once with Frafan and once with Klestra. She knew where that path led...to the Farm of Cages.

She had heard Ephran say to Frafan, "If you know where one place is, and want to get to another, simply go the other way." Though that didn't sound quite right, she convinced herself that would be the way to find home...to Jafthuh and Odalee...to Corncrib Farm. Quite simply then, she would set off in the other direction, away from Rocky Creek's path.

"I must eat first," she told herself aloud, being as calm and serious as she could. "If I'm to travel I must fill my stomach as full as I can." She had heard Ephran talk like that too.

Janna turned on the branch and ran back along the edge of The Pond. She curled in Ephran's nest and finished the walnut she'd dropped. She found another. It was bitter. She ate it anyway. She tried to ignore her feelings, but fright and excitement caused her heart to pound in her ears. She told herself she could do it. Home wasn't so far. She would see places she'd recognize...places that would help her find the right path.

She left the nest, turning once more to look across the frozen water toward Klestra's tree. An almost overwhelming urge to stay right here came over her. Her eyes felt sleepy. Visions of snowstorms raced through her mind. Badgers with red teeth and rabbits with scarred faces filled her imagination.

But she knew she could not stay here. Despite the dread that filled her chest, despite the fact that there was plenty to eat, she could not stay. She had been here too long already. She might not starve, but her breath would cease from sheer loneliness.

She began running, tree to tree, up Great Hill. Now, all by herself, traveling once again during the wrong season, she wished she'd listened more closely to Frafan and Ephran when they spoke of finding their way in the woods. It occurred to her that what she was doing was almost exactly what Ephran had done: setting off through the woods without experience, companions, or a sure destination. Only he'd had the advantage of starting out at the end of the cold season. Now, as far as she could tell, it was far from over.

By the time she reached the crest of Great Hill, Janna's legs felt heavy. She rested in a massive hackberry tree for a moment before setting out again.

Going downhill was much easier. A brook appeared ahead. Klestra had spoken of this quiet stream, on the far side of Great Hill. It was called Bubbling Brook. It was not bubbling now, of course. It was good to find anyway. Waterways made good paths, she knew that much. Like Rocky Creek, which she and Frafan had followed to The Pond. If one got really lost, a brook was an easy thing to follow back to your starting point.

She'd not traveled far before she came to a place where no trees grew on the other side of the brook. Instead, there was a large barren meadow, surrounded by an orderly placement of thick sticks sprouting from the ground, all connected by a thorny vine. Snow covered the short brown grass within the vine. She knew what this was...a place to keep cows. But the enclosure was deserted now, the snow unbroken.

Janna was about to move on when her eye caught a bright red blotch against white snow, partly hidden by a small oak tree at the corner of the meadow. A fox perhaps? Too small for a fox. Perhaps a late-falling oak leaf laying on the snow. No, whatever it was, was not on the ground. It seemed attached to a branch. Too large for a leaf.

Her breath left her all at once. A squirrel! She was looking at a squirrel. A red squirrel, no doubt, but a squirrel nevertheless...sitting motionless on the lower limb of the oak.

"Klestra!" she was about to shout. But, before the words reached her lips, she realized this squirrel may or not be Klestra. He or she was too far away to be sure. How wonderful anyway! Someone to talk to!

She ran as fast as she dared, until she scampered to the end of a branch on a small ash tree that stood right next to the red squirrel's oak.

Breathlessly she said, "Hi there!"

The little red squirrel, a female with a thick and lovely pelt, must have seen Janna coming. If her eye moved, it was the only part of her that did. Her lips certainly did not.

"I said hello," Janna repeated.

"Are you talking to me?"

Janna looked around. There was not another breathing thing in sight.

"Of course I'm talking to you. My name is Janna. I can't begin to tell you how pleased I am to find someone else out and about. I was beginning to think I was the only squirrel in this part of the woods. Bitter Berries! It gets so lonesome after a time! You know what I mean?"

The red squirrel looked straight ahead and said nothing.

"Are you ignoring me?" asked a shocked Janna.

The red squirrel snorted through her nose and said, "I'm doing my best. It's not easy. You are a chatterbox. And grays accuse red squirrels of making too much noise!"

"I beg your pardon," said Janna, "I was only trying to be friendly."

"Friendly? What sort of nonsense is friendly?"

"Nonsense? What do you mean 'nonsense'? What is nonsense about stopping to spend a little time with another creature in this cold and lonely forest?"

"Are you blind? Can you see what color I am?"

"I can see very well what color you are...oh, I understand. Red and gray."

"Exactly. You must be looney. Be on your way then."

Janna sat on her branch for a moment, then folded her tail around her. "You want me to leave?" she asked.

The red squirrel turned toward Janna. Their eyes met. The red squirrel's lip quivered. Her eyes looked puffy. It struck Janna that she'd been crying.

"Not really," the red squirrel said...so quietly Janna could barely hear her.

"Are you lost?"

"Yes. You?"

"Nearly."

"Alone?"

"Pretty much. How about you?"

"Totally." The red squirrel took a long breath. "You said your name is Janna. Mine is Lylah."

"Hello again, Lylah." Janna cleared her throat. "I know of a warm nest not too far from here. With lots of food. Would you like to come there with me?"

Lylah tilted her head, as though trying to look through or behind Janna. "You're serious, aren't you?" she said.

"Of course I'm serious. The only creatures that might joke about food during the cold season are crows. Do I look like a crow?"

"No, you don't," answered Lylah with a giggle.

"How about it, then? Why don't we keep one another company in a warm place? Besides, you may be interested in meeting a friend of mine who spends a lot of time around these parts."

"Thank you, Janna."

CHAPTER VIII
OLDER AND WISER, TIMES TWO

Rain and warming sun had melted most of what snow was left. Fewer and fewer white patches could be seen, following the curves of hillocks and valleys, intermixed with matted brown leaves and occasional brave and bold green shoots. There were tracks in the few shrunken drifts that remained. Rennigan could see his own, here and there. Foxes.' A red squirrel's. Deer and rabbit tracks, as always.

The grizzled fox squirrel gazed at the bare trees, standing like lonely sticks. He saw no gray squirrels in the branches. There had been only one all day, that a female. He'd stopped and talked to her for a while. She'd heard of Ephran, but knew only that he was "a different sort." And she did not seem especially interested in talking. That was the story of his search, really. Nobody had much to say. They'd all heard of Ephran. Some had looked for him, some hadn't. Some offered the opinion that his breath must be gone. Thundersticks were fatal things. But, if he hadn't been carried off in the paw of a Many Colored One, and if he wasn't in his nest at The Pond, then nobody could say for sure where he was. There had been nothing seen or heard of him since that terrible day he fell.

Far off, in the very top of a tall green ash tree (which was anything but green right now), and yet far below him and his perch on High Hill, were two crows, fluffed against the chill in the air. They were silent, as was the entire woods. He'd had no success in getting information from crows. They either ignored his questions or gave garbled and unintelligible answers.

Rennigan sighed, long and deep. Then he shivered once and crawled through a tight hole in the tree and into one of his leafy nests.

What to do next. Where to go. Was there any hope at all? And why did he bother? Animals of the forest disappeared all the time. He sure knew that. He'd been around this old woods long enough to have seen plenty of them snatched away. Usually in the claws of a hunter.

Rennigan tossed and turned. Too much to think about. Too frustrating to try and figure where to look for a treeclimber who may well have left the woods on a duck's back. Where should he start? Might Ephran and that mallard duck have flown far away, to warm water and trees always green? Just how far could a mallard carry a fullgrown gray squirrel? And, if he had indeed seen a squirrel astride a duck, how could he know that squirrel was Ephran? The air had been full of big snowflakes that day. Maybe one of those gorgeous, irregular flakes, resting for a moment on his eyelash, had made him think he'd seen a furry tail growing from the duck's back. Who could know?

Snorting and shaking his head, he pretended the drops of water in his eyes did not exist. Ah, lost friends, young and old. Dingbinged whippersnapper of an Ephran had gotten under his fur, that was the problem. Lost, like that, when he was such a young 'un. Cute little critter he'd been, with his bushy tail and bottomless stomach. Such a curious little cuss. Had to know about everything. Asked about things Rennigan hadn't even thought of. Clever too. Rennigan had learned that Ephran's talk had not been all "braggin'" when he said he'd outsmarted a fox, an owl, and a cat. And brave...no question of that. He'd seen and heard enough proof of his young friend's courage.

He rolled over again. This nest was definitely not among his more comfortable ones. It was lumpy from rolled-up leaves and broken sticks. Drafty besides. Rennigan finally sat up, twitched his nose, and decided to sit outside on a branch and watch the sunset.

As he spread himself out on a thick limb, Rennigan smiled and sighed. This was his favorite time of day. It had been Ephran's too. Maybe sunrise was as spectacular, but he never had believed in getting up early enough to really judge the matter.

The sun, seeming to move at a snail's pace through the bright hours, now sank so rapidly past the edge of the earth that he could actually watch it disappear. Streaks of red colored the snow. Bare trees threw long angular shadows far down the hillsides. Tiny gray clouds, for an instant, assumed a fire and glory they would not see again. Blazing red slowly cooled to orange, then pink, and at last became a gentle glow. Not now, but during the warm season, birds of all kinds would bid the sun farewell with their most pleasing and harmonious songs.

Just as the sun rode over the edge of the world, Rennigan felt the fur on his neck stand straight up. No time to think. And no need. He swung all his weight, as quickly as he could, off the side of the limb. Nearly falling, he gripped the underside of the big branch for an instant. Then he scrambled, heart pounding, around the trunk and into the hole.

Rennigan felt, more than he saw, a big bird sail on by, sharp claws extended. By the time the owl turned and fluttered back to the tree, Rennigan was safe inside.

"Whooo!" it hooted. "Missed again."

"Winthrop!" Rennigan shouted from inside the hole, "y'old dusty bundle a feathers! Is that you?"

"Whoo? You? Of course it is I. What other owl would dare hunt my territory?"

"Shoulda figured," said Rennigan, poking his nose out of the hole. "Why do ya keep doin' this?"

The big white owl tipped his head at Rennigan. "Doing what?"

"You know full well what yer doin'," said the squirrel. "Tryin' to scare the breath outa me with this swoopin' nonsense. Why? Ya know I'm too big t'carry and too tough t'eat."

"Hmmm. You are correct, of course. No mistaking you for a plump young cottontail. But I need the exercise, you see."

"Exercise, schmexercise. You just like t'bug me. To see me scramble."

"Well, I suppose that might be part of the fascination," agreed the owl with a smile. "But there is a contest here, you understand. I want to prove something to you."

"If yer callin' this a game, I won it a long time ago," said Rennigan. "You musta missed me twenty times if ya missed once."

"True. I have missed. The possibility exists that I've wanted to. But this is a game where only the last point counts."

"Last point counts? What's that s'posed to mean?" asked Rennigan.

"You know very well what I mean. You are getting older and slower every day," sneered the owl.

"Ah. And I s'pose you think yer gettin' younger and quicker. Great Green Grasshoppers, owl, yer easier to git away from now than you was two seasons ago."

Winthrop lifted a wing and scratched under it with his beak. "I told you, I've been toying with you."

"Catch me anytime you wanted to, eh?" said Rennigan, and he moved his forelegs out of the hole.

"Absolutely."

"What would you do if you caught me?"

Winthrop gazed over at Rennigan with bright yellow eyes. He opened his beak, as though to bite. Then he laughed. "Let you go before you chewed both my legs off, you grizzled, bug-infested, worn-out old branchjumper."

"You got that much right," Rennigan laughed back, and crawled entirely out of the nest.

They sat in the tree, nighthunter and treeclimber, unmoving among the branches, while the sun sunk lower and the sky became darker and darker. Finally Winthrop said;

"Do you still search?"

Rennigan's head swiveled toward the owl.

"Search?"

"Yes. No need to act surprised. I know you are looking for something. And I have a fairly sound assessment of what it is you search for."

"Wowee! You must be one smart ol' owl. Tell me whut I'm lookin' for."

"For your friend. You're looking for that tricky little imp that escaped me by jumping into the snow. Was a night much like this. An escape much like yours. You know the one, the same gray squirrel that nearly caused the loss of my eyes to a pair of crows."

Rennigan shook his head slowly. "Yep. Guess you do know. And guess I am lookin.' How'd you know?"

"You've been asking a lot of questions in the woods," said Winthrop. "Word gets around."

Rennigan squinted at the owl. "Why'd you bring Ephran up?" he asked.

"Oh, I don't know. Just interested perhaps."

Rennigan said, "I think yer more'n interested. I think you know somethin' I might like to know."

Winthrop flapped his big wings and laughed. "Me? A simple old white owl know something wise old Rennigan does not know? Highly unlikely, is it not?"

"C'mon, y'old thief. What you hidin' under those itchy feathers of yers?"

"I'm quite certain that I have no obligation to tell you anything," said the owl.

Rennigan sighed and his shoulders slumped. "S'pose you don't."

"Then again," continued Winthrop, putting a wingtip to his beak, "that young treeclimber outsmarted both me and Maltrick. He caused Blackie to quit hunting altogether. Maybe he's worth keeping track of after all. If, for no other reason, so that I know where to hunt and where not to."

The fox squirrel sat up on the branch, muscles tense.

Winthrop cleared his throat. "A screech owl friend of mine nests at the edge of the Many Colored Ones warren," he said. "Never could understand why he thinks it's such a wonderful place. He says a lot of mice nest there. Personally, I don't care that much for mice. No accounting for taste, I suppose..."

"C'mon, c'mon!" said Rennigan. "Quit stallin'. Tell me if you're gonna tell me. Keep still if you ain't."

"Control yourself, old fellow. I am uncertain if what I heard means anything. This friend of mine just says he witnessed a most unusual thing. A thing involving gray squirrels."

"And what sorta thing was that?" asked Rennigan, growing more and more impatient.

"He said he heard a few gray treeclimbers from the deep woods spent the cold season in the park on the far side of the warren. He has no idea how they got there. Or what they were doing there. In any case, he said some sort of bad feeling has developed between them. Between the warren squirrels and those from the deep woods."

"Bad feelin's?"

"Yes. Bad feelings. You know. Bad feelings like those between foxes." Winthrop smiled. "Or owls."

"Ah, I know what ya mean. Territory. No room for strangers or their ideas, eh?" said Rennigan.

"Seems that way," agreed Winthrop.

"So the warren treeclimbers want the newcomers out. Right?"

"Well, that's the reason I thought you should know. That's why I thought I might give you a direction to search." Winthrop looked directly into Rennigan's eyes. He said, "See what that goofy young treeclimber's done to us? Here I am, a reputable great white owl, telling a fox squirrel, of all worthless creatures, where to go to perhaps lend a paw to a gray squirrel that might badly need it! Makes no sense..." Winthrop shook his head.

"Yeah, yeah...go on. So the deep woods folk'll move on. Well 'n good. Suspect this is the direction they'd wanta come anyway. Why should I stick this old, bruised snout inta this business?"

"Yes...well...things are not quite that simple. It seems those warren squirrels are not interested in a simple departure of the woods squirrels from their warren. They plan to, pardon the expression, tear them into small pieces."

CHAPTER IX

MEMORIES

No, I'm afraid that branch will not serve the purpose," Cloudchaser said, doing his best not to laugh.

"Why not? What's the matter with it?" Elgan, the male grouse, was balanced precariously on the stem of an elderberry bush. Barely thicker than his leg, the slender twig bent and shuddered under his weight.

"If you're going to try and build a nest for two fullgrown grouse, you have to start by finding a branch much sturdier than that one. And, don't forget, you have to take into account the weight of the nesting material as well," said Cloudchaser.

Deela, Elgan's mate, lay on the earth. She rubbed her beak in the fallen red and yellow leaves, looked up, and asked, "What I'd like to know, Cloudchaser, is why you feel so strongly about nests in trees. Since when do mallards nest in such places?"

"They don't, Deela," said Cloudchaser. "But they do protect themselves by putting deep water between their nests and the hunter. That might do for you too, but I know you prefer trees to water. Besides, other birds put their nests in trees."

"So do squirrels and raccoons, but that doesn't make it right for us," pouted Elgan.

"Indeed, some animals nest in trees," said Cloudchaser, "and I have no intention of forcing you to do anything you don't want to do. However, you seem so certain that a fox will eventually find your earth nest I thought...well, speaking of foxes... Deela!...Quickly!...up here!"

The female grouse knew a warning when she heard one. She exploded from her earthen perch and fluttered up to the big drake. A red fox squirted through the underbrush, sliding to a stop right where Deela had left the ground warm. The fox seemed surprised to find himself all alone.

"Good day, Mr. Fox," said Cloudchaser.

Elgan became so excited at the prospect of talking to a fox that his slender perch once again swayed wildly, and he, too, was forced to spread his wings. He flew to join his mate and Cloudchaser.

The fox frowned and looked up. The sight of a mallard, perched in a tree with two grouse, made him close his eyes for a moment and shake his head. The hunter said, "I don't believe I've ever seen anything like this before. I have to speak to you. I have to ask. What brings such unlikely feathered ones together...and what are you all doing up there in a tree?"

"Trying to find a reasonable place for a nest, if you must know," said Deela.

The fox laughed. "A nest? For whom?"

"Why, for us," said Deela.

"Grouse nesting in a tree? Who ever heard of anything so foolish? And a mallard up there as well. Now that I think of it, what is a duck doing anywhere, tree or otherwise, when every bit of water in these parts is frozen solid?"

"The mallard is giving us advice on how and where to build," said Elgan, puffing out his breast feathers.

"And, not that it's any of your business, but he is here because he was ill and got left behind," said Deela.

The fox sat down. "This gets better all the time. Where did the mallard learn how a tree nest should be built?"

The grouse turned to Cloudchaser. "Good question. I suppose from other birds," said Deela.

"Actually," said Cloudchaser, "a treeclimber and myself had a number of discussions concerning the construction of dens... both water and tree dens."

"A treeclimber?" said the fox. "Let me get this straight: You had discussions about the finer points of den-building with a squirrel?"

"That's a matter of fact," said Cloudchaser. "I think he was pretty good at building tree nests. And his mate was better. Perhaps you've heard of them, though they nested a long way from here...."

"I don't want to hear about them," the fox said loudly. "You are, quite obviously, one crazy duck. Who ever heard of a duck and a squirrel talking about how to construct dens? Squirrels eat duck eggs. And, if those grouse build a nest in a tree, I think they're as crazy as you are."

"Since you can't climb or fly, I would have guessed you might disapprove," said Cloudchaser. "This kind of craziness among birds, if it spread too far, might lead to a permanent fox diet of mice and grasshoppers. And, for your information, not all squirrels raid duck nests."

The fox sat for a moment. "I'm not going to waste my time on you." He slowly got to his paws and trotted off.

"Well," Cloudchaser said, "there's one visit by the fox that left all of us whole and full of breath."

"Kind of fascinating," said Elgan with a lopsided grin, "talking nonsense with a fox like that. Our youngsters would have fainted to see me jawing with a hunter."

"How did you know the fox was about to pounce?" asked Deela.

"Another advantage of trees," said Cloudchaser. "I hope you noticed that the fox didn't bother to look up, a common failing among most earth creatures. So he didn't know I was here. On the other wing, from up here I could clearly see him sneaking along behind the bushes."

"The idea is interesting," said Elgan, "but tree-nesting is not grouse-like. I really doubt that I'd be comfortable sleeping in a tree."

"Nor I, I suppose," agreed Deela.

"All I wanted to do was to show you an option. Someplace safer. At least from foxes."

"Thank you, Cloudchaser. That was thoughtful. It may be, however, that grouse must be grouse, safe or not," said Deela.

"And ducks should be ducks, I suppose," said the big drake. "The time for flying is come. My mind grows impatient. My thoughts turn always to Marshflower...and my young ones."

"I understand," said Deela. "It is not good to be away from loved ones. Especially when they don't even know breath is still strong in you."

"Do you feel fit enough to fly?" asked Elgan.

"I think so. I think I am ready."

"If that be the case, I will hope for fair winds behind your wings," said Deela.

"I will always be grateful for the help you gave. I will not forget cloander seed and grouse who care."

"Grouse who had to learn to care," corrected Deela.

"Hope you find your mate," said Elgan.

His takeoff from the branch was awkward, but Cloudchaser lifted himself over the trees, quacked twice at the grouse below, and turned his face toward the place of warm air.

He'd tried his wings only twice since that frightening day that he'd fallen from the sky, stomach knotted in pain. Deela's cloander seed had almost certainly saved him. And he found the grouses' diet of catkins and buds from small plants, protected from the cold season under fallen leaves, to be quite delicious. When he had recovered a bit, they'd gone together, on foot mostly, and raided a nearby Many Colored Ones' field for leftover grain. Now that was his kind of food! Over the next few days he felt his strength rapidly return.

He had learned a valuable lesson about what not to eat. He decided that, if he had the chance to fly again, he would watch for grain fields. The Many Colored Ones almost always left a great deal behind after They took what They wanted. It was not good to depend totally on ponds and marshes for food.

As it turned out, the only really troublesome thing about the days he spent with Elgan and Deela was that his chances of catching up to Marshflower were even slimmer than they'd been when he started out. But he was so much stronger than he'd been when he left the Farm of Cages that he felt somehow the whole adventure, terrible cramps and all, had been worthwhile.

Cloudchaser adjusted his wings to a slight shift in wind

direction. His heading was far from where he wanted to go, but a fairly stiff breeze blew from his right side. If he did not fly at an angle, into the wind, he would be blown a long way from his destination.

He lifted himself higher and higher. A thin veil of clouds spread out below him. The earth became hazy. There was little to watch or to think about. Cloudchaser let his mind drift, back in time, away to the big lake where his parents always spent the cold season, the place where the air and water were always warm.

In his mind he saw himself, young and curious, flying for the first time that exhaustingly long flight to the warm lake. He recalled wishing that he had the bright green head, the full breast feathers, and the mature voice of the older males. He distinctly remembered how very tired he was after that test of wings and wit. Youth would not admit weariness, of course, but he was relieved to see his parents set their wings and begin the final descent toward blue water.

He was proud he'd made it so far, and happy that his entire family — mother and father as well as his brother and sisters, had survived the tiring journey from the cold country. Not all of their friends had.

The place mother and father had come, season after season, was a wonderfully warm and private area. The lake was huge, dotted with many small islands and thick with a wonderful variety of waterfood. Many mallard families came here to make their nests. Other kinds of ducks too — teals, gadwalls, wood ducks, and pintails. There was room for everyone, though the different families kept pretty much to themselves.

One particular day, that first season in the warm lake, would always stay in his memory. He had decided he would try a new spot to feed, a quiet little bay he'd noticed when he and his brother were returning from a short flight before darktime. To find a new feeding place would prove he was an adult. So, early the next morning, while everyone else slept, he paddled quietly away from his family, spread his wings, and lifted into the still air.

When he swung around a grassy point, into the cove, he found that his secret feeding place was no secret after all. A young female mallard was already there, dunking beneath the surface, pulling up crispy white and green tubers. At first he was irked that anyone would dare invade his spot.

That feeling disappeared quickly when he noticed that this young hen was one he'd had his eye on. Her family nested a short distance from his. He had hoped he'd get a chance to talk to her, and tried to think of a way to impress her. It seemed his chance had come. He slid into the water. She looked over at him. He pretended to ignore her. He swam, head held high, into deeper water. She was still watching. He could feel her eyes.

She broke the silence. "It's too deep out there."

"Think so?" he answered airily.

"Yes. I tried it. The food under the water looks good, but it is too far down to reach."

"Not for me," he said, fluffing up his breast as big as he could. Then he took a deep breath.

He tipped below the surface and stretched his neck. The appetizing plants were indeed a lot further down than they had looked through the clear water. He stretched more but could still not reach them. Maybe he'd have to dive after all. How embarrassing!

He pushed himself to the surface to catch a breath. If he had to, he'd submerge completely. He'd show this bright-eyed female a thing or two about food-gathering!

He glanced at her, prepared to smile. The female's eyes were intense. She was saying something, loudly. He could not understand her. He sat in the water, dumbly, looking at her, trying to clear his ears. Now she was screaming! Suddenly she flew directly at him, wings spread wide and feet out. What sort of crazy duck was this? She was attacking him!

Cloudchaser jumped from the water to meet her mad charge. Just as he did so, the water beneath him foamed and frothed wildly. An open mouth, row upon row of tiny jagged teeth, appeared just under his tail feathers. Then the backfin of a huge fish slid by.

He and the female met with a soft "Thud!" Feathers floated to the water. They both managed to stay in the air. He fluttered after her, a short distance down the shoreline, where they settled down into shallow and safer water.

She smoothed her feathers. He put his beak in the water, as though searching for something. The water felt cool against his hot face. After a while, when he was almost out of breath, he lifted his head.

"Thank you," he said sheepishly.

She smiled. "It's not very easy to get your attention."

"The water was too deep for feeding," he said, mainly because he couldn't think of anything else to say.

"And unfortunately, just about the right depth for that very large fish," she said.

"Yes. I wonder what it would have done with me."

"Almost got a mouth full of tailfeathers," she laughed.

He laughed too. "Doesn't sound very appetizing, does it?"

They giggled and looked at one another. "What is your name?" he asked.

"I am called Marshflower," she had said. "And you are Cloudchaser. I have to admit that I have been asking about you."

"The water...foamed
and frothed wildly."

The memory of Marshflower made his eyes water. He could not put her from his mind. She had been so lovely. So open and honest. And she had saved him. "Ah, my dear," thought Cloudchaser, "those foolish and carefree days seem so long ago. Where are you now? I need you."

The sun was sinking low in the sky. He'd been up here a long time. Once again he had an empty stomach and heavy wings. Far below, a small patch of water, nearly iceless, shimmered in the last rays of light.

"Ducks on this little pond," he thought. "Look like pintails, not mallards. It means I am catching up though. And it looks like there might be food here."

As he sailed over the glistening water he glanced down, looking for a good spot to settle. Among the reeds, in the shallow water ahead, were another small group of birds he hadn't noticed from higher above. There were seven of them. It was growing dark and hard to see, but the ducks in the reeds did not appear to be pintails. Too large for teal, too small for snow geese.

Mallards! "Good!" Cloudchaser thought wearily. A place to rest among his own kind. Maybe he could learn something here. Perhaps there would stragglers from earlier flights.

A graceful hen, partly hidden in high weeds, looked up. He saw her at the same moment she saw him. Her eyes grew wide, closed, and opened wide again. Cloudchaser tried to quack. The sound caught in his throat. He settled into the water, unable to take his eyes from hers. His landing was every bit as clumsy as that which had so frightened Deela and Elgan. This time, though, there were no stomach cramps. There was a different feeling — a feeling so strong, so deep, so intensely happy — that he would never be able to describe it. Never.

He fell forward, onto his breast, skimming the water. He hardly noticed. His gaze remained fixed on her. He righted himself. He swam toward her and she toward him, neither of them able to make a sound.

One of the young hen mallards looked up quizzically. Her mother's eyes were flooded with tears! She cocked her head, the question for her mother in her beak. Why did mother swim so rapidly toward this drake...? Then she knew.

"Father!" said the young hen, "Oh...my father!"

CHAPTER X

SUCCESS WITH A DIRTY FACE

A re you certain...," said Payslee.

"...that this is...," said Flutterby.

"...the way to The Pond," finished Peppercorn.

"Y'bet I'm sure," said Fred confidently. Then, mumbling under his breath, "Purty sure, anyways."

The pigeon sisters, perched on a thick aspen branch, wore concerned looks. The yellow-haired dog flashed them a big smile. Then he continued along the waterway, sniffing at clumps of weed or wood, digging in the sandy soil as if he wanted to see exactly where each and every scraggly plant stem was attached.

Air bubbles could be seen in the streambed, moving along beneath a thin, opaque layer of ice. Sun and warm air would soon turn it all to water.

How come, Fred wondered, nobody had any faith in his ability to find what he was looking for? How come nobody gave him any ding-binged credit for being able to learn? After all, hadn't the best searcher in these parts given him lessons? Hadn't Ephran taught him a few tricks about using wind and sun and trees and waterways to find what had to be found? And hadn't he proved how clever he was by showing the pigeon sisters how to loosen the vine that fastened him to the tree? Never mind that the knot was poorly tied.

For a moment he wished he was back at The Farm of Cages. Who knew how many wonderful meals he was missing? But there was important business to attend to. He needed help. More precisely, he was convinced that Ephran, Frafan, and Kaahli needed help. And where would he find help for treeclimbers? Not in the warren of Many Colored Ones, that was for sure. He'd have to seek help from Ephran's friends. And he understood there were plenty of those around The Pond.

Stale Bisquits! These pigeon ladies, dear though they be, were just getting him confused. He was more than a mite pleased with himself for having found and followed what he figured had to be Rocky Creek. And he was immensely proud of remembering that Rocky Creek was supposed to lead directly to The Pond. So what was the pigeons' problem?

They flapped to another tree, moving ahead, up the stream. One by one they turned to face the dog.

"If this is Rocky Creek," said Flutterby.

"Then why isn't it full of rocks?" asked Peppercorn.

"Supposedly, that's how it got its name, you know," said Payslee.

Fred did not break stride. "Small matter," he said, with as much disdain as he could muster. Rocks and water. Water and rocks. Ephran had never mentioned using rocks to find the right path. Such silliness.

"We should have..."

"Reached Rocky Point..."

"By this time."

"We think you...," said Peppercorn.

"Are following your stream...," said Payslee.

"In the wrong direction," said Flutterby.

"Blather," muttered Fred, softly enough so that the birds could not hear him.

But just around a gentle bend he could see where the stream ended. And it did not end, like Rocky Creek was supposed to, in a big puddle of water. Instead it ended in countless trickles and rivulets, erupting like gooseberry branches from a small hillock thick with bushes.

Fred sat down and began to scratch his flank. The pigeons exchanged glances.

"Well, Fred, you might as well confess," said Payslee.

"That we're on the wrong end of the stream," said Flutterby.

"And that we best set out the other way," said Peppercorn.

Fred sneezed and rubbed his nose. Wrong way, huh? Maybe. Then again, maybe not. Though his mistake was now obvious, no embarrassment showed on Fred's face. He was too busy thinking. This place looked awful familiar. More proof, of course, that it wasn't The Pond — he'd never been to The Pond.

Wait a blinkin' minute! Last time he came this way he got only as far as Rocky Point before he met Frafan, Klestra and Janna. They'd turned around then, and headed back toward the Farm of Cages. That's why it seemed like he'd been here before. He had been! Fred collected himself and stood tall.

"Ladies," he announced solemnly, "whether you think we come the wrong way or not, we come this way fer a reason."

"A reason?" they said together, and looked curiously down from their tree.

"'A course. A reason. Ol' Fred always got a reason."

"Well, ol' Fred...," said Peppercorn.

"Would it be too much trouble...," said Flutterby.

"To let us in on why we find ourselves on the wrong end of Rocky Creek?" said Payslee.

"No problem," said Fred. "Reason is that a gentle male gray squirrel makes his nest here 'bouts." He smiled broadly up at the pigeons once again.

"So — there's a gray squirrel nearby," said Peppercorn.

"Considering that this is a woods...," said Payslee.

"Having squirrels here and there is not particularly unusual," said Flutterby.

"Ya don't understand," said Fred. "This here gray squirrel's a friend. Papa of Kaahli, Ephran's mate."

"Very nice," said Flutterby.

"So this treeclimber happens to be a relative of one of those for whom we search," said Peppercorn.

"We still don't see what good it will do to find him," said Payslee.

"That's cuz ya don't know him." Fred wiggled his nose. "This here treeclimber's sumthin' else when it comes to clever. Knows lots about the woods, about where to look fer other squirrels, where to find friends."

"Ah!" said Payslee.

"I see," said Peppercorn.

Flutterby eyed Fred. Then she shook her head and smiled.

"I'll give you the benefit of the doubt, Fred. Lead on. Let's find this wise treeclimber of yours."

Fred puffed out his chest and coughed importantly.

"Right up over this here little hill, I 'spect," he said. And he set out, marching over the wet leaves and up the incline soaked with insistent trickles of water.

The cold season had not yet surrendered its grip on the woods. Under a covering of very slippery leaves and slick brown mud was a layer of still-frozen earth. This combination did not lend itself to solid pawholds.

Fred suddenly realized that the terrain under him was not the most dependable, especially for uphill travel. But he'd come this far and had convinced his companions that they'd reached an important goal, even though it was not the intended one. He was too proud to admit another mistake, retreat, and go around the hill. He was, come Bare Bones or Spoiled Milk, going to convince these pigeons that he was a confident and dependable leader. Then, just as he was nearing the top of the hill, and despite ever-so-carefully placed steps, he found his paws sliding out from under him.

"Wow! Wow!" Fred barked, as his hindlegs slipped backward and his forelegs went sideways.

"WHUMP!"

Fred's floppy ears sailed like wings. His chin met the muddy earth at the same time his belly did. Black ooze splattered onto his face. He tried to right himself, too quickly. He barely got his paws under him when he lost his balance and slipped again, this time falling over sideways. He rolled over and over, all the way back down the hill.

"Fred!" shouted Payslee.

"Are you hurt?" asked Flutterby.

"Can you stand up?" inquired Peppercorn.

Fred lay there, on his back, looking up through half-closed lids, at thin clouds high in the sky. Maybe he should stay right where he was, pretend he was asleep. Or like his breath was gone. Maybe, if he didn't talk or move, the pigeons would tire of staring down at him. Maybe they'd just fly off. Maybe they would shake their heads, say "Poor old dog," and leave him and his embarrassment to themselves.

But they didn't. They sat there, saying nothing, waiting for Fred to get up. It was terrible lying there, trying not to show you were breathing, feeling cold water running across your tummy, feeling mud drying and itching in your ears. It was no use. He was quite sure he could not lay still any more.

"Fred, you haven't changed a bit."

Fred lay on the ground, paws in the air, keeping his eyes tightly closed. Whose voice was that? Sure didn't sound like no pigeon. Had Flutterby become hoarse?

"Come on, you faker," said the voice. "It's quite obvious you couldn't have been hurt sliding around in that soft goo."

"Aden!" he cried, as he struggled to his paws.

Through a vague brown cloud he saw the pigeons' attention shifted to a gray squirrel, seated on the branch of a young linden. He wiped the mud from his eyebrow and the scene cleared considerably.

"What brings you to The Spring again, Fred? And who are your feathered companions?" asked Aden.

"These here are the pigeon sisters," said Fred, carefully sidestepping away from the muddy little streams, and onto solid earth. "Flutterby, Payslee, 'n Peppercorn."

Aden nodded and the pigeons nodded back. "A pleasure, I'm sure," he said, and they murmured,

"Of course."

"Likewise."

"Absolutely."

Fred smiled sweetly, his face splotched and thick fur caked with mud.

"Well," said Aden, after watching Fred grin at all of them in turn, "I'm happy to see you, Fred. But I'm a little puzzled as to what you're doing out here in the woods again. The last time we met, you were headed downstream to visit Ephran and Kaahli. Are you trying to find The Pond again?"

"Oh sure. A course," said Fred. "Me and these here birds come lookin' fer The Pond...I mean, we come lookin' for you. Got news, ya see."

"News, you say..." Aden cocked his head.

"Yeah. Well, actually, had a few bones ta chew the other time too. Didn't get 'em chewed, I guess," Fred said, realizing he hadn't told the old gray squirrel all he knew the last time he visited Spring Hill.

"Before you do a whole lot else, I'd suggest you break the thin ice on Spring Creek and wash yourself up. You look like one big clod of mud," smiled Aden.

"Sure thing," said Fred. "First class idea." Then, to the pigeons, "See. Told ya he was clever."

Flutterby turned to her sisters with a shake of her head. "Just as we thought," she said, "this isn't Rocky Creek at all. It's called Spring Creek."

Fred ignored the comment. He walked slowly to the frozen bank of the creek and gingerly broke the ice. The water was bitterly cold. He stuck his nose under the ice, woofed loudly, and rubbed the mud from his snout. Little by little he washed himself clean. The job took considerable time, and was accompanied by a lot of jumping and dancing and woofing. The pigeons began to fidget on their perches.

"Fred! For Sweet Clover's Sake, tell us...," said Flutterby.

"...What is it that you know about Frafan and...," added Payslee.

"Why you have us all sitting here in these cold branches waiting for your next words," finished Peppercorn.

Aden interrupted. "Frafan?" he said to Fred. "Isn't that Ephran's younger brother? The one who loves to explore? What does he have to do with why you're back in the woods?"

Fred shook himself vigorously and looked up at the gray squirrel.

"Has quite a bit t'do with it, Aden," he said. "Ephran 'n Kaahli been missin' from their nest by The Pond fer some time now. Frafan went lookin' fer 'em. I did too, fer a ways."

Aden's jaw dropped. "Ephran and Kaahli missing? Who says? How? When? When you told me you were going to visit them I thought it was a strange time to be wandering around the woods. But it was you, so... Anyway, were they missing then?"

"Musta been. But I didn't want to git ya all perturbed 'bout nothin," said Fred. "Heard a rumor that Ephran was missin'. Nothin' sure. Didn't really trust whut I heard. Came ta the woods then to find out fer m'self."

Aden took a deep breath and said, "I have to hear the whole story."

"And so ya will, but first I gotta tell these pigeon sisters that the reason I know somethin' about Frafan and where he ended up was I listened real careful to those gray treeclimbers that nests by m'old master's den. This time I kept m'mouth shut and m'big ears wide open." A smile broke out on Fred's face, pleased with the sound of his own words. So he repeated them. "Yessir, mouth shut 'n ears open."

Payslee said, "Well, go on..."

"By all means," said Flutterby.

"Don't stop now," said Peppercorn.

"Okay, okay," said Fred. "Well, them squirrels were like you, all excited. They was talkin' about some deep woods treeclimbers that were nestin' in a place with lots a trees and grass, right in the middle a The Many Colored Ones warren. They said these newcomers were sayin' strange words and doin' stranger things. Said they were tryin' t'get the warren squirrels t'come out here and nest in the deep woods."

"And you think one of these deep woods treeclimbers was Frafan?" asked Aden.

"Heard one of 'em was real small. Skinny tail. Curious sort. Full'a ideas about diggin' and savin'."

"That does sound like Frafan, all right," agreed Aden. "Were there others? Forest squirrels, I mean?"

"Sounded like it. A male 'n female," said Fred.

Aden's eyes grew wide. "You think Frafan found Ephran and Kaahli?"

"Can't figure who else," said Fred.

"Is it possible...," said Peppercorn.

"That they might try to find their way...," said Payslee.

"Back to The Pond?" said Flutterby.

"Sure would think so," said Fred. "That's where I figure they'd git to. If they kin git."

Aden frowned. "What do you mean, Fred, if they kin git?"

"Well," said Fred, "I think them other squirrels meant ta follow the forest squirrels."

"Why would they follow them?" asked Aden. "Did some decide to take the forest squirrels' advice, to come to the woods and find a place to nest?"

Fred's expression turned grim. "Not really. Sounded t'me like they was gonna try and catch 'em. Ya know? Thought we better round up some friends from The Pond. That we ought try an' meet Ephran and Kaahli and Frafan afore those other treeclimbers do. Because the last thing I heard 'em say was they meant to stop those forest climbers and their crazy ideas. Meant to make sure they never got back t'the woods."

CHAPTER XI
WAITING

*T*he days were yet cool, but each seemed a bit warmer and longer than the one before. The occasional snowflakes that fell from the sky turned to water as soon as they touched the earth.

Waiting was the hardest part. The gray squirrel named Frafan, his older brother Ephran, and Ephran's mate, Kaahli, had many long discussions about which route would have the greatest chance of success, about how they must avoid contact with the Many Colored Ones as best they could, about the prospects of ending up where they wanted to end up. And exactly where they wanted to end up was the first, and perhaps the most difficult, decision of all.

"Are you certain, Ephran, that you really want to go back to The Pond?" Kaahli watched his face, searching for emotions he might not want to show — signs that he was hiding his true feelings. Knowing her mate as she did, she knew he would go where she and Frafan wanted to go — regardless of how the destination might terrify him.

"Kaahli, my dear," he said, "I would be lying if I told you I do not seek the deep woods without fear. I don't know what to expect anywhere anymore. But The Pond is home. It was when we left it, and I can only hope it will be when we return."

Frafan said, "There was no sign of Many Colored Ones anywhere around The Pond while Janna and I were there with Klestra."

And so the decision was made, the destination set.

Ephran and Kaahli had spent the entire cold season in this little piece of forest The Many Colored Ones had set apart, this place the other squirrels called "park." Neither of them had any clear recollection of the trip from the Farm of Cages in the blue van. Ephran had been recovering from terrible wounds inflicted by a thunderstick. Kaahli was far too concerned for her injured mate, and frightened by the noisy and smelly van itself, to worry about where it was taking them.

Some time later, while searching for his brother, Frafan found himself at the very same farm, in the very same barn, and stowed away in the very same van as Ephran and Kaahli had. Luckily, Frafan had picked up valuable habits from both Ephran and from Blackie, the farm cat. Without even realizing he was doing it, he'd made note of where the sun was that morning the van had sped away from the Farm of Cages. Mostly the sun had sent long shadows pointing in the direction they were traveling, which meant the sun was behind the van. That was of some help. At least they knew they had to travel toward the morning sun to reach the woods.

But that was all they knew — a general direction. They would have to run on the earth at times, when the distance between trees was too far for jumping, or when who-knew-what threatened them. They would have to plan on help: perhaps from landmarks and from wind, clouds and sun. And they would hope for advice from animals and birds they met along the way.

Crows flapped over their nest now and again. Ephran and Frafan had tried to converse with them, but gave it up. Once Frafan actually chased after them, across the park, so desperate was he to get some sort of message to those who waited and wondered in the deep woods. But the crows would not talk to him. One time Ephran tried getting their attention by shouting, "I am Ephran!" It almost worked. One crow had circled around, looked down, and before it flew off said, "Eeyah! Shud pek yur eyes out, liar. Ephran gone. No more Ephran."

The park, though no place to build a permanent nest, had been a decent place to prepare for the trip home. There were few hunters and food was plentiful. The trees, however, were too widely spaced for keeping jumping skills sharp.

Because of this, on days when the air was reasonably warm, Ephran thought of a useful way to fill some of the daylight hours. They exercised. He led his mate and his brother in longer and longer sprints across the still-frozen earth. He made them practice jumping, using branches in the same big tree. He drilled them on constant vigilance for hawks and foxes.

At first they felt silly. The park squirrels watched them, smirks or looks of puzzlement on their faces. But, little by little, the fat beneath their fur became harder to find, and their muscles became tighter and thicker. After runs, which got longer every day, their breath came easier and easier.

Late one morning Ephran, Frafan, and Kaahli lay resting on a wide branch. They had been practicing long jumps in the limbs of a maple. Work had finally become tiresome and degenerated into a game, with the three squirrels shouting and laughing and racing one after the other.

When Frafan's breath returned he said, "When we leave, I can only think it would be wise to avoid the terrible part of The Many Colored Ones' warren I saw through the van's window."

"You mean where no trees or grass grow? Where their dens are close together...the place They tend to swarm?" said Kaahli.

"Yes. I don't know how any creature, other than Themselves, could possibly find its way through there."

Ephran nodded.

Kaahli readjusted her position on the branch to face her mate. "Explain to me again, Ephran," she said, "how we will know which way is home."

Ephran smiled at her. "Do you remember how we set out to

Corncrib Farm after we found your father and brother?"

Kaahli closed her eyes. Then her face lit up. "Yes, I think I do! You said that since we'd traveled so far in one direction, we should not have far to go in the other." She hesitated and frowned. "I'm afraid I still don't know how it's done though."

"When I had tried to find my family earlier, I had traveled sort of cross-current, between where the sun rose and the cold wind blows. In our search for your father and brother we traveled a long way toward where the sun rises. So I knew that, to reach Corncrib Farm, we would have to turn toward the cold wind. Nothing really complicated about it. Do you understand?"

"I think so."

Frafan said, "I do. But if we have to go cross-current again, shall we travel toward the mouth of the cold wind...or the warm?"

Ephran shrugged. "Either will do. Hopefully, if we keep our wits about us, we should be able to remember to turn the right way when the chance to correct our path arises."

"How about my guess?" asked Kaahli.

"Even better," smiled Ephran. "If memory serves correctly, it was your 'guess' that led us from Spruce Hill to Aden and Laslum's cage."

"You mean Kaahli had to direct you to the place of the great rescue?" Frafan asked, an incredulous look on his face.

"That's right, Frafan. Kaahli knew how to find Aden and Laslum when I was out of ideas. What do you say, my dear? Which way? Toward the home of the cold wind or the warm?"

"No question in my mind," said Kaahli. "I'll take warmth anytime."

"It's settled then," said Ephran.

* * * * *

The amount of corn left at the food cage seemed larger than it had been before the bitterly cold time. Part of the reason was that a big bully of a squirrel named Wytail did not keep most of it for himself — or waste it — as he had in the past. Part of the reason was something none of them cared to think about: there simply weren't as many squirrels as there had been before those cold days. While The Many Colored Ones had not made their desperately-needed corn deliveries, squirrels had quietly frozen in their nests.

As for Wytail himself, it seemed he'd changed his ways. Since the day Ephran, with some unwitting help from a group of young Many Colored Ones, faced Wytail down at the food cage, his manners had improved dramatically. No longer did he keep the other squirrels away until he was done eating. He'd gone to the other extreme. Now he didn't approach the food until everyone else had eaten their fill. He'd sit on a nearby hill, tail wrapped around himself...and simply watch. When he finally ate, he spoke to no one. Ephran tried to get him to talk, but questions were answered with a grunt.

Frafan did not like the idea of taking Wytail along, back to the deep woods. His confidence in the big squirrel's motives was not strengthened when he happened to see Wytail talking quietly and privately to a squirrel named Scaffer.

To Frafan's mind, Scaffer was even less trustworthy than Wytail. Scaffer bore watching. Scaffer had been one of the most outspoken and hostile critics of Ephran's offer to lead the park squirrels to a new home in the deep woods. He'd made some nasty comments about "those weird longtails from the deep woods," referring, of course, to Ephran, Kaahli, and Frafan. Since Ephran had made his offer, Scaffer had not spoken directly to any of Frafan's family. And he would sneer in their direction anytime they all happened to be at the food cage at the same time.

Later, when Frafan asked Wytail what Scaffer wanted, Wytail said, "Uhhh...nothin'. Just...ah...Hey! Just askin' a few questions about when we're leaving...stuff like that."

"Why does he care?" asked Frafan.

"Don't know. Maybe he's thinkin' of comin' along," said Wytail with a crooked smile.

That night in the nest Frafan said to his brother, "Ephran, Wytail is one strange squirrel. I don't know what he's thinking. Do we have to take him with us? And his hanging around with that malcontent, Scaffer, really bothers me."

"I invited everyone," Ephran said, "and he was the only one to accept the invitation. We don't have any reason to deny him the chance. I don't think who he picks as friends should be a factor. I guess it would go hard with me in some quarters if everybody judged by that standard."

It was true. Ephran had invited all the gray squirrels in this place to come along: to the clean air, the freedom, the peace and joy of the big woods. When Wytail had been the only one to accept, Frafan had been sure he would eventually change his mind and back out, and that others would decide to come along. So far he'd been wrong on both counts. He'd wondered aloud if the fact that Wytail was coming kept others from doing the same. Ephran had solemnly nodded. It was possible. But it didn't make any difference. Wytail had been on his best behavior ever since Ephran drove The Many Colored Ones away from the food cage. Wytail had every right to find a place for himself in the woods.

Why in this wide world of tall trees, green grass and clear water had Wytail decided to come in the first place? What did Wytail want that the other squirrels didn't? What did Frafan or Kaahli or Ephran say that convinced him to tag along when none of the others would so much as hint they were thinking over the proposal? After having been embarrassed in front of everyone by Ephran's bravery and his own cowardice, could there be another motive?

At first Frafan spent a lot of time trying to unravel the puzzle. But he tired of worrying about something he could do nothing about. He decided time would be better used reviewing and increasing his knowledge of The Many Colored Ones.

And so he took to visiting the edge of the trees to observe The Many Colored Ones in their warren. Ephran agreed that it was a reasonable thing to do. Sometimes the brothers went together, and sometimes Frafan went by himself. Kaahli tagged along once or twice but, more often than not, found watching The Many Colored Ones boring. She soon quit the little jaunts saying, "I hope that the two of you knowing about Them is enough."

There were certainly plenty of Many Colored Dens to investigate. But their favorite, and the one they kept returning to, was a den with many large windows. The family of Many Colored Ones inside was likewise sizeable, numbers-wise. Two big Ones and four smaller Ones nested there.

The den was a two-level affair, located right next to the park. Luckily, tall elm and ash trees grew closeby. Having had experience at this sort of thing, Frafan quickly found a number of comfortable branches, each of which afforded a view of different parts of the den. He found it enjoyable to educate his older brother about those habits of The Many Colored Ones with which he was familiar. Fred and Blackie had added to his knowledge and he could tell Ephran the names of many of the things they saw through the windows.

Most squirrels would have been shocked or puzzled by Frafan's keen interest in these Creatures. Ephran was no longer among them. And there was plenty of new information for Frafan himself to absorb. The group nesting near the park possessed some objects, and did some things, he had never observed when he watched the old couple at Corncrib Farm.

"Amazing!" said Ephran, seated next to Frafan on a high branch one bright day, peering through a large window. "Two of Them. Exactly alike."

Frafan said, "Are you sure there are two, brother? Watch."

A very delicate Many Colored One, almost certainly a female, better than half-grown from what Frafan could tell, stood on Its hind legs in front of what seemed her twin. Every time She made a move, the twin would copy it. Every single action, from adjusting the wrinkles in her pelt to running a thorny branch through her long dark hair, was imitated in every detail.

"What are They doing?" Ephran asked. "Is One making fun of the Other?"

"You are still asking before you think it through. Watch some more."

"Well," Ephran snapped, "I don't know why I should be expected to understand why They do what They do."

"They...," said Frafan, "are not They at all."

Ephran squinted at Frafan. "Are you trying to be funny?"

"Not at all, brother," he smiled. "Look carefully. Think about what you are seeing."

Ephran looked back. He frowned as the Twins leaned close to one another, faces almost touching. He tried to ignore what They were doing...something crazy again...smearing bright red goo on their lips. Then he realized one Twin stood well out into the nest, while the Other was up against the wall. Flat against the wall, actually. She had no depth. His face lit up.

"Reflection!"

"Exactly!" said Frafan. "There is only One. It watches Itself, just as we can watch ourselves in calm water."

"But what reflects is not water. Not standing upright like that, against the wall."

"No. It has to be made of stuff like the windows, something that plays tricks with light, something that can let you see what's in back or what's in front, but not both at the same time."

Ephran nodded soberly. "Yes, Frafan. Not both at the same time. It must be. Very clever."

On some of their visits they found the den empty, but there were still many things about which to wonder. Ephran repeatedly expressed his amazement at how much room there was inside. When The Many Colored Ones were there, their actions were often fascinating. Sometimes, though, They just lay on their backs, facing a large wooden box for hours on end, or sitting on their tailless bottoms, gazing at a sheaf of square white leaves They held in front of their faces.

Frafan delighted in watching his brother's reactions to the little suns They lit and unlit, the way They donned and shed pelts of all colors and kinds, the way They prepared their food from brown packages called boxes and bags, and put it into bright roundish containers called dishes and bowls. Ephran could only shake his head in wonderment at the way They used fire to heat food before They ate it, the way They made water to run from little silver branches in the wall, the way They slept in nests within a nest.

One day, after feeding at the food cage, Wytail followed Frafan and Ephran to what they had come to call their "Watching Tree".

"Hey! Whatd'ya find so interesting?" he asked, perched on a

"Reflection"

branch below them.

"Most everything," Frafan answered.

"What good do you think it's gonna do you, watchin' like this?"

"Who knows?" answered Ephran. "Maybe no good. Maybe a great deal."

"The Ones you're watchin' are just like all the rest, you know. Not worth thinkin' about. They all do crazy things that don't mean nothin'. No way to figure. No way to predict."

"You may be right, Wytail," said Ephran.

As the days grew warmer and warmer, Frafan grew more and more impatient. The first robin had appeared some time ago. There was a hint of sweetness in the air and of promise in the earth. Tiny green stems sprouted in the most unusual places, even in the fissures of The Many Colored Ones' black path.

One evening, as the sun set, they sat on the earth near their nest and chewed on corn and a few tiny green buds Kaahli had discovered. Frafan said, "See this, Ephran? Kaahli found buds today. The warm season is here. Surely the time is come to find our way home."

He was so used to Ephran putting him off, telling him to eat as much as he could, to store up energy, or else just smiling and saying, "Soon, little brother, soon", that his mouth dropped when Ephran said, "Yes, Frafan. The time is come. Tomorrow we leave this place. Tomorrow we turn our faces to the woods."

Frafan closed his eyes and breathed deeply. He opened them to see Kaahli hugging her mate.

"We must sleep now. We'll need our rest. We should be able to find something to eat on the way...I hope," said Ephran.

"Surely we will get help," said Kaahli. "The squirrels who live among the dens of The Many Colored Ones will show us where food might be...and perhaps will know of a path to the woods."

Frafan sighed. "After what I've seen of the squirrels in this place, I think we'd better plan only on what help we can provide ourselves."

Ephran said, "We'll try not to worry. There's always someone around. Someone to help make luck. A Rennigan or a Mayberry. Maybe even a Maltrick."

They curled into the dry leaves and grass, while the last red beams of the sun still colored the greening grass below their tree.

Frafan stood up suddenly. "Wytail!" he said. "I suppose we'll have to find Wytail and tell him we're leaving."

Without lifting his head Ephran said, "Wytail has many eyes and ears in this place. He knows we're leaving."

CHAPTER XII

MAT AND WILLIE

he sun had not yet appeared over the edge of the earth when Frafan found Wytail standing at the base of Ephran and Kaahli's tree.

"Hey! Up there!" the big squirrel shouted. "Let's move those bushy tails! Time t'go."

Kaahli yawned and stretched. Frafan mumbled, "What's his big hurry? He has no idea where he's going or what he's getting himself into."

"We'll be right down," Ephran called back, shaking the sleep from his head.

As always, Ephran and Frafan looked to the sky as soon as they left the nest. A smattering of high and wispy clouds lay motionless above the trees. Calm air was dry on their noses. Countless tiny green and brown buds were forming on the branches, thick and fuzzy in the early morning light.

"Ready t'go?" asked Wytail, as Ephran, Kaahli and Frafan ran down the trunk of the little tree. Frafan thought the big gray seemed nervous. Maybe he should be. He would be totally dependent on them to learn how to survive in the deep woods. His search would begin where theirs ended.

"Soon," Ephran said.

"Before traveling, Ephran insists on eating," said Kaahli.

"Hey!" he said. "If you're thinking of eating, there won't be nothin' yet. No corn by the path for a while."

"I noticed a few buds on some bushes near Queesor's nest," said Frafan.

"And there will be yesterday's leavings at the corn cage. Green buds and yellow corn go well together."

On the way to the corn cage they passed a group of budding bushes. Ephran, Kaahli and Frafan each put a bud or two in their mouths. Then they scampered along the cool earth to the hill overlooking the black path. Frafan noticed that Wytail's eyes were constantly moving, as though watching for something. For hunters? Strange thing to be doing now. He had not seemed to worry about such things before.

"Hey! Still a little corn here," said Wytail.

Golden kernels, left over from the previous day, weren't the best. Obviously stored over the cold season, and shortly before new corn would be growing in The Many Colored Ones' fields, the kernels were brittle and stale. But the fresh buds they ate with it, under greening bushes, made it taste much better.

Wytail ate only corn. For a moment Frafan thought he should say something about getting used to eating buds if one planned on nesting in the deep woods, but he thought better of it.

Very few park squirrels were up and about. They slept later than they used to and wandered to the corn cage only when their stomachs told them to. There was no longer any rush for corn. They no longer had to squabble over Wytail's leavings. All the more reason for the squirrels who had either ignored or faulted Ephran's arguments about nesting in the deep woods to feel smug about staying right here, thought Frafan. He and Ephran and Kaahli were doing them a big favor. They were ridding them of a very large and furry problem. They were taking the bully Wytail away with them.

"Has everyone had enough to eat?" Ephran asked.

Kaahli said, "I made sure I had enough. I'm going to try and avoid unnecessary swims this trip." She winked at Ephran who smiled back at her. Frafan and Wytail nodded that they too had eaten their fill.

"Well, then, I suppose the time is really come," Ephran said. He turned to Kaahli...then to Frafan. He stood on his hind legs and looked all around him, in every direction.

"So we say farewell to this place of puzzlement called a park. This place that belongs to Them, yet They leave it to us. I still don't understand it. Maybe our travels will bring understanding."

He lowered himself to all four paws. His eyes sparkled and his grin grew wide.

"Set your paws to the branch," he said. "We are going home."

They ran swiftly along the earth, across the black path, past the likeness of the Many Colored One astride the horse made of rock, to the edge of the park, where older and taller trees grew close enough for branch jumping. Ephran led the way up the trunk of a thick oak, followed by Kaahli and Wytail.

Frafan hung behind. The fur on the back of his neck tingled. At first he didn't know why. The air was not cold enough to cause such a feeling. Then he understood. Someone or something was watching. He looked behind, from where they'd come. He saw no one.

He listened for strange sounds, but his senses had been dulled. Strange sights and sounds might occur at any moment in this place. He had become accustomed to it. It was when he turned to follow Wytail up the tree that his eye caught a flash of gray. There... behind the trunk of a tiny black ash...a face peered back at him. Only for an instant, then it disappeared behind the treetrunk again.

Scaffer! Was the unfriendly squirrel following them? Why was he trying to keep out of sight? Frafan would have sworn Scaffer had been watching Wytail, and with an angry look on his face. Should Frafan shout a greeting? Should he ask Scaffer if he wanted to come along? Bad idea, he decided. Didn't they have enough of a puzzle on their paws, with the old bully Wytail running through the branches with Ephran and Kaahli, as though they were the best of friends?

Frafan looked up to see Ephran already three trees ahead. He decided to put Scaffer out of his mind. He'd never see him again. He'd probably been watching out of sheer curiosity. Maybe he wanted to be sure Wytail was leaving. With Wytail gone, Scaffer might very well have thoughts of taking over as the new park bully.

The sun's first rays were still off the horizon, near the thickest collection of Many Colored Ones' dens. That was the area they would try to avoid.

The trees were closer together than Frafan had remembered. It made for easy travel. Maybe it was a favorable omen. Maybe the path would be smoother than he'd thought. They traveled down a long row of elm, made a gentle turn toward where warm air is born, and the park faded from view. The line of elm followed one of the black paths, this one nearly deserted. Every now and then a car or truck whizzed past, round legs hissing. Across the path were rows of huge dens.

Very few Many Colored Ones were out and about. From what he'd observed, both here and at Corncrib Farm, Frafan guessed that most of the inhabitants of this warren were still asleep. He thought of asking Wytail about their sleeping habits, then decided not to. The big gray wouldn't know anything about those sort of habits anyway. Wytail ran in his own tree, a good distance from his traveling companions, as though he'd rather not be thought of as actually being part of their group.

Kaahli's voice caused Frafan to turn toward her. "Look there!" she said, pointing to the earth below her.

Ephran and Frafan's eyes followed hers to a Many Colored One, small for their kind, still huge...at least four taillengths from head to hindpaws. It was blue mostly — with a pure white chest and back, and small white hindpaws. A shock of pale yellow fur topped its round head.

It tottered across a grassy patch, apparently following a robin who, by intermittent hops and short flights, easily kept out of reach. The small Many Colored One held its forepaws straight out in front as It wobbled along, smiling and making soft sounds at the robin all the while.

"Is It stalking the robin for breakfast?" muttered a puzzled Frafan.

"I don't think so," said Kaahli. "Probably just curious. It appears to be a young One. Actually, very small and young to be wandering around by Itself." She turned to her mate, who was watching the small Creature in silence. "What do you think, Ephran?"

He shrugged. "I don't know. I'm not sure I care. Just so It doesn't get the robin."

At that moment, the bird, probably tired of the silly game with this slow and unsteady Many Colored One, took wing and flew over a thick hedge. The Many Colored One watched it fly away. Though its plump little face was lit by a huge smile, Kaahli's wore a frown.

"Very strange. It worries me," she said.

"What worries you, Kaahli?" asked Frafan. "You think It will catch the robin later?"

"No. I doubt that One is a hunter. Actually, I wonder if It is even supposed to be alone. The day is barely begun...and the air is still cold."

"Excitement's over. Let's be on our way," said Ephran. "This business is no concern of ours. I will say, though, that if that One plans to hunt It has a lot to learn."

Ephran and Frafan set out again, branch to branch, tree to tree. Kaahli hung back, watching the small Many Colored One, as It wandered off on a crooked path. She finally sighed and turned to join the others. They crossed patches of close-cropped grass and black paths.

Wytail continued to follow his own line of trees, parallel to theirs, ignoring them as though they were invisible. They traveled a considerable distance before Ephran stopped to rest. Frafan was grateful. He wasn't used to all this running. Despite their exercise program, the bounce in his legs was fading rapidly.

Ephran sniffed the air and wrinkled his nose. Wytail, at last, ran through the trees to join them.

"What is it, brother?" Frafan asked.

"A strange smell in the air, Frafan. Wytail, can you tell us what that odor is?"

"Hey! Don't know. In the warm season, sometimes when the air was movin', I could catch a whiff of somethin' like this now and again."

"There is some fire," offered Kaahli, a tense look on her face.

"Yes, a little," agreed Ephran, "but it's more than that."

Frafan said, "Whatever it is, it certainly isn't plum blossoms."

"Should we go around it?" asked Wytail.

"Around a smell? I don't think we can start doing that," said Ephran. "We'll never reach home if we steer around every strange thing we hear, see, or smell."

"Let's find out," said Frafan, "after we rest our legs a bit. Whatever the smell is, it lies directly in the path we've chosen."

With the passing of every branch, the odor grew stronger... and more unpleasant. Kaahli was right, part of the smell was fire. But it did not smell like especially hot fire. It was mostly of smoke. Putrid smoke. Abruptly, they came to the end of the trees.

They sat there for a while, in the branches of a young hackberry tree, mouths open.

"What is this place, Ephran?" Kaahli finally asked in a hushed voice.

Across a weedy field, perhaps the length of two end-to-end oak trees, a tortured and torn landscape sprawled in their path. The place looked as though it had been the battleground, possibly a to-the-last-breath showdown, between all the enemies in the woods. The place had been terribly gouged...one massive, ugly, rolling scar. A jagged hole, more like a deep trench, had been scraped out of the ground. It was immeasurably long, as wide across as a cluster of large spruce laid end to end, and as deep as a five-season maple. It was surrounded by piles of gray and black dirt...and a jumble of mostly unrecognizable objects, things they could never name. Square and round objects, black, red, blue, gray, white, crushed, mangled...some of it half buried in the earth.

Nary a tree, bush, or blade of grass was to be seen. And from every here and there came wisps and streamers of acrid smoke that burned their noses every time they breathed.

"Hey! Look over there!" cried Wytail.

He directed their gaze to two animals, slowly picking their way along the top of piled-up earth and debris.

"What are they?" asked Kaahli.

"Don't know. About our size. They look a little bit like Fetzgar," noted Ephran, as puzzled as his mate.

"Black, though. Or almost black," said Frafan. "What about it, Wytail? Do you recognize those kind of creatures?"

"Hey! Those critters aren't black, they're just filthy." Wytail's face wore an obviously disgusted look. "You never saw rats before?"

"No, we've never seen rats. Among many other things, I guess. Look at their tails," said Ephran.

"And the way they move. They don't look like they could climb if they wanted to," noted Frafan.

"Should we go down and speak to them?" Kaahli asked.

"Of course we should," said Frafan.

"What for? Nobody talks to rats," said Wytail. "Anyway, there's no trees over there."

"Wytail, we have to take every reasonable chance," Ephran said softly, "to learn all we can. Who knows what or who will help us follow the right path."

Wytail shook his head. "Hey! Not me. I'm not traipsin' around on black dirt to talk to no rats. I'll stay right here."

"Your choice," said Ephran, and he ran down the tree.

Once again Frafan, Kaahli, and Ephran found themselves on the earth. There was really no place for a hunter to conceal itself, so scampering across the open field, full of scattered weeds, was not as frightening as it might have been. Halfway to the rats Ephran fleetingly considered the possibility of being cut off from behind. Though no danger was visible right now, what if, while they were trying to communicate with these unusual animals, an enemy should come between them and the trees? Well, it was his own voice that he heard saying that they would have to take chances. It was too late to turn back anyway. Little Frafan had almost reached the torn earth and the rats. Kaahli was close behind him.

"Hello!" said Frafan loudly.

"Whoops!" said one of the surprised rats.

"Wow!" said the other, flinching away from Frafan.

"Sorry. We seem to have startled you," said Kaahli.

"Well, I guess! Sneaky, sneaky, sneaky."

"We didn't mean to frighten you. We just want to talk," said Ephran.

"Sure. Gray squirrels wanting to chit-chat with rats. Since when? Don't try to shorttail me, bright eyes. You're looking for trouble, for our food, that's what you're doing. And trouble is what you're going to get." The rat bared its horribly yellow teeth.

"Hold on!" said Frafan. "We're looking for information, not trouble." He looked around and wrinkled his nose. "And certainly not food."

"Listen, my name is Ephran and..."

"Ephran, Sneefran," said one rat, squinting at him. "What does this sneaky old Ephran want to talk about?"

"We're trying to find our way home. We could use a little help," answered Ephran.

"Let me get this straight. You're lost and you want to ask directions? Is that what you treecreeps want?"

"Well, yes."

Frafan said, "We were curious too. About you folks. Nobody like you in the deep woods."

"We wondered what happened to the earth here, too. What tore it so badly apart?" added Kaahli.

"Hey, Mat!" said one rat to the other. "You listening to this? Ever hear such a bunch of ninnies? They got more questions than you got fleas."

The rat named Mat snickered and said, "You jokers never seen a rat or a Trash Hole before? Where you been hiding? Willie's right about you being ninnies. Maybe being up in them branches all the time makes you dizzy in the head."

Ephran said, "Our nest is in a place of many trees, cool streams, and tall grass. We are only trying to find our way back. If you aren't interested in talking, just say so."

The rats gazed at the squirrels for a time, quizzical and somewhat amused expressions on both dirt-smeared faces. Then one turned to the other and said, "Well, what'd you think, Willie? They telling the truth, you think?"

"Look and act too simple for otherwise," said Willie, wiggling her nose.

Ephran ignored this insult too, but it was becoming more and more difficult. "This other male is my second brother, Frafan. The female is Kaahli, my mate."

"We know the general direction we want to go," said Frafan, "but it would be very nice to know of any obstacles or dangers in our path. Might you know the easiest way to get to the woods from here?"

"Whooee! You folks are really far out! But harmless enough I guess. Don't fault me for it, but I'm actually beginning to like you. I'm called Mathilda. This is my sister, Wilhelmina. Mat and Willie to you."

"Pleased, I'm sure," the squirrels mumbled.

"Don't worry about being pleased. Not much of anybody cares about pleasing rats," said Willie.

"Yeah," said Mat, "not much of anybody. Anyway, I'll tell you this; ain't no trees in this direction. The way you came is the way of trees. Now why don't you get back to your trees. We're busy here."

"Busy? You like it here?" asked a disbelieving Kaahli. "You have no desire to leave this...uh, Trash Hole?"

"Leave? What for?" asked Mat, vigorously scratching her bottom.

Frafan mumbled, "For one thing, I'd think you'd want to get away from the smell."

"Who's insulting who here?" asked Willie, cocking an ear toward Frafan. "What's the matter with the smell?"

"What's the matter...why, it's terrible!" said Kaahli.

"Hold on there!" said Mat. "We talkin' about the same thing? You talkin' about the smell here in Trash Hole?"

"Of course I am," said Kaahli, "can't you smell it? Fire and horrible odors, all mixed..." And it suddenly occurred to her that maybe they couldn't. That maybe their noses were built different, like their tails.

"Look around, cutie," said Willie. "The chow is great. More stale bread than you can imagine. Good moldy stuff. Even find an orange rind now and again. This is trash. Tasty trash. We love trash. Believe me, this place is a find. Best Trash Hole we've found in umpteen seasons. And it smells just fine."

Ephran decided to try a different track. He asked, "How did it come to be so torn...and burned. And so filled with these piles and piles of...whatever this stuff is." And he kicked at a piece of translucent material, something that looked very much like a chunk of ice, only far lighter — and not in the least bit cold.

"They did it," said Mat.

"Who did it?" asked Kaahli.

"Them, of course," said Willie, and pointed a filthy paw toward one of the far-off Many Colored Ones' dens.

"But why?"

"They love us so much that I suppose They just wanted to give us one dandy place to feed our faces," said Willie. At that comment the two rats broke into gales of high-pitched laughter, dancing to and fro on the earth, flicking their ugly tails at one another.

Ephran said, "I can't understand why They would make such a mess right in their own nesting place."

"Yes," agreed Frafan, "They are so clever in some ways, so neat and clean. And then this. No squirrel or rabbit, not even your friend Smagtu, would so pollute their nest..."

Suddenly, Willie's high-stepping stopped. She let out a high squeal. "Oh! Oh!" she squeaked, "Run, Mat, to the hole!"

With astounding speed for such ungainly-looking creatures, the rats disappeared into an oblong hole beneath the trash.

"What got into them?" wondered Kaalhi.

Her question was answered by a snarling bark. She turned to see three large dogs racing toward her, muscles bunching beneath their fur. Their long white teeth glistened with saliva. Ephran's worst fear was fulfilled. The line of trees was behind the dogs. The escape route was cut off.

CHAPTER XIII

SWEET SMELLS AFTER SOUR

Fred...?"

Frafan's question, asked of no one in particular, was more of an out-loud wish than a real question. He was hoping one of the ferocious-looking animals racing toward him was Fred. But none of these dogs faintly resembled their special friend.

"Shall we follow the rats?" asked Kaahli. She spoke with amazing calm, as though she was asking whether her mate and his brother preferred a hazel nut or an acorn for lunch.

"I'd rather not," said Ephran. "I noticed a hole in the earth...just over there."

The dogs, tongues out and teeth bared, bore down on the squirrels. Frafan and Kaahli turned toward where Ephran pointed. A yawning black hole faced them from the side of the small hill they'd crossed. It was as frightening as it was large. Frafan scolded himself for not noticing it earlier.

This was a strange hole, not only because of its size. It did not dive straight down into the earth like most holes, but entered sideways, much like that of a squirrel den in a tree. Across its gaping darkness was spread a large web, like that hard netting around the cages in the big red barn. The mesh of this web, however, was far thicker than that of the cages. And, fortunately, the gaps were also larger, big enough to allow a squirrel passage.

"Oh my," sighed Frafan. "Do we have to go into the earth? Is there any other choice?"

"If you think of one, let me be the first to know," said Kaahli, and she ran toward the hole.

Ephran raised his eyebrows at his brother. "I want you to know this is the same female I had to save from skystones by dragging her into a hole under a stump."

"And the same female who had to save you from fire by leading you into a fox den," Kaahli shouted over her shoulder.

Frafan was the last one in. He squeezed through the cold, hard grating and turned to watch the dogs race to within two taillengths of his whiskers, yapping and growling, stretching their long legs through the mesh.

After watching their frantic scraping and drooling for a moment, he turned and ran along the tunnel. There was light ahead, and he could see Ephran and Kaahli scampering into the light and out the hole at the far end.

Kaahli, back out in open air, could hear the dogs. They were out

91

of sight, behind the rise in the earth, barking wildly, the sound coming to her more clearly through the earthen tunnel than through the air.

"We fooled them," she said. "They look for us at the other end. But they can't squeeze through the mesh."

"All well and good," said Ephran, brushing his fur clean, "unless they come romping over the top of that hill."

Frafan said, "You're absolutely correct, brother. If they catch sight of us, the chase will be on again. Let's get into those trees."

The tunnel they'd run through crossed beneath the grassy earth at an angle, back toward the line of trees, but a goodly distance from where they'd set out. They ran away from Trash Hole, without stopping, to the nearest tree — a maple — and into its thick branches. From there they could see the dogs, still barking and digging.

"Where's Wytail?" asked Frafan. He looked around, suddenly delighted at the thought that maybe the disagreeable big gray squirrel had gotten restless or frightened, that he might have run off, back to his nest in the park.

Kaahli squinted down the line of trees. "I think that's him, way down there," she said. "I wonder why he moved."

"He didn't move," said Ephran. "He's right where we left him. We came out of that tunnel a long way from where we went in. We'd better get back. He'll be worried."

Wytail was laying on a branch, attention riveted on the scuffling dogs. The brow of the little hill Ephran, Kaahli, and Frafan had crossed shielded their escape route from his eyes. He did not notice them as they approached through the branches. As he ran, Frafan eyed the old bully. He wished he could see the face more clearly. He could not decide if Wytail was grinning or scowling at what he saw.

At that instant he noticed Ephran.

"Hey! Oh! Wow!"

Wytail jumped up so quickly that he nearly fell from his branch. "G...good to see ya! Figured ya musta 'scaped. Hey! Can't figure how ya did it. How'd ya get away from them mutts?"

"Under the earth, Wytail. Under the earth," said Ephran.

"What? How's that?"

"A tunnel. A tunnel beneath the grass," said Kaahli.

Wytail sneered. "You're joking."

"No joke," said Frafan, eyeing Wytail closely.

"Hey! Never heard of no gray squirrel using no tunnel in the earth."

"Old red squirrel trick," said Ephran.

"Red squirrel...?" Wytail asked.

"Yes," said Ephran, "we have a red squirrel friend."

Kaahli did not give Wytail a chance to respond. "We better

forget the dogs and plan our next steps. Mat and Willie made it clear that no trees grow along the path we wanted to follow."

"More than that," mumbled Frafan. "We know a bit more about The Many Colored Ones than we did before." In an even lower voice he added, "And maybe something about our traveling companion as well."

They settled into two large elm. Frafan and Ephran found places on a thick branch. Kaahli curled next to Ephran. Wytail lay on a nearby limb, eyes wide open, every so often looking back through the trees, as though waiting for someone.

"I'm not fond of changing our plan," said Frafan.

"Nor am I," said Ephran. "It was basically a good plan. Kaahli felt comfortable with it too. Do you have any idea how we might get around this place, this Trash Hole?"

Frafan rubbed his nose with the back of his paw. "No," he said, "I'm sure the blue van did not take this path."

A short discussion convinced them there was no way they could pursue their planned course. Flat, treeless fields stretched to the horizon. Earth travel was out of the question: Dogs obviously roamed the area, dogs who were true hunters.

"We have to follow the trees," said Ephran.

"Well then, if trees there must be, it's back we go," said Kaahli. "But even if we get past the big warren, are we sure we can find trees in the direction of The Pond?" asked Kaahli.

"I wish I knew," said Frafan. "I should have watched more carefully during the trip in the blue van. At the time I wasn't thinking of someday wanting to find a way back to the woods."

Ephran said, "There should be trees for running through the warren of Many Colored Ones. Luckily, Frafan knows something about such places."

"I wish I felt confident that I knew enough," said Frafan.

They set out then, back through the elm, Ephran leading the way. They moved slowly, through towering trees that bordered the wide black path. The path was now busy with slow-moving cars and trucks.

The squirrels traveled in silence, finally coming to the place from which they had set out that morning. Ephran led them past the park, then turned into a line of trees stretching toward where the sun could now be seen between the big dens.

Frafan heard and felt his stomach growl.

"Anybody getting hungry?" he asked.

"Hey! Sure am," said Wytail.

"Too bad. I see no promising trees or bushes," said Ephran.

Kaahli, raising her nose high in the air, said, "The bad smell is out of my nose." She sniffed again. "As a matter of fact, now I smell something wonderful."

"You do?" Frafan sniffed as hard as he could.

"Hey! I smell it too," said Wytail.

Then, on a whisper of a breeze, they all smelled it — sweetness, like the wind across a wide expanse of flowers. Only the smell was more than sweet. It was warm, comforting, mouth-watering.

"Where is it coming from?" asked Ephran.

"Right over there," said Kaahli.

They watched in hungry silence as a Many Colored One far below them, almost totally green in color, unloaded sweet-smelling bundles from a van parked at the side of a very large flat-roofed den. Fred called those things "bags". Inside the clear bags was what at first appeared to be wood, pieces of wood nearly as long as Frafan plus his tail, but almost perfectly round. They were even thicker than Wytail's body.

"What is that delicious smell?" Kaahli looked at Wytail.

"Don't really know," he said.

"I think I might have an idea," offered Frafan.

"I should have known that you'd have an idea," Ephran smiled, patting his smaller brother on the back.

"So now comes the reason for it, the good of spying on Many Colored Ones in their dens. Is that it?" laughed Kaahli.

Frafan smiled back. "It is indeed. I have seen this before. These bundles are only the color of wood, but not the taste or texture. They are soft and white in the middle. Those Many Colored Ones who nest in the white den at Corncrib Farm eat a great deal of it. Blackie called it "bret"...something like that. I could not smell it through the layer of ice-that-does-not-melt, their windows, but I could see that They ate it."

"Hey! So it's food," said Wytail.

"Yes. At least it's food for Them," said Frafan.

"Good point," said Ephran. "We know well enough that not all things that are food for Them are food for us."

"The smell of this tells me it has to be food for almost anybody or anything," said Kaahli.

As she spoke, the Many Colored One disappeared through the entrance of the big den, carrying a load of the wondrous bret. It did not return. The squirrels sat. An occasional car or truck went by below them. The entrance to the den beckoned them. It blew sweet breath at them. It pretended it was harmless.

"Who is going with me?" asked Ephran.

"Me," said Frafan.

"I am," said Kaahli.

"Hey! Why not?" Wytail said.

The door stood wide open. When the squirrels reached it, sweet

94

warmth flowed over them. There were many odors, all mixed together, one better than the next. Wondrous odors in noses and growling in stomaches blotted out caution in heads. Any thought of staying in the trees dried up and floated away.

It was bright inside the den — bright as the finest and clearest morning. Soft melodious notes filled the air, almost like Janey the wren, Mr. and Mrs. Robin, and the mourning doves all singing together. But where the sound came from was not easy to imagine. The green Many Colored One, the One with the mouth-watering bret, was nowhere to be seen.

The place was huge, bigger than the barn on the Farm of Cages. As far as Frafan could see were things he'd learned the names of: stack upon stack and row upon row of shiny round cans of all sizes. There were big bags, little bags, squarish and oblong boxes, roundish clear and colored things called bottles and jars, mind-boggling in number and variety. Everything was evenly spaced and well kept, like rows of corn in a field.

"So this is it," breathed Frafan.

"What do you think, Frafan? What is this place?" asked Ephran. Kaahli and Wytail leaned close.

"This is their food place," Frafan said, "This has to be where They get the things They don't grow in the earth themselves, things They bring back to their nests."

"Yes," said Ephran, "Fred told us They brought food from somewhere. It had to be from here."

"Hey! Could be," Wytail allowed. "Not a bad idea. Let's find out if what They eat's any good."

Wytail ran down a wide aisle, stopping now and again. He leaped up onto a wide white shelf containing row after row of long, flat boxes. As Ephran, Kaahli and Frafan watched, the big gray nudged one of the containers off the shelf. It tumbled to the floor, landing softly on one of its sharp corners. Wytail jumped from the shelf and seated himself next to his prize.

With sharp teeth, Wytail ripped the box open. Out spilled a bunch of thin, yellow-colored wafers. Kaahli watched as he sniffed at one of them, then bit into it.

"Hey! Good!" he said. "Not like corn. But good."

Kaahli picked up a broken fragment and nibbled at it. "Not bad...," she said, "if you're hungry enough."

She dropped the wafer and ran off to follow Frafan and Ephran. The brothers were moving slowly down the next aisle, looking first to one side and then the other, at the massive stacks of food on both sides, towering high over them.

"Look, Frafan," said Ephran, "these containers are like Them, many colored."

"Yes. I've seen them before. I think the colors mean something to Them. And, look there." He pointed to rows of small jars. "Those jars have...ah, something like reflections on the outside. Reflections of berries. Raspberries and blueberries at least."

Ephran pointed to a large box, standing beside others of its kind on the smooth floor. "See the color and outline on this one? What does it look like?"

Frafan moved closer. "I haven't been this near before. I don't know what it is, but I bet what's inside looks just like the outside."

With that, he tore open the box with his front paw. What came out looked like the round legs of the van. A whole pile of them. Only they were tiny copies...and not black, but tan. One of them rolled across the floor, right up to Ephran. He picked it up, smelled it, and took a bite.

"Good!" he said, "Really good. Tastes a little bit like corn. Maybe a touch of walnut."

Frafan cocked his head and ran over to the box. He put his tongue out, and licked the likeness of round legs, nestled in a dish on the outside of the box. Ephran watched his brother with a puzzled smile. Then Frafan picked one of the little round things up and took a tiny nibble. "You know," he said, "what you see on the outside is what the inside looks like. But, for food, that's not the important thing. It tells nothing of how it tastes or smells."

"These slender black scratches, Frafan," said Ephran, peering closely at the box. "They have to mean something. The Many Colored Ones use them all the time."

"Like on Fred's collar...," said Frafan.

"Ephran! Frafan!" Kaahli called softly, from far down the aisle.

"Look here," she said as they ran up to her. She pointed to rows of little bags, like those in the barn, only much smaller, hanging from thin silver branches above their heads. These bags could be seen through, like windows, and they were stuffed with nuts! The only ones Ephran recognized were walnuts. Kaahli jumped onto a larger box, then leaped to one of the slender silver branches. To Ephran's surprise, the branch did not break or bend. The nuts did not fall. That slowed Kaahli for but an instant. She clutched a bag in her forelegs, holding to the silver branch with her hindlegs. She tore a hole in the bag with her teeth. Nuts tumbled out on the smooth floor.

"Wonderful idea, Kaahli!" said Ephran. He jumped up beside her and began to open bags of nuts with his teeth.

"It's raining nuts down here!" giggled Frafan, taking a bite from one kind of nut, then another. Ephran and Kaahli joined him on the floor.

"How does that one taste?" asked Kaahli, as Frafan chewed a long and curved kernel.

He thought for a moment and said, "Amazing flavor, once you get that salty stuff off."

"Oh, you have to try this one!" said Ephran, holding up a very large white nut.

"The one I'm eating is wonderfully rich and sweet," said Kaahli.

"I wonder where They find nuts like this. If we could only find a grove where all these grow," said Ephran.

"Corn will never be the same treat it used to be," said Kaahli.

They sampled one kind of nut after another, each picking their favorite, arguing playfully about which had the best texture or the best flavor. Finally Ephran sat back and rubbed his stomach. He said, "I'm getting very full."

"So am I," agreed Kaahli.

Frafan realized they hadn't seen their Wytail for a while. "Say," he said, "what happened to...?"

Just then came a thunderous noise from the other end of the huge den. Though stacks of food hid the maker of the sound, they all knew what made that sort of noise: It came from the mouth of a Many Colored One.

Wytail suddenly appeared at the far end of the aisle. He skidded around the corner, tail straight up, eyes full and wild.

"Hey! Move it!" he shouted to them.

Almost atop Wytail was a huge Many Colored One, a male. The Creature seemed as wide as It was high. Its forelegs grasped a long stick, capped by a bunch of bristles, like quills on a porcupine. The Many Colored Ones at Corncrib Farm had used a stick just like this. They had swung the bristles back and forth on the wooden planks that led to the entrance to their den, sweeping dirt unto the ground.

"Whoops!" said Frafan. "Time to find a tree."

"Stay together," Ephran said quietly.

They turned, toward the part of the den that seemed the brightest, where the morning light spilled through huge windows. They could hear Wytail behind them. "Oh, Whiskers!" they heard him mutter, as he swerved to follow.

The Many Colored One, too clumsy to make the turn as neatly as Wytail did, and afraid He might lose its chance, took a wild swing at Wytail with the long stick. The swing undid his balance. CRASH! The stick smashed into the very center of a delicately balanced display of clear bottles.

The struck bottle split like an overripe melon. Two other bottles, supported by the broken one, collapsed into the ones beneath. Bottles tumbled in all directions, breaking into shiny pieces. Golden juice, smelling of ripe apples, flew in grand sprays and flowed across the floor.

The Many Colored One was unable to stop. Hindpaws lost their

grip in the unexpected juice and chubby legs flew high in the air. He grunted as He hit the floor, barely missing one of the broken bottles. The bristled stick twirled through the air, end over end. It settled, hairy end down, bouncing once, against a shelf filled with yellow and red and green fruit.

"Let's go!" said Ephran. The Many Colored One groaned as He struggled to get his hindpaws under Him. But He kept slipping and sliding in the wonderful-smelling juice.

The squirrels followed Ephran to a hidden place, behind a line of low shelves.

"Ephran," said Frafan breathlessly, "we have to find a way out. I'm sure the One who chased us is telling the Others about us being in here."

"Yeh," gasped Wytail, "not safe. Not at all." Ephran could not have agreed more. It was time to leave. But where? How? The door they'd entered was on the other side of the huge den. Even if they were lucky enough to make it that far, there was no guarantee it was still open. Were they trapped?

"Ephran!" Kaahli whispered loudly. "Look."

As she spoke, he felt a draft of fresh and brisk air against his whiskers. At the far end of the shelf a Many Colored One had opened a large window-like door. Outside the den was a herd of Many Colored Ones.

"Some of their hungry friends want to come in," said Ephran. "First food-collectors of the day."

"Hey! They can have it...," breathed Wytail. "Now that we're done."

Ephran looked quickly at each of his companions. "Are you ready to run?"

They all nodded. As the entrance swung wide, and the Many Colored Ones began to walk in, four gray squirrels squirted through long legs, amidst a chorus of shouts and screams, down the smooth pathway, and up a tall elm tree.

CHAPTER XIV

GREEN LIGHTS, RED LIGHTS

ytail was winded. "Hey!" he managed, "That got the old fur standin' up."

Ephran nodded his head. "For me too. I suppose Father would say what we just did was very foolish."

"With that smell tickling your whiskers, who could think what might be wise and what might be foolish?" said Frafan. "And who knows, maybe we learned something that will turn out to be important."

"I hope something worthwhile comes from it," said Ephran. "Besides a full stomach, that is."

"We didn't even taste bret, the thing that tempted us in the first place. But we escaped with our ears and tails and I'll settle for happy endings," said Kaahli.

"Frafan is right though," said Ephran. "We should try and remember everything we see. We don't know what might be useful."

"Well," sighed Frafan, "dens of food or no dens of food, I'm ready to see the woods. Which way, Ephran?"

"As we decided earlier," said Ephran, "we have to follow the trees. There's no use going back the way we came, toward Trash Hole with its discards, dogs, and bad smells."

"Hey! Could go back to where we started from," said Wytail. "Always corn at the park, ya know."

Frafan and Ephran looked at him as though the words he uttered were in a strange and unknown language.

Kaahli said softly, "I don't think a permanent nest in the park will ever be part of our plan, Wytail."

Wytail shrugged.

They set out again, Ephran leading the way, closely followed by Frafan and Kaahli. Wytail stayed back, always two or three trees behind.

Frafan mumbled, "What's he waiting for?"

"Who knows?" answered Kaahli. "Maybe he's still thinking about returning to his nest."

Many Colored Ones passed beneath the squirrels every now and then. They did not so much as look up. Ephran began to feel more secure and sure of himself with every leap. Branch after branch, tree after tree, they were making definite progress. The thing he feared most — the end of the trees — was not in sight. After they'd traveled a considerable distance, he stopped to rest in a tall elm bordering a wide black path.

Frafan's attention rested on the path for a long while. He turned to Ephran and said, "Brother, have you noticed the cars below?"

"What of them?" asked Ephran. There was no shortage of cars.

Many cars, and trucks as well, passed beneath, rumbling along on plump round legs.

"Doesn't it seem strange that they are all traveling the same direction?" said Frafan. "Every other place that I've seen these noisy things, they seem to be trying to go in all directions at once."

Ephran nodded. "Yes. I see what you mean."

Kaahli listened closely, looking from her mate and Frafan to the cars and trucks below and then back again. While they talked, Wytail caught up to them.

They all sat on their tails, watching the cars. Ephran finally said, "I think I know why."

"Do you really understand why they all move the same way?" asked Kaahli, her nose twitching.

"Look over there." Ephran pointed to the nearest corner, where two black paths intersected.

In the brown grass stood a tall stick. It rose straight out of the earth, about the height of a one-season oak. Though much like the sticks the Many Colored Ones placed around the meadow where They kept their cows, this stick was different. Fastened to its top was a large, flat white plank. On the plank was the likeness of a car, totally black. Across the black car, at an angle, was a swatch of red...like a smear of the thick red juice.

"Are you pointing at that stick in the ground?" asked Kaahli.

Ephran nodded.

"I see it, but I can't imagine its purpose," said Frafan.

"Remember when we watched through the window of the Many Colored Ones' den?..." asked Ephran. "The time I thought that there were two of Them. And then you made me understand that One was only a reflection?"

"I remember," said Frafan, scratching his chin in puzzlement. "What does that have to do with this?"

"Well...?"

"Well what?" said Frafan impatiently.

"You told me to look again. You told me to think about what I was seeing."

Then, in an instant, Frafan understood. "I see! None of Them dare enter this way! That's why They are all traveling the same direction."

Ephran smiled.

Kaahli said, "I still don't understand."

"The stick, my dear," said Ephran. "It gives The Many Colored Ones a message. It tells Them not to take their cars and trucks along the path if They are traveling the other way."

"Aha!" she said. "They would bump into one another."

"They communicate with sticks and symbols," breathed Frafan. "A stick crossing an image means that whatever is imaged is forbidden."

"Also, I think three crossed sticks and a circle means 'NO,'" said Ephran.

"Astounding," said Frafan. "I guess the scratches on Fred's collar did have meaning after all. When he told me that those markings could tell Many Colored Ones where his nest was, I thought the roots of his brain had come loose."

"They communicate on boxes of food, too," said Ephran.

Even Wytail's ears perked up. He gazed intently at the picture of the car and the red slash.

"Like Them or not, you have to give Them credit," said Kaahli.

Frafan said, "What They manage to put together with their delicate paws — cars, huge dens, containers of food, lights that go on and off — boggles the imagination."

"Let's not forget thundersticks, as well as torn and trashed earth," said Ephran. "They build some fine things. And some horrible."

"Speaking of trash, don't look now," Wytail interrupted, standing up on his branch, "but we got company."

Sure enough, a number of gray squirrels were moving through the branches, directly toward Ephran. There must be at least ten. He had not seen so many squirrels, all together in one place, since the reunion at Corncrib Farm. The sight was even more startling when he realized they hadn't encountered a single squirrel since they left their nest earlier in the day.

Ephran smiled. Was this, at last, the help he'd been hoping for? Had some of the local treeclimbers decided to accompany the four of them back to the deep woods after all? Might they know a safe path? They would almost certainly have some ideas. My goodness, he thought, where would they find nests around The Pond for so many squirrels?

As they drew closer, Ephran recognized their leader. An icy feeling grew in his stomach, replacing happy questions. There was no mistaking the jerky movements, the scraggly fur, or the hostile jut of the chin. The squirrel was Scaffer.

Before Ephran could think of anything to say, Wytail chattered, "Hey! Scaffer! Out for a little exercise?"

Ephran thought Scaffer might have winked at Wytail then, but he could not be sure. Maybe it was only a stray breeze that stung his eye, causing it to blink.

"Where you headed with these misfits, Wytail? You left the park in an awful big hurry," Scaffer answered with a sneer.

Wytail was silent. Ephran heard Frafan, on the branch just behind him, murmur, "Oh-oh. I smell trouble."

The squirrels were males. Scaffer was the only one Ephran

recognized. They fanned out in the branches, along the line of elm, placing themselves in a half-circle. All routes from the park were blocked by gray squirrels.

"Ephran," Kaahli whispered in his ear, "what do they want?"

"I'm not sure," he said quietly.

"You...Ephran," said Scaffer loudly. "You know who I am?"

"I know who you are," said Ephran.

"These treeclimbers here, who nest around this warren, and me too — we want to know where you think you're going."

"You know very well that we're trying to find our way back to the deep woods."

"Going about it in a pretty round-about way, aren't you? Looks to us like you're taking a trip around the Many Colored Ones' warren...like maybe you was looking for something right here." Scaffer leered at Ephran.

"We're just following the trees," said Frafan.

"Wasn't talking to you," Scaffer snapped at Frafan. He turned back to Ephran. "What about it, Ephran? What you looking for?"

"I've told you. We're looking for a way home," said Ephran. "What are you looking for?"

Scaffer sneered again. "You got one thing right anyway. We were looking. For you."

"You found me. Not that I was hiding. What do you want?"

One of the other male grays jumped to Scaffer's branch, his flushed face only a few taillengths from Ephran's.

"We know what you're up to," he said gruffly. "You're after the young ones, and the females, those who can't figure things out for themselves."

Ephran's brow furrowed. Kaahli said, "What do you mean by that? Your words make no sense."

"Oh yes, little female, we know you and the scrawny male are in on this plan too," said the squirrel. "You're all in it together. And you'll all go down together."

"What makes you think we search for your young and your females?" asked Ephran. "What would we want with them?"

"Sure, play dumb," said Scaffer. "You're not fooling anyone."

"Scaffer told us all about you," the other squirrel said. "All about your crazy ideas. You can't mislead us. But the young ones — they might be silly enough to listen to stories about clean air, endless trees, and bizarre friends."

Another squirrel spoke up. "You'd try to convince them to come with you, to either starvation or certain destruction by hunters in the deep woods. We're not going to let you do it."

"And we're not going to let you sweet-talk us into thinking

you're innocent either," said yet another.

"What my friends are saying," said Scaffer, "is that you buggers have to be destroyed. Now. Before you can do any more harm." Scaffer took a step toward Ephran.

"Hey!"

Wytail had been sitting quietly in a nearby tree. His voice was full of authority, like it used to be, when he'd given his orders to the squirrels around the food cage.

"Listen up! You smart-talkin' toughies got mouths bigger'n your tails. You come gallopin' through the branches like you got some breathe-or-don't-breathe job to do. How about me? Whatd'ya think I been travelin' around with this motley crew for?"

A wicked smile spread across Scaffer's face. "I think he got something to say, fellas. Listen to Wytail."

All heads turned to the big gray squirrel.

"Hey! I got a score to settle here. Every one of you knows what this here Ephran-character did — in front of everybody. Made a blasted fool of me. Figured a way to use Many Colored Ones. Mighty strange thing for a gray squirrel to do, all right. No wonder he's got mallard and red squirrel friends. Anyway, I owe him. Leave him to me. I'm gonna take the hide off his bones."

Everyone's attention was focused on Wytail. Ephran cast quick glances at his mate and his brother. Wytail's words had caused their mouths to drop open.

"Now!" Ephran whispered sharply. Two pairs of glazed and frightened eyes turned to him. "Run," he said soundlessly with his lips.

Ephran, Kaahli and Frafan turned as one, and raced up the branch, jumping from one to the next, not looking back. Frafan would not have imagined he could run so fast or jump so far. In every step Kaahli felt a heavy sadness that there was reason to be running at all.

If anyone could have seen Ephran's face, they would not have missed the anger there. He would have liked nothing better than face these so-called "brothers," bent as they were on destroying their own kind. All for lack of understanding. He would have liked to knock Wytail from a branch, to bite Scaffer's ear off, to make the thick red juice flow from some noses. But that would be no help. It would serve no purpose, even if it were possible. And it wasn't. He couldn't fight all of them. Any more than he could have fought off Winthrop the day the big white owl attacked Truestar. Any more than he had any chance against the hawk in the water. Little Frafan, brave as he was, would be little physical help. He could not bear to think of Kaahli being hurt.

He could hear them running in the branches...getting closer, but seeming to be in no hurry. He stopped. Kaahli was right behind him, but Frafan had dropped back. Ephran turned and waited for his brother.

Kaahli rested beside him, breathing heavily.

"Oh no, Ephran...," Frafan sputtered.

"What is it?" asked Ephran.

"Look," said Frafan, pointing over Ephran's shoulder, then laying down on the branch, totally winded.

Ephran looked down the line of trees. Then he understood why Scaffer and his pack didn't seem to be running as fast as they were able. And he understood why they had blocked off the route by which they'd come. This warren was their place. They knew what they were doing.

Because, just ahead, the trees ended. Actually, they didn't end. But they might as well have. Separated by a wide black path, there was no chance of jumping across. No need for Scaffer and his gang to run fast. They had pushed their quarry into the trap.

Ephran looked at Kaahli. Her eyes said good-bye. He smoothed the fur on his brother's heaving back. Wytail stopped on a branch a short jump from Ephran's. He held his paw up and the following pack of gray treeclimbers came to a halt.

"End of the trail, Ephran," he said, with a strange and sad sort of smile.

After all this, Ephran thought. After learning so many important things. After coming to understand that making and helping friends is what it was all about. After realizing that those he loved, most especially Kaahli and Frafan, were the real treasures. After falling into such depression, then recovering and so wanting to see The Pond again...now it was all going to end. Right here in the warren of Many Colored Ones, where at first he'd been convinced things would come to an end by different paws.

Before he turned to Wytail, to prepare for violence he wanted no part of, he happened to glance once more toward the end of the trees.

That's when he saw the vine.

His first visit to Corncrib Farm flashed through his mind. He saw Blackie, and the vine he'd crawled along, upside down. The vine he saw now, running between those same kinds of trees with a single pair of limbs, was thicker than the one he'd used at Corncrib Farm. It would be easier to balance on. The two branches, growing straight out of the top of the tree were thicker too. The vine crossed directly over the wide black path below, spanning the distance between the trees. "Why not?" he thought. A vine had saved him before.

Wytail had looked back, at those who followed, and said, "Hey! Stand back, fellas. This ain't gonna be pretty."

Ephran wasted no time. While Wytail's head was turned, Ephran leaped to the next tree. "Come on!" he shouted to Kaahli and Frafan. "Follow me!"

When they saw their intended victims running off, two or three of the gray squirrels shouted, "Stop them!" and "Don't let them escape!" Wytail shouted back, "Take it easy! They can't get away."

A large maple grew close to the tree that held the thick vine. Ephran raced to it, ran out on a thin branch, and jumped to the top of the strange tree. Kaahli and Frafan stopped behind him, one looking more puzzled and frightened than the other.

"Jump!" Ephran shouted. Kaahli hesitated. Frafan nudged her. She jumped and landed next to Ephran. Frafan came next. He nearly jumped too far, and Ephran caught him with his paws before he could skid off the far side of the branch.

"Don't tell me we're going to cross the black path on this swaying vine," Frafan said breathlessly.

"That's what we have to do," said Ephran. He licked Kaahli's face. "Are you up to it, little one?"

"Do I have a choice?" she asked, her voice barely a whisper.

"Sorry. No reasonable one I can think of," he said.

They started across the vine: Ephran in front, Kaahli next, Frafan in the rear. It was slow going but, Ephran was delighted to realize, it was possible to keep one's balance on this thicker vine. They would not have to travel upside-down. Besides, their pursuers would not be able to go any faster up here. If he could just get the three of them to the trees on the far side of the path, maybe they would have a chance.

He heard Wytail shouting. At the same time he looked down at the smooth path below. There were still no cars or trucks. Strange, he thought, there had been none since they'd started across. He looked to his right. No cars that way. One of those "one-way" paths maybe. He looked to his left.

There they were! Two rows of them. Cars and trucks. Not one of them moving. All just sitting there, huffing and puffing, big shiny eyes staring down the black path, right at him. Then he noticed two strange trees, standing at the corners of the black path where the rows of cars waited restlessly. They were a shiny silver color and not particularly tall...about twice as high as the cars. No branches. Just a line of three circles at the upper end of the trunk, like big eyes. Only one eye was lit. He could see the reflection in the windows of the cars. The color was red.

"...Vine's too slow," Wytail was saying. "We'll cross on the black path. Greet 'em when they reach the other side. Hey! Finish 'em off right there..."

"What about cars?" Ephran heard a voice ask.

"Look for yourself. No cars on this path. We got plenty of time." said Wytail. "Come on then."

Ephran realized he'd made a horrible mistake. The trip across the vine took far too much time. They would be caught after all. This

"You got things
figured out now, Ephran?"

time the earth offered the quickest and safest path. He had doomed them all. He stopped in his tracks.

At that moment, a change in color caught his eye. A different reflection. The red eye in the trees at the end of the path had turned green. At that moment, as one huge beast wakened from a long sleep, all the cars began to move toward him at the same time, growling and squealing.

Wytail, having replaced Scaffer as the leader of the longtails, had led them down the trees, right to the edge of the black path. He motioned to those behind. Looking up at Ephran he called, "Hey! We got 'em! They realize their mistake now."

Most of the other grays were grinning. Some were focused on Wytail and the black path, some on the squirrels balanced upon the vine high overhead. None paid any heed to the cars and trucks that bore down on them at tremendous speed.

Wytail was more than halfway across the path when he glanced at the cars, turned back to Ephran, and called out, "Hey! You got things figured now, Ephran? You're not the only one got special ideas and ain't afraid of Many Colored Ones, you know. Watch me."

Suddenly the air was filled with the screech of round black legs on black path, the terrible hooting and squealing voices of the cars and trucks, and the screams of squirrels. Ephran, Kaahli, and Frafan watched in horror. Cars swerved crazily. Squirrels scattered in all directions. Wytail dodged two cars, a careless sneer on his face. But a large truck, careening wildly, surprised him, and he went down beneath its front leg. Scaffer disappeared under a small green car. Before he closed his eyes, Ephran saw at least two other squirrels crushed beneath the terrible weight of shiny cars. Red juice ran thick on the path.

One squirrel made it, nearly flying onto the grass on the far side of the black path. He did not look back. He ran, as though a fox was at his tail, until he was out of sight. Ephran could only be sure of two or three that managed to reach safety on the side of the path they'd started from. They too ran off into the trees.

"I feel sick," said Kaahli.

"So do I," agreed Frafan.

When my enemy is helpless
He is no longer my enemy.

Winfindahl:
"All Is Silence"

CHAPTER XV

COMFORT FOR THE ENEMY

hat was the most terrible thing I've ever seen," Kaahli whispered.

She lay in the branches of an ash tree, next to Ephran and Frafan. Each knew the others' thoughts, the fervent wish that the scene they had just witnessed could somehow be erased from their minds. They knew the attack was not deliberate. The cars and trucks had not meant to crush the squirrels. They had honked, swerved, tried to stop. It had turned into a nightmare nevertheless. Nobody spoke for a long time.

Finally Kaahli said, "Why did he do that?"

"Why did who do what?" asked Frafan in a weak voice.

She cocked her head at Frafan. "Wytail, of course. I don't understand why he turned on us like that. Was he pretending to be a friend? He said he wanted to go with us to the deep woods. Why did he lie? Why did he want to see us destroyed?"

"I thought maybe you wondered why a squirrel who should know better could make such a stupid and fatal blunder."

"Do you think he actually understood that the cars would start moving when that little sun on the stick changed color?" Kaahli asked.

Frafan shook his head. "I can't say for certain. I would think so. He's nested in this warren of Many Colored Ones since birth. Cars and trucks were an old story to Wytail. So were their paths and habits. I would think he must have seen them stop for the red light many times."

"He seemed confused, though, when you and Ephran were talking about the strange little tree, the one that told the cars to travel only in a certain direction."

"True. At least he acted as though he didn't understand." Frafan turned to Ephran, who had been laying silently, head on his paws. "What do you think, brother?"

"I don't know," Ephran said, very slowly. "I don't think any of us ever will. No more than we know why Wytail went to look for Queesor that day we faced him down at the cage of food. I wondered then; did he go to taunt him? Or when he noticed Queesor wasn't in the crowd could he actually have become concerned? Is any treeclimber all good or all bad?" Ephran rubbed one paw over the other and said, "All I know is that Wytail saved our breath. Whether he intended to or not will always be his secret now."

"'Intended to or not...?'" Frafan murmured.

"I hadn't thought of that," Kaahli said softly. "It didn't even occur to me that he might have meant to help us."

Ephran stood on his branch and said, "Time to move along. There is nothing we can do here, and the sun sinks quickly. We have to find a place to spend the dark hours."

They set out, away from the corner where red and green eyes continued to regularly and automatically blink off and on, as though nothing had happened because of them, as though the black path was not smeared with gray fur and thick red juice.

Once again trees stretched out ahead, lining the black path along their way. Traveling felt different now. No longer did a big gray squirrel shadow them in the branches. It gave Frafan the most unusual sensation...one of mixed sadness and relief.

Beneath the sun, which was dipping low over the trees, a bank of heavy purple clouds lay against the curve of the earth. Their ragged edge burned with a glorious red and yellow light that colored the branches and roofs of the dens of Many Colored Ones. Long shadows slid over greening grass and down the long black paths, which were almost deserted now. Bright suns on high, limbless trees suddenly popped on all over the warren.

The rumble of thunder came to their ears. Three sets of paws picked up the pace, toward an old box elder tree that leaned wearily over a gravel path. The tree had a large hole, above a branch in the rotted trunk. Frafan was the last one in, tail barely beating the torrent of raindrops that accompanied an earth-shaking clap of thunder.

It rained as hard as any of them had ever seen it rain. Maybe harder. The nest was damp and drafty, but there was no thought of looking for a more comfortable one. With every flash of light, and the following thunderous crash, Kaahli curled more tightly against Ephran. Rain poured down all night long, and well into the early morning. They slept fitfully and woke later than usual. Heavy eyelids opened to a shaft of light pouring through the hole. The last of the dark, black clouds had scuttled away.

Their spirits lifted with the sun, as cheerful and warming light spilled across the warren of the Many Colored Ones. Bright beams helped them forget yesterday's tragedy, but did little to stop complaining stomachs. Their last meal had been in the Many Colored Ones' Den of Food.

"Are we still on the path to The Pond, do you think?" Frafan asked Ephran, as they passed from branch to branch.

"We haven't traveled far from where we started," said Ephran. "We have to put some distance between us and the park today. Given a choice, I would travel directly toward the rising sun, but we have to stay with the trees. Anyway, we're as close to the right path as we can get."

They moved along, looking as much for food as to follow the path toward the sun. Without thinking, they veered toward an unkempt and large thicket where a ragged-looking bunch of oak and hickory trees grew. Perhaps there would be nuts there, buried in the thick green and brown grass. A few scraggly elm and prickly ash pushed their branches above clustered bushes.

Kaahli and Ephran, having descended to the lower branches, searched for likely-looking areas on the earth, open places that might have been used as a burial place for nuts last warm season.

Ephran ran ahead, eyes glued to the ground. He stopped when he heard Kaahli say, "Frafan, what do you find so interesting?"

Frafan was seated on the branch of a small green ash tree, attention riveted on a large bush beneath him. When he did not answer Kaahli asked again, "Frafan, what do you see?"

"A mound of some sort. Can either of you see it? Under the branches of that big bush."

"I can't see anything from here," said Ephran.

"Come closer then," said Frafan.

"Frafan," said Ephran impatiently, "What is so important about a clump of bushes? I thought we were looking for food."

Frafan gave his brother a most curious look. What he saw was, in his opinion, worth investigating. Ephran asked no more questions, and he and Kaahli ran to join Frafan.

When they reached his tree, Frafan silently pointed again. Sure enough, from here they could see a bump in the earth, colored blue and white, mostly hidden by overhanging leaves.

"What do you think it is?" Kaahli asked.

"Come now! What's gotten into you, Frafan? We've all seen how They leave trash everywhere," said Ephran. "It's just another pile of their discards. Besides, we're all hungry. Let's be on our way and save our curiosity for more important things."

"It moved," Frafan said softly.

"A trash pile moved?" said Kaahli.

"Are you sure?" asked Ephran, frown suddenly gone.

"I'm sure I saw it move."

"Well...," said Ephran slowly, now intent on the dirty blue and white mound, "I guess a few more minutes won't make a great deal of difference. If they've waited this long to find out what happened to us, our family and friends can wait a bit longer."

They nearly crept through the branches, ever so cautiously, lower and lower, in single file: Ephran in front, then Kaahli, then Frafan. The pattern of dappled sunlight on the lump, filtered through new leaves, suddenly changed.

"There!" Kaahli chattered excitedly, "I saw it too! It moved!"

The bundle curled under the bush was exactly what Kaahli feared it would be. "It's the small Many Colored One, the One we saw yesterday. Remember? It was chasing a robin."

The little creature lay facing the squirrels. Its golden hair was tangled and filled with twigs and brown leaves. A pinkish-white face was scraped and smudged with dirt. One of the closed eyelids was blue and puffy. Thick red juice had dried on a long scratch that ran down one side of its face.

The blue and white pelt, fresh and clean the day before, was torn and wet. It was so grimy that, in the shade, its true color could hardly be discerned. One hindpaw was a scuffed but smooth white. The other was pink — pink as sunbeams filtered through high, thin clouds. The paw had five tiny toes with even tinier claws. Actually, thought Ephran, the little Creature was dirty enough so that if It had been lying in any different position, the squirrels would not have noticed It at all. It would have been mistaken for a large clump of dirt and leaves.

"I'm going down to take a closer look," said Frafan.

"Stay clear of its paw," said Kaahli.

Knowing how much he feared Them, she expected Ephran to remain in the branches. But he did not. Limitless curiosity overcoming fear, he followed his brother down the treetrunk. She left her perch too, and joined the two males in the grass. They seated themselves directly in front of the Creature's face.

Big eyes were closed, tiny forepaws clenched tightly on its chest. It was breathing. They could see that. And, every so often It shivered and sighed in its sleep.

"All right," said Ephran in a low voice, "are we all satisfied now? It is indeed the small Many Colored One we saw yesterday. It's taking a nap. Good for It. We have a long way to go. Let's move."

"Ephran," said Kaahli, reaching out to put a paw on her mate's shoulder as he started to move away, "this One is not just taking a nap. It should be in a den with its parents. It is hurt and sick."

"What of it?"

"I think It will stop breathing unless something is done," she said.

Ephran looked closely at the little Many Colored One. "Yes," he said, "you may be right. Too bad, I suppose. Come along now. This is not our concern."

"Ephran!"

"Kaahli, what would you have me do? You understand, don't you, that this is one of Them? One of Those who felled the big oak, who set fire free in the woods, who took the breath from Marshflower's young drake, who tumbled me from the high branches? You do understand that, don't you?"

Frafan spoke up. "Also, my brother, one of Those who helped Laslum — and you — when you were injured."

"We've talked about this before. Those on the Farm of Cages are misfits," said Ephran. "We cannot depend on Them. Let's not get into another of those discussions now."

"No, wait," said Frafan, as Ephran ran through the grass and began to climb a tree. "I've given this a lot of thought. I'm not at all sure that The Many Colored Ones on the Farm of Cages are the misfits. Did you ever ask yourself why They took you and Kaahli to the park?"

"You know what I thought at first," said Ephran.

"Yes. That it was just a big cage to hold us in. A place to keep us until They were ready to hunt. To use us for food. What do you think now?"

"I...I don't know. I try not to think about it. After we'd decided to leave the park I put the whole puzzle from my mind. We're on our way home, in case you two have forgotten."

They all held their breath while the small One shuddered and groaned in its sleep. Then It lay quiet again.

Frafan said softly, "The little Creature does not have much time. Listen, Ephran, don't you think that those gentle misfits, as you call them, took you to a place filled with trees and ponds and other squirrels because, in their minds, it would be a better place for a treeclimber's recovery than a cage inside a dark barn? And, since you were weak and barely able to climb, might They think you'd be far safer in the park than in the deep woods? No foxes or hawks in the park, you know."

"I suppose it's possible," said Ephran. "Maybe They were just doing what They thought was best." He squinted at his brother. "So what's the point? I already agreed that Those on the Farm of Cages might be caring and gentle."

"Ah," said Frafan, "then take the thought another step. What of the place you were taken to? The place set aside? Who is it for? And who put it there? Who built the nest, shabby or not, that you slept in all those nights? Who, in their caring ignorance, at least brought corn to feed us? Not realizing treeclimbers would become dependent on it. And, finally, who never made a move to harm any of us?"

Ephran swallowed and licked his lips. He closed his eyes and nodded his head slowly. The three squirrels sat that way for a while, on the cool and damp earth. The small One coughed weakly.

Kaahli scampered close to its face and chattered. Eyes, brilliant blue eyes, like the most beautiful sky imaginable, on the brightest day of the early warm season, opened. But there was a mist over them, like the sun setting.

"Let's find some nuts," said Ephran.

Kaahli spun to face him. "Please, Ephran, we can't think of ourselves now. This One has parents. They must be worried sick. Just as our parents are worried sick about us. Did you not understand what Frafan was trying to tell us? We have to help."

"That is exactly what I'm trying to do, my love. Do you have

"A tiny smile curved
it's bruised lips."

any better idea for feeding It? Do you think we dare try to get into, and back out, of the Many Colored Ones' den of food?"

She smiled, turned to Frafan, and said, "Come, Frafan. Let's see if we can't smell out a few nuts."

They worked as hard as they ever had, or harder. They found a reasonable number of nuts, but many were spoiled. They brought the good ones to Ephran, who made a small pile very near the small Many Colored One.

Finally, about the time Frafan was so tired he thought he'd drop of exhaustion, Ephran said, "Okay. That's enough nuts. Let's start opening them."

Cracking shell after shell, they took the food from inside and began to make two little piles, one of shells and one of food. Hungry as they all were, not a morsel was eaten. Ephran kept his eyes on the small One. It had not stirred for some time.

"Kaahli," he said. "Wake It up."

Kaahli moved as close as she dared, stood on her hindpaws, and chattered loudly. The little One opened its eyes and looked directly at her. A tiny smile curled its bruised lips. The eyes slowly closed again.

Once more Kaahli chattered. "Wake up, little One!" Ephran picked up a small walnut and ran up to the small One's face. He dropped the nut right in front of its nose, turned as quickly as he could, and scampered away.

The small One did not move. It closed its eyes once more, shivered mightily, and heaved a great sigh.

Ephran ran back. He sat down, half a taillength from its face. He picked up the nut and, with his paws, gently placed the food directly on the small One's mouth. The lips did not move. The nut fell to the ground.

"It's no use, Ephran," said Frafan. "Either It is too weak or else It does not understand that nuts are to eat."

Ephran shook his head sadly.

Frafan's ears went up. "I think I know what the problem is." To Ephran and Kaahli's puzzled look he said, "I've watched Them through the windows at Corncrib Farm, you know. They drink a lot. I wonder if It might want water."

"Water?" said Kaahli. "How strange."

"Strange, maybe. But This is no squirrel," answered Frafan. "And I don't know what we can do about it anyway. I have no idea how we can get water to It."

"I do," smiled Ephran.

He ran back, around the side of the bush, where he'd noticed something the others hadn't. The small One had lost the covering for the bare hindpaw. Ephran had found the thing while looking for nuts. Last

117

night's rainstorm had filled it with water. He dragged the pawcover back, through the grass, by a piece of very pliable vine woven through it. He was careful to spill as little of the water as possible. It was difficult though. He lost nearly half of it. He pulled, while Kaahli pushed, and they managed to get the pawcover up to the little One's mouth.

Its eyes were wide open now. One forepaw moved the tiniest bit and all three squirrels scattered, Frafan making it all the way to a tree before looking back. The small One drew the paw back.

Kaahli said, "It is very young. It won't hurt us."

Despite her words, they returned to their work cautiously, watching for any sudden movement.

After much experimenting, and a few sharp words about the best way to proceed, Ephran and Frafan managed to lift the hindpaw covering. Kaahli leaned against it, adding a little to its weight, but making it considerably more stable. As the two males lifted, Kaahli gave instructions.

"Lift a bit more," she'd say. "Now...tip it...slowly...no, slowly, I said! There...perfect..."

A few drops of water rolled over the edge, and trickled down the lips of the small One. The lips opened and the tip of a tiny pink tongue poked out. The tongue licked wet lips, and the lips opened wider. Water ran slowly from the pawcover and into its mouth.

When the water was gone, Ephran dragged the pawcover away. The small One was wide awake now. It stared openly at the squirrels, a smile on its face. It cooed at them, sounding almost like a mourning dove. It reached out with one little pinkish paw.

"What does It want?" wondered Kaahli.

"More water perhaps," said Ephran. "But now that It's awake I don't trust It. It might be dangerous to get too close."

Kaahli watched the tiny creature for a time. Then she said, "It means no harm. It is still very nearly helpless. Just like a newborn squirrel. The nuts are too big. Maybe if they are in smaller pieces..."

She picked up a shelled nut and moved close. The small One slowly reached out and touched Kaahli's full and soft tail. She ignored it, breaking the nut into small pieces with her paws. Then It touched her head and slid its paw slowly down her back.

"Uuue...that tickles," Kaahli giggled.

"Kittie," It said.

Kaahli put a few tiny pieces of nut on the small One's lips. The little pink tongue came out and pulled them inside.

"Hooray!" shouted Frafan.

"Good for you, Kaahli," smiled Ephran.

Kaahli, Frafan and Ephran took turns putting food in the mouth while the others cracked and pulverized nuts. The creature gulped down the food as fast as the squirrels could provide it. Soon only a scattered pile of shells remained. Intermittently the small One petted each of the squirrels, ever so gently. And every so often It sneezed. At first Ephran avoided its touch but, eventually, even he found himself smiling and laughing at the pleasant and unusual sensation of having the soft pink paw run over his fur.

At last the small One seemed satisfied. It closed its eyes once more, breathing deeply and slowly.

"I think its color is better," said Kaahli.

Frafan laughed. "That depends on your taste in color, and exactly what color It choses to be, I suppose."

They sat for a while, watching the little Creature sleep peacefully. Then Ephran said, "Here we are, on the earth, not even paying attention to whether or not hunters might be nearby. Let's get up into the trees."

They scrambled into the branches, settling on one that gave them a clear view of the little One.

"What now?" asked Frafan.

"We've done what we can," said Ephran. "We have to be on our way."

"We can't just leave It here," said Kaahli.

"Do you have any ideas?" asked Ephran. "I don't believe we can drag It to one of their dens. And It seems either too weak or disinterested in getting up on its own legs."

"It's sick," said Kaahli. "It will stop breathing if we don't feed It."

Frafan shook his head and said, "I watched this kind long enough to know that It can't survive on nuts. They eat many sort of things. And It will need water or the juice from fruits. Besides, It desperately needs shelter from rain and cold nights. It's already spent one night in the rain."

"What can we do? We can't stay here forever," said Ephran.

"Maybe we won't have to," said Frafan. He pointed toward where the cold winds came.

There, in an open field on the other side of the trees, was a crowd of Many Colored Ones. There were nearly as many as the rabbits in Great Woods Warren. They walked in a long irregular line, spread out across a wide expanse, eyes on the earth.

The variety of color was less than usual. Though there were some red, and sky-blue, and mauve, a number of the big creatures were green in color, and almost as many brown. They moved slowly, like a ponderous thunderhead, bodies turning to and fro, seeming to search around every tree and every depression in the earth.

"What are They doing?" asked Kaahli. "Is it some sort of

119

game?"

"I'm not sure," said Ephran. "But I don't believe it's a game. I think They might be looking for this small One."

"Oh, how wonderful!" she said. "And They are surely moving this way."

The squirrels watched as the long line of Many Colored Ones drew nearer and nearer. Then, for no apparent reason, They stopped. A group of Them clustered together, chattering softly to one another. After a short time the line shrunk into a tighter group, turned, and began to walk slowly away.

"They can't do this!" cried Kaahli, and she chattered as loudly as she could at their retreating backs. "Come back!" she shouted.

Ephran began to chatter too, but The Many Colored Ones ignored the squirrels as though they weren't there.

"Oh, please!" begged Kaahli.

Suddenly, without a word to his companions, Frafan bolted from the branch. Down the trunk and through thick grass, to the small One's pawcover. He grasped the vine attached to the pawcover in his teeth and set off, toward The Many Colored Ones.

Ephran and Kaahli watched in amazement as Frafan closed the gap between himself and the searchers, pawcover bouncing along beside him. He scampered right through the legs of the tallest One. Directly in front of Them, Frafan spun around, stood on his hindlegs, and tossed the pawcover in the air. It was too large to throw very high, but he got their attention nevertheless. The Many Colored Ones came to a stop so sudden it was as though They'd run into a solid oak.

Frafan did an amazing backward flip, picked up the pawcover, and ran back, once more through the legs of the tall One. The entire group pivoted to follow him. Frafan sat for a moment, in plain sight, playing with the pawcover. He then took the unraveling vine once more in his teeth and ran back toward Ephran and Kaahli.

The Many Colored Ones' steps were no longer slow and deliberate. They ran. Kaahli's mouth dropped open. Ephran didn't know whether to laugh or cry. The sight of a tiny gray squirrel, running through the grass with a white pawcover, chased by a whole herd of Many Colored Ones, was as funny as it was terrifying.

Frafan bolted through the trees, dropped the pawcover under the small One's nose, and ran up the treetrunk. Neither Ephran or Kaahli had moved since the beginning of Frafan's amazing performance. Frafan was totally out of breath. He lay down next to his brother, huffing and puffing like he wanted all the air in the world for his own.

Like the big and clumsy creatures They were, The Many Colored Ones came crashing and stumbling through the trees and long grass. They did not bother looking up. It took only a moment before a Female

"Frafan...tossed the pawcover in the air."

with long yellow hair, and wearing a red and white pelt, spotted the small One.

She screamed wildly, as though injured, and ran to where the little One lay beneath the bush. She picked It up in her forepaws, with great tenderness, and hugged It to her chest. Others gathered around her, crooning and making soft and comforting sounds. A tall One, a Male with short hair, blue hindquarters, and a white front, ran to Her. The Others made way for Him. He put one forepaw around the Female and the other around the small One. He lay his head next to the small One's.

After a moment, the tall Male bent down. He picked up the white pawcover. He began to straighten up but stopped suddenly, studying the earth in a half-bent position. Then He stooped down once more...and picked up a pawful of empty nutshells. He held them out to the Female. And then to the Others, who looked at the shells with quizzical expressions. Finally He turned his face to the high branches and searched with his eyes until they rested on Ephran, Frafan, and Kaahli, all watching silently.

It was not too far to see the tears running down His face. Her's too, standing next to Him, tears sparkling like fresh rain on cottonwood leaves.

He held his forepaws out toward the squirrels, extending them as far as they would go. The paws were unclenched, and open to the sky.

CHAPTER XVI

RAFTS, RATS AND ROUGH RIDES

A s the many colored ones walked away, chattering softly among themselves, Kaahli turned to Ephran and said, "The events of these last few days have to be among the strangest any treeclimber could dream of."

Ephran nodded. "Maybe things will settle down now. It appears we've reached the end of their dens."

Frafan grinned and said, "How wonderful! Toward the place of the rising sun I see nothing but trees and open country. Let's be on our way."

Kaahli said, "I'm glad for what we did here — helping the small one. Aren't you?"

"Yes, I am," said Ephran.

Frafan said, "I have to say I am especially pleased with your attitude, Ephran. I know it was not easy for you to be concerned for any of their kind."

"Ha!" said Ephran. "Don't try to make me the hero. You're the one who showed the streak of genius and bravery with the pawcover. You saved the little one's breath."

They set out then, stopping now and then in trees especially laden with fresh green buds. As they ate, they found themselves watching, a bit anxiously, for squirrels. None appeared. A flock of crows passed them, traveling the same way they were, but out of earshot. The dens of the many colored ones faded behind. Ahead, the trees parted. Between them flowed a wide and wild river of water.

What had been a peaceful little stream was terribly swollen. Last night's rainstorm had pushed to it to the tops of its banks. Raging water growled and hissed, carrying all manner of debris along. As far as the eye could see, up and down the waterway, branches did not meet across the water.

"Our path lies across that creek, doesn't it?" Frafan asked in a tense voice.

"I'm afraid so," said Ephran. "Maybe it won't be a problem. The trees on the other side look close enough for jumping."

"I hope so," said Kaahli. "I cannot see the end of the water in either direction. Now I'm glad you insisted on jumping practice back in the park."

Frafan and Kaahli followed Ephran onto a sturdy ash branch. Directly across was an elm. They tried not to look down; to the tumbling, snarling, dirt-brown water.

Ephran licked his lips. "I think this is about as close as the branches grow. I'll go first."

They back-tracked, to the trunk of the ash. Kaahli ran to a lower branch while Frafan clung to the side of the tree. Ephran took a deep breath, blew out a puff of air, and raced down the limb. Kaahli held her breath. His leap was smooth. His forepaws grasped a small elm branch. He swung in the air for a moment, then scrambled up the little branch to where it grew wide and solid.

He turned and shouted back, "Your turn, Frafan!"

"That's what I was afraid of," mumbled Frafan.

He followed Ephran's example, backing up as far as he could go. He closed his eyes for a moment, opened them widely, and ran as fast as he could. His lighter body soared through the air. He caught the same branch Ephran had.

"Come on, Kaahli," they called to her.

She had watched them carefully, deciding how to manage her jump. There was a heavy feeling in her belly. She could not tell if it was real or imagined. She picked out what appeared to be a better angle, one that led to a sturdier branch. She smiled sweetly and said, "Watch this. I'll show you a little something about jumping."

She took a short run, aiming for a much larger branch than the males had. Falling the extra distance was a bit scary, but her paws grasped the branch solidly.

Then, suddenly, Kaahli found herself in a predicament every treeclimber dreaded. The branch she'd grasped was not attached to the tree! It must have broken in the wind, fallen from higher up, and caught among solid branches. It was too late to reach for another. From the corner of her eye she saw Ephran's and Frafan's appreciative smiles turn to grimaces of horror. She fell through the air, grasping the branch as though it was her last and only hope.

Even before the water touched her, Kaahli cried out, a yelp as much of frustration as of surprise. At first she was not frightened. There was no more time for fear than there was for reaching. And, without really thinking about it, she expected the water to be warm, as it had been the other time she'd found herself swimming. This time, though, her body shrieked in pain at the intense cold. Worse, her legs were not long enough to reach the bottom of the stream, and her sharp claws were of no help against the strong and insistent current.

As she spun helplessly, she saw Ephran and Frafan, running down the trunk of the elm. Frafan was shouting at her, his words lost in the snarling and gurgling of the water. She told herself that they would get her out, find a way to rescue her. Ephran and Frafan were clever. They were full of ideas.

She looked up, trying to ignore how very cold she was, how much she hated the feeling of water soaking through her fur, to see tree branches sweeping past overhead, the muddy bank of the creek flying by at amazing speed. Ephran and Frafan were going to have to run very fast to catch her.

She paddled as best she could, struggling to keep her head above water, trying to stay calm, trying to catch a glimpse of her dear mate and his brother.

Then, like sudden night, everything was darkness. For a long minute, Kaahli did not breathe. Was it over? Had her eyes stopped working so suddenly? Was sight the first thing to go...even before breath and thought ceased? No, it couldn't be. Water still tumbled around her, echoing in her ears. It yet held her in a steady and icy embrace. All had not ended. Not yet.

As suddenly as it had left, bright sunlight reappeared, and with it, a feeling of relief, however small. She looked back and saw that the stream had spurted under one of the many colored ones' black paths, through a long silver tunnel, and back out again. Despite the sun overhead, Kaahli shivered. She preferred to think it was because of the cold. But the claws of hopelessness began to creep into her mind.

With the kind of understanding that comes a while after a serious accident or a bad surprise, when at first you don't understand that something truly terrible has happened, Kaahli realized she was in big trouble. Her body told her that her heart would not beat long if she stayed in the water.

She had to do something. She must not just lie here until she fell asleep and sank beneath the surface. Kaahli used her paws to face the bank of the stream. It seemed a very long way. She tried to swim, the strong current pushing her insistently sideways, giving her the feeling that she was getting nowhere. Water splashed into one eye and ear, the ones toward the current. A stick rose out of the water and hit her in the nose, causing both eyes to cloud over. She gasped and almost swallowed a mouthful of dirty water.

She let herself float again. It was the easiest thing to do. Swimming crosscurrent was very difficult and risky. Besides, the bank was simply too far away. She could not swim so far. She would tire long before she got there. She gave up the struggle and let herself be carried relentlessly along.

A matted cluster of sticks and leaves, held afloat by a few shiny round containers, bottles like those she'd seen in the huge food den of the many colored ones, bobbed next to her. Something else surfaced next to the floating pile. Something ugly and alien. Something big and brown. A bag or a box? A mink? No, please, not a mink! A paw rose slowly from the water. Kaahli gasped.

As she tried to understand this new danger, she found the swirling water had turned her into the sun. All she could make out was a fearful outline, an animal pulling itself out of the stream, up onto the pile of rubbish. The thing rose up, cutting off the sunlight. Her mouth opened, to scream or to beg she did not know. And, with that, she sucked in some of the muddy creek after all. She coughed and choked. The animal climbed higher and loomed over her. There was no escape.

"For weird, lookit the soaked treeclimber," came a squeaky voice. "You look better now, more like me. Sister, I suggest you get your tail up here before you drown."

Kaahli blinked desperately. One of her eyes cleared long enough to see the creature that spoke. It was a brown rat. A brown Willie-kind of rat. She tried to speak.

"Oh, for pity's sake," said the rat. "Don't just look at me and gargle. Are you hopeless or what? I suppose I'm required to help a lamebrain. Grab my tail and get up here."

With that, Willie turned her back to Kaahli and whipped her long, skinny, and snake-like tail almost into Kaahli's face. Kaahli winced and wrinkled her nose. But she knew what had to be done. There were no snapping turtles underpaw today, to lift her out of the water. Coughing and snorting, she grabbed Willie's tail with both forepaws.

"Wow! Easy! That's no numb willow branch you're digging into," howled Willie.

As gently as she could, Kaahli eased herself up the floating debris, onto an empty translucent bottle, trying not to sink her claws into Willie's tail. She shivered again, violently.

"Spread the old bod out," said Willie. "Spread the old bod. Like this." And Willie lay down, spreading front and rear legs wide. "Let the sun get a clear shot."

Wise words. But first Kaahli had to take a quick look up and down the wildly rolling stream. There was nothing familiar except an occasional floating branch which, like her, was out of place here. Her raft was a loose bundle of trash. It rocked back and forth, making her feel nauseated and dizzy. The water was terribly dirty. On both banks, bare bushes and thick clumps of brown weeds rushed by. Ephran and Frafan were nowhere to be seen.

She shook herself, trying to rid her fur of as much of the cold water as possible. Before she lay down she said, "Thank you, Willie." She coughed and rubbed her nose. "I don't think I would have known what to do if you hadn't been here."

"That's obvious. You treeclimbers are so amazingly addled when it comes to water."

"I suppose it's true. We generally avoid water. How did you come to be in it?"

"We like to take a swim once in a while," said Willie. Kaahli thought a look of embarrassment crossed the rat's face.

"In a cold and wild torrent like this?" asked Kaahli. "I have trouble believing that."

"Well, got to admit, this was a little more of a swim than I bargained for," Willie said.

"You got swept away as I did, didn't you?"

Willie said nothing and started licking her tail.

"Didn't you?"

Willie wrinkled her nose.

"Where's Mat?" Kaahli asked.

"Yeah. How about Mat? Well, old Mat talked me into rescuing some moldy trash from the water. Knew I'd fall in. Ratty Matty is most likely back there, eating all the goodies I'd been saving up," said Willie, showing her yellow teeth. "That's what gets me. Besides, I think the dirty rat gave me a nudge."

"What? Mat push you into the water? Mat wouldn't do that. Would she? You are sisters, aren't you?"

"Mat got no family feelings," said Willie. "No honesty, no charity, no looks. Ever notice her beady red eyes?"

"Her eyes are just like yours," said Kaahli.

Willie ignored the comment. "Suppose I better get back before everything I worked for is gone."

"Can you find your way back?" asked Kaahli.

"Don't know as I can. Don't know as I want to anyway."

"I thought you just said you'd better get back."

"Better get back. Didn't say I wanted to."

"Surely, despite the way you talk, you want to see your sister again!"

"What for? She's just a dirty old rat, and who likes dirty old rats," Willie giggled. "Except maybe other rats, of course. How about you? Where are your two equally dull-witted friends?"

"They're not friends. I mean...one is my mate..."

"Sure not a friend in that case," Willie nodded solemnly.

"Oh, you know what I mean," said Kaahli. "One of the males is my mate and the other is his brother. And, by the way, I'll ask you to mind your tongue. You're full of insults. What makes you think you're so much better than squirrels?"

"Didn't say I was better. Just smarter. Cuter too."

At that moment, the raft made a sudden turn, almost throwing both of them back into the creek. Gripping a waterlogged stick, Kaahli realized the stream was splitting in two — right under them. A large branch surfaced ahead as it was pulled into the eddy. It rolled slowly over in the deep water, and appeared for a moment as though its groping limbs might swamp their floating junk pile. What happened instead was that a smaller branch, attached to the larger one, appeared from below and gave them a gentle nudge — just enough to send them into the smaller of the two streams. It was a stroke of luck, and Kaahli knew it immediately. This stream was sort of a backwash, quiet and almost without current.

Yellowish foam had disappeared, and the gurgling ceased. Willie and Kaahli found themselves floating slowly toward a grassy shore. The pile bumped the earth and fell into pieces.

"Here's where I get off," said Willie.

"Me too," said Kaahli.

They jumped to shore. Willie immediately put her nose to the earth and shuffled away.

"Where will you go, Willie?" asked Kaahli, running alongside the rat. "Can you find your way back to Trash Hole?"

"Told you, I don't care if I do find my way back. All I want to do is find some nice rotten stuff to chew on. Should be no problem. Should be all kinds of junk laying around after a rainstorm like that. Want to get out of the sun, too. Once I'm dry I hate that sun."

"Can I help you?" asked Kaahli.

"Can a lowly squirrel help a wondrously intelligent rat? You're for laughs. Leave me alone. You're safe now."

Kaahli stopped running alongside. She watched as Willie scratched and clawed herself into a dense patch of weeds. Then the rat was gone. Kaahli looked around. Willie had said she was safe.

She understood that without Willie, insults and all, she would almost certainly not be here on dry land. Very likely she would be at the bottom of the swollen stream, bumping along like another piece of debris, without sight or breath.

"Thanks for your help, Willie," she called out, toward where she'd last seen the skinny tail disappear in the long grass. There was no answer.

Kaahli took in her surroundings. A few trees scattered here and there, not a great deal more than in the park. Lots and lots of dry weeds and stunted bushes. No sign or sound of squirrels. Or other animals. A few red-winged blackbirds, a long way off, perched precariously on delicate stems of last warm season's cattails.

This open field was a lovely spot — a lovely spot for any hawk searching for a bite to eat, that is. She glanced up fearfully, at the clear sky, then at thick bunches of bushes. Not a bad spot for foxes to hide either. She would have to get up, off the earth. She would have to look after herself. Ephran must have been left a long way behind. She looked for the nearest tree.

Because, despite what Willie said, Kaahli did not feel one bit safe.

CHAPTER XVII
DESCENT INTO DARKNESS

The muscles in Ephran's legs stretched like they'd never stretched before. He flew at blinding speed down the trunk of the tree, stumbled, rolled head over tail, and came up on his paws. Frafan was right behind him.

Ephran's tongue seemed frozen, but Frafan shouted, "Hold on, Kaahli! We're coming!"

She had fallen almost directly into the middle of the angry stream. The broken branch had been swept away. She was looking back at them, only her head and the tip of her tail above the ripples and the foam, terror and surprise on her face.

Between trees and stream the land dipped gently. The low area was filled with long, shimmering, shallow puddles left by the rainstorm. Ephran and Frafan raced through, water splashing, trying to judge their approach so that they would arrive on the banks of the stream close to where they'd last seen Kaahli.

As they slid to a stop at the top of the embankment, Ephran's heart sank. In the few moments it had taken them to get here, Kaahli had already been carried far downstream. He could barely make her out, sweet face bobbing along, floating rapidly with the flotsam and jetsam in the water. He doubted that she could see him at all.

"Let's go, Frafan," he said, his throat still so tight he was surprised he could speak at all. "We have to catch her."

And so they ran again. As fast as they could. Ephran gritted his teeth, heart filled with panic once more. Terrible visions returned: he, escaping from Maltrick, up a butternut tree. Kaahli and he, running from the terrible wind and skystones, and later trying to out-distance the roaring forest fire. Klestra and he, along the base of Great Hill, looking for Kaahli. Then the three of them, running for their very breath again, away from Wytail and their own kind, those who should have been their friends. Running...always running. Where would this stop? Would it ever stop?

Breathless, Ephran and Frafan came to a place where the stream dived into a bank of earth, a hole like the one they had used to escape the dogs near Trash Hole. Only this hole wore no mesh and was full of roaring water. Ephran hesitated. Frafan fairly flew by him, up the slope above the hole, and into a thick bunch of weeds.

Just as Ephran started up the hill, he heard a loud "Oooff!"

At the top of the bank Frafan lay, rubbing his nose with both paws and gasping for breath.

"I'll be back for you, Frafan," Ephran said, crawling over his brother. "I have to get to Kaahli first..."

"No...," Frafan managed. "No further..." He held out a paw and pointed.

The path was blocked. For as far as he could see in either direction, Ephran's eye beheld what his brother had stumbled into. Here was the mesh after all, the stuff of which the many colored ones made cages. The holes in this mesh were too small for a squirrel to squeeze through, even one as small as Frafan.

Immediately Ephran tried to climb. He kept slipping. Tears of frustration welled up in his eyes. Then, as he neared the top, the flimsy mesh bent toward him and backward until he was nearly upside down. He tried to reach the top, to pull himself over. He fell to the earth, struggling back to his paws. The mesh sprung back to its original position.

Trying to get his breath, Ephran looked both ways again, for a stick in the earth...the mesh must be attached somewhere to a stick...as it was when it surrounded cows. Then he saw one, far away, too far to run, and climb, and then run back to the stream. It would be too late. It was too late now. Ephran slowly sat on his tail and put his face to the mesh.

Through the weeds and the deserted black path on the other side of the mesh, the stream flowed steadily along. Kaahli was nowhere to be seen. Down the hazy sun-splashed grassland, down the long and curving path of the water, there was no sign of her.

Frafan looked at his brother's eyes for a moment, then lowered his gaze to the earth. They walked slowly back to the stream. A little yellow flower, perched serenely atop a very long and narrow stalk, grew near the water's edge. Its petals were soft and filmy, and covered with a golden powder, fine as dust. A single drop of water lay at its core, sparkling in the sunlight like a lost firefly.

Ephran walked to the blossom and, very gently, took the stem in his teeth and bit through its green tenderness. He stood on his hindlegs and lifted the flower high in the bright, clear air. Then he dropped it into the water. It hesitated for a moment, turning slowly in a graceful circle. Then it tipped on its side and rushed off, down the waterway. Tears rolled from Ephran's eyes.

Frafan could not think of a single thing to say. He was heartsick. He could only imagine what his brother was feeling. He watched the flower disappear into the dark hole, just as Kaahli must have...

The idea smacked him on the side of his head like Jafthuh's paw. Of course! The flower rode on the water, just as Kaahli had! Just as waterbugs do...

"Ephran!" he shouted. "The water!"

Ephran's tear-stained face registered a puzzled and almost angry expression.

"I mean...the water will carry us...like the flower...like Kaahli.

No need to give up yet."

"Of course," Ephran whispered hoarsely, his brows lifting. "Good thinking, Frafan."

"And look," said Frafan, pointing upstream, "as though we ordered it, here comes our ride."

A massive chunk of wood, an uprooted tree stump, bore down on them. It floated on the dirty water with a sort of heavy majesty, bumping and pushing smaller and lighter objects out of its way. Broken-off roots pointed in all directions, like Fetzgar's furry head when it was wet and he'd been absentmindedly scratching it.

"You go first, Frafan," said Ephran. "I'll run alongside and, as soon as you're settled, I'll jump on."

They stood on the bank, muscles tense. The stump came nearer and nearer. Frafan crouched and, as he jumped, Ephran broke into a run, keeping pace with the wood. Frafan quickly scrambled to the far side of the stump and called, "Now, Ephran! There is room."

Legs churning, Ephran did not break stride. He only turned a bit toward the stream and took a long and graceful leap. He landed solidly, very near Frafan.

"This is wonderful," said Frafan, bright sunshine and clean air in his face. "We are traveling almost as fast as the blue van. We will catch up to Kaahli in no time."

Ephran frowned. "It does feel good, riding so fast and effortlessly. And this was a fine idea. But Kaahli must be traveling as fast as we are. I'm not so sure how quickly we'll catch her."

"I hadn't thought of that," said Frafan, moving his paws for balance as the stump wobbled. His smile returned. "But the water has to stop somewhere."

"I suppose," agreed Ephran. "Or perhaps she will come ashore at a curve in the water. Better yet, wouldn't it be wonderful if this stream finds its way to The Pond?"

They did not share it with one another, but the terrible thought occurred to both of them at the same time: there was hope for her if she could keep above water, if she was able to do what they did, if she was able to find something on which to climb. Otherwise, Kaahli's unwanted swim might very well be the last swim she'd ever take.

Ephran stood, forepaws on one of the broken roots, one that pointed straight up. From there he thought he might better search the shoreline for Kaahli, should she have somehow made her way to the bank. They bounced smoothly along, Frafan's eyes glued to one shoreline, Ephran's to the other. Clumps of brown bushes and red dogwood sped by. Here and there a big rock lay, challenging the rushing water. The stump roared by a quiet sidestream and for a moment Ephran panicked. What if she'd gone that way? Then he calmed down. How

"They bounced
smoothly along"

could anything work its way free of this insistent current?

An occasional blackbird or robin could be seen along the way, looking for bugs in the wet soil or for edible debris the water had deposited along its path. Those were the only creatures they saw. They swept through a tunnel, beneath another of the many colored ones' black paths.

After a long while Ephran, with a grim face, said, "No sign of her. And no sign that the water intends to slow down and settle into a lake or..."

His words stopped so suddenly it caused Frafan to look over. Ephran's eyes were glued to a big tree, the only big tree, they'd passed in a long while.

"What is it, Ephran? What do you see?"

Eyes unmoving, Ephran said, "Gray squirrel. Running up the trunk of that big tree back there. Just caught a glimpse."

"That tree's in the middle of nowhere," said Frafan. "What gray treeclimber would be..." He swallowed...and stood on his hindlegs to look himself. "Kaahli! You think it could be Kaahli?"

"It has to be! Frafan, she's safe! She's on dry land. Better yet, she's in a tree."

"Hooray!" Frafan shouted. "Let's get off this stump then."

A smiling Ephran's eyes were fastened on the tall tree. Frafan tilted his head and picked up his ears. Had there been a change in the sound of the water? Yes...a far-off rumble, a sort of soft, yet fearful, roar. Thunder? The sky above was empty of clouds. He strained, trying to tell where it was coming from. He could detect no change in the landscape around them. As far as he could tell, the water continued to flow at the same speed. "What could it be?" Frafan whispered to himself. He looked ahead, through the spike-like roots rising from the water-soaked stump. Then he said aloud, "Ephran..."

"What is it, Frafan?"

The rumbling sound had become very loud. Ephran turned to face ahead, following his brother's gaze.

No more than a five-season oak treelength ahead, the stream they rode could no longer be seen. It was not that it took a sharp turn behind a big tree — or that overhanging vegetation hid it. No, it simply disappeared.

The roar became louder. The stump moved with increasing speed. Then they could see...a gaping and jagged hole in the earth...the water falling into it, howling as it went.

"Jump!" Ephran shouted.

But they were too entangled in the roots. And they were moving far too fast. The tree stump, carrying its two astounded passengers, plunged into the yawning mouth of the earth.

CHAPTER XVIII

DREAMS OF PEACE

Kaahli scurried back to the stream. The water had not slowed. She kept well away from it, looking up and down the weedy shore, alert for any danger that might lurk there.

Should she follow the water back the way she'd come? Where she'd fallen in would be a long run upstream. There were few trees along the way. Most of her running would be on the earth. What if she met another mink? Or a dog? Kaahli shuddered. Would Ephran and Frafan be where she left them anyway?

What, she asked herself, would they have done after they saw her swept away? Most certainly they would not have stood there, calmly waving good-bye. They would have followed her. If that was true, where would they be now? How could they guess where the creek would take her? Would they, with their knowledge of wind and sun and clouds, find a faster and surer way? How could they possibly imagine where she and Willie had finally come ashore?

She decided she'd better find a good tree, something with high and sturdy branches. She would have to think...to consider her next move. And that would be easier if she could see what sort of country lay about her.

Across the stream a big green ash stood by itself. The upper branches of ash trees made for good resting and fur-drying places. And from there she would be able to see a great distance in all directions.

Downstream, the creek widened, separated by a narrow bar of sand. Kaahli ran toward it. She kept constant watch, in the grass and around bushes. She made herself ignore the rushing water, concentrating on her leap. The sandbar was a bit over half way to the other side. She must not think too long. After all, too much planning, concerning branch-jumping, had caused her present predicament. She backed up, closed her eyes to slits, and ran toward the water. Her paws barely met the wet sandbar before she jumped again. It crossed her mind that, lovely as branches were, there was something wonderfully solid about the earth.

Kaahli turned sharply and ran to the big tree. She did not look back. Just then, a large stump floated around an upstream bend in the creek. Two gray squirrels rode the stump, standing on their hindlegs. By the time Kaahli climbed the ash, and found a high branch that suited her, the stump had traveled down the waterway and tumbled into a massive hole in the earth.

When she reached the highest branches, Kaahli looked upstream, from where she'd come. There was no sign of Ephran and Frafan. The warren of the many colored ones was barely visible. She was astounded at how far she and Willie had ridden their pile of trash. Where they had washed ashore was mostly tall grass...few bushes and fewer trees. It was not the ideal spot for a treeclimber to start any sort of journey.

Her luck was not all bad though; big juicy buds grew everywhere. Kaahli put one in her mouth and bit down. It was moist and sweet, and filled her with a sense of the new warm season. Her spirits lifted.

She faced away from the stream, toward the edge of the earth where the sun rises. The sun was the only beacon she had, and she knew it. An idea occurred to her.

If The Pond lay toward the rising sun, then why not make a plan that would keep her running the right direction? Why not pick a landmark, say a big rock or an unusually-shaped tree, as far away as she could see? She would choose something located a little toward the cold side of where the sun came up. Once the landmark was reached she would simply wait until the next sunrise. Then she would pick a new landmark and set her destination the same way. That way she could not be fooled.

A chill passed down Kaahli's tail. She sneezed and shook herself. She told herself that she must not panic. She must be brave. She'd been alone before. She had a good plan and she would follow it.

A good part of the day was gone, so Kaahli chose her first landmark close enough to reach before the sky grew dark. That landmark happened to be a cluster of linden trees, standing on the other side of a small meadow. She would have to work her way carefully across the field but, as long as she kept the linden in sight, next morning's light should find her on the right path. And the linden themselves would give her a place to spend the darktime.

There was an immediate problem: Before she could even start her journey she'd have to conquer a familiar and frightening obstacle...one of those wide black paths for cars and trucks lay between her and the open field. Even now she saw a car speeding away from her, round legs hissing on the smooth surface.

She slowly approached the black path. A ditch lay between her and the path, dotted with little puddles of shimmering water. She sat, for some time, among long brown weeds.

Finally she stood on her hindlegs. Not a car or truck was in sight. She listened as hard as she could. There was no sound save the buzzing of insects and the songs of birds. Kaahli knew she should run now. But she hesitated, heart pounding in her chest. She did not want to cross the path. Visions of Wytail disappearing beneath a truck popped into her head.

A far-off rumbling came to her ears, growing louder and louder.

She lay down in the weeds, hugging the firm earth, as a huge silver and red truck with rows of big black legs sped by. The ground shook. In the truck's gusty wake, dust and pebbles flew everywhere. It was almost as frightening as the day she and Ephran hid beneath the earth from the skystones.

As suddenly as it appeared, the truck was gone. It swooshed down the path and out of sight.

Kaahli turned back the way she'd come. There had to be an easier way than this. She stopped and bit her lip. There would be no easy way. She felt something move in her belly. If she ever wanted to see Ephran again, if she wanted to curl in her nest by The Pond, to have and raise her and Ephran's young, she would have to cross this terrible black path. This was a time for going forward, not for shrinking back. Every bit of courage summoned, she raced through the ditch and started across the path.

Her legs could not move fast enough. She nearly stumbled twice, but at last crossed the long white stripe that ran down the far side of the path. Safe, at least from cars and trucks, Kaahli lay down in the short grass at the path's edge and closed her eyes. Her mother's face appeared, smiling and nodding, wearing the wonderful expression of praise and encouragement always bestowed on her young ones when they had completed a difficult task. Kaahli opened her eyes and smiled. The panicked feeling was gone.

By the time Kaahli reached the linden, the sun had sunk low in the sky. Its color had changed from brilliant gold to bright pink. She climbed into the lower branches and quickly found a shallow hole in the trunk. She would barely fit. A pawful of buds made up the last meal of the day. She ate, facing the sinking sun, hope and fear struggling in her heart.

She crawled into the hole as shadows grew long. The wind began as a whisper, then grew to a whistling night-monster. The tree groaned and swayed with the uneasy air. A brittle branch broke above her hole and crashed to the earth. Kaahli shivered and drew her tail closer around her. She was sure she would be unable to sleep, that there was far too much noise, too much fright, too much to think about. She was wrong. Kaahli was sound asleep before worries could form in her mind.

She could not know that almost directly beneath the roots of her ash tree, in a huge underground cavern, the one she loved most was also curled in fretful slumber. Their dreams, bright and real in a world beyond their understanding, hovered close to one another in the singing air.

She saw herself falling again, and moaned in her sleep. But, before she struck the cold water, she was swept away by the wind. She was flying! Not on Cloudchaser's back this time. The air itself was carrying her, like a maple leaf caught in a squall.

Sailing over the warren of many colored ones, she recognized the small many colored one, blue and white pelt restored to its original brilliance. The creature was seated in short green grass, throwing a bent twig as far as it could with its pudgy forepaw. A robin, seated so close to the small one she hadn't seen it at first, took wing. It flew to the little stick, picked it up in its beak, and flew back to the small one. The bird perched fearlessly on the small one's leg. The small one laughed happily, took the stick from the robin's mouth, and gently rubbed the bird's feathers with a soft white paw. The robin warbled its happiest rainy-morning song.

Suddenly a huge oak loomed in her way, a gray squirrel scampering up its trunk. A tear formed in her eye when she recognized Queesor. Then she saw a larger squirrel, chasing Queesor up the tree. It was Wytail! A warning came to her lips. But Queesor's smile and laughter told her to hold her tongue. Wytail touched the smaller squirrel's tail and the chase reversed. Wytail ran off, through the branches, Queesor in hot pursuit, both of them laughing loudly.

She floated away, mouth agape. It grew darker. Another squirrel appeared below her, this one apparently sound asleep on an outcropping of rocks. Ephran! Could it be Ephran? She swooped lower. It was too dark to see clearly. She came closer yet. Too close. She scraped along the earth, stumbling on the uneven surface. She rolled over, right next to the sleeping squirrel. When she looked up, he was looking into her eyes. It was not Ephran. It was Rennigan!

Kaahli woke suddenly and totally.

"Well, I'll be dignabbed!"

"Rennigan!" She nearly fainted with relief.

"How ya doin', Kaahli?"

"Oh, Rennigan! Oh, Rennigan! I can't tell you how happy I am to see you!"

"Good ta hear. Feelin's mutual, y'know."

"Where did you come from, Rennigan? How did you manage to find me? Oh, I still can't believe it! It's really you!"

"Come from High Hill, Kaahli. Actually, got to admit I wuz about lost. Headed too far toward warm season's nest. Not much other excuse fer treeclimbers ta be away from the woods, in the middle a nowhere."

"Where were you trying to go?" Kaahli asked.

"To find you. And that whippersnapper of a mate a'yers. Heard there was some nasty treeclimbers from the many colored ones' warren after ya. Which brings us ta Ephran and his second brother. Where are they?"

"The story about unfriendly squirrels was true, Rennigan. But they didn't catch us. We were saved, I think, by a most unusual squirrel..." Kaahli began to shake like a cottonwood leaf in a windstorm.

"Hold on there, Kaahli. Don't come undone now, m'dear," he said, and put his paw around her. Then he laughed loudly. "Not quite so quick, anaway, after this ol' buck-toothed branch-jumper managed ta find a little luck."

CHAPTER XIX

TIGHT SQUEEZES

Frafan awoke with a terrible headache. Gingerly, he put his paw to his brow. He winced. A rock...must have hit a rock. The way he'd been flying down the tunnel, it wasn't surprising that there'd be a few bumps to show for it. What was amazing was that he woke up at all.

The fur above his eye was wet. Was he leaking thick red juice? It was too dark to tell, and he hesitated to put his paw to his mouth to see if the sweet salty taste was there. Then he realized he was wet all over, not just his head. Actually, he was soaked. Water dripped everywhere. Except for the dripping, and for the far-off murmur of a stream, all was quiet. A very hollow sort of quiet. Like the big deserted barn on Corncrib Farm. Frafan most definitely did not like this sort of quiet.

Should he try to get up? He knew of the dangers that lurked on the earth — in tall grass, behind bushes, in the clouds. But now he was beneath the earth. What sort of hunters might nest here?

He reached out and felt around. He was laying on smooth and sandy earth, next to water. How much water he could not tell. He remembered being thrown from the tree stump as it dived into the sinkhole. He remembered too, the amazed look on his brother's muddy face as he flew past him, down the black tunnel. There had been just enough light left, coming from above, to see where the tunnel bent, where his body would slam against the rocky wall. There was no place to jump, no sweet branch to grasp. After that the light was gone. What rotten luck! Now he had no idea where he was.

On the other paw, maybe this luck wasn't all bad. Foolish as it sounded, having the sense knocked from him may have saved his breath. Limp and relaxed, instead of tense with panic, he had survived a very rough trip. He had obviously washed ashore after being in the water for some time. A frantic branch-runner, finding himself in deep water, might have swallowed enough of the cold liquid to force the air from his chest. Instead, all he had was a few bumps and bruises. He could breathe, move all his legs, and he could hear and smell. Things could be a lot worse.

The only physical problem (and he tried not to think about it), was that the darkness was so complete he could not tell if his sight might be gone. Such loss, of course, for any animal of the woods, meant the end of things.

Slowly and carefully, Frafan got up. He was able to stand. Though he could not see his legs, there was feeling in them. He lifted one paw, ready to take a step. It occurred to him that any step, in any direction, meant the possibility of slipping and sliding off into another deep tunnel...or into the claws of a horrible waiting enemy...maybe a slimy, scaly thing with damp skin and yellow teeth. He slowly put the paw back where it had been.

Fear crawled into his mind so unexpectedly that, without thinking, he chattered loudly: "Ephran! Where are you, you rascal? Where are you hiding in this ridiculously dark place?"

There was no answer. He hadn't expected one. But, answer or no answer, shouting made him feel better! At least there was a voice in this horribly dark and lonely place, even if it was his own. He decided not to worry about waking monsters. And the sound served more than one purpose. He was delighted to find that his chatter, echoing and rebounding from ceiling and walls, gave a definite impression of what surrounded him.

He chattered again. "Hey! Who wants to go for a swim?"

Yes, indeed! Echoes bombarded him. He understood he was in a cavern, nearly round, like the individual rabbit dens in Great Woods Warren. Only much larger. The ceiling was low, maybe five taillengths above. He was at one end of a big underground hole. At the far end no echoes had returned. He tested his theory.

"If you can't swim, don't worry. We can drown together," he shouted.

Again, no echoes returned from the other side. And, now that he listened carefully, the place of no echoes was where he heard the muted sound of running water. There had to be an entrance. It must be the way he came in, washed into the cavern stunned, and deposited on the sandy shore.

"So....," Frafan thought, "now I know the way out of my dark and watery cage. But how do I get over there?"

The distance between himself and the hole he'd been carried through was considerable. And the gap was filled with water. He'd swim if he had to, but he'd rather not. He had learned he could drink the stuff and now he knew he could float on it. It had brought him to a safe resting place. Nevertheless, he did not relish the thought of lowering his body back into that cold, black liquid. What other creatures might float or swim beneath its black surface?

Maybe there was another way. After all, if there was sandy soil on this side, perhaps...

Slowly and cautiously Frafan felt his way along the edge of the water. One paw after the other. It was very hard to keep from running. And it seemed a long time before he could tell that his heading was changing — ever so slowly — toward the entrance. The pool of water must be circular.

Every so often he would chatter aloud, to check his position and progress, to be sure he hadn't followed the water's edge into a deep side-

142

cavern. He would shout things like:

"I thought I'd seen some dark and gloomy days in the woods, but this is ridiculous!" or:

"If you're hiding around the next corner, Ephran, I'm going to bite your tail like you won't forget!"

The shouting, the thinking, the physical activity of feeling his way along, all made Frafan feel much better than he had when he first woke up. He was able to consider what was happening more of a fascinating experience and less (at least a little less) a breath-threatening disaster. He smiled grimly to himself in the dark when he almost heard Jafthuh's voice saying: "Cheated a little on your first Alone Time, didn't you, son? Not so easy cheating this round, is it?"

The dull ache in his head had nearly disappeared. His heart slowed and the knot in his stomach loosened.

At one point he had to shuffle along a thin ledge, cold rock wall on one side and colder water on the other. Each step had to be carefully placed. Who knew where there might be another hole to fall through?

He could feel open space ahead. Like waking on a rainy morning in the nest at Corncrib Farm, moist air moved through his whiskers. Where he had ridden a rainstorm-swollen torrent (how long ago, he wondered?) the tunnel now held only a trickle. It gurgled softly, almost under his nose.

All right, then! First goal reached. But what now? Which way to go?

Frafan turned his head in the direction from which the water flowed. Then the other. Air, fresh air, was coming from the downstream tunnel. And he got the impression of a faint glow, far away. Were his eyes deceiving him? Were his eyes of any use any more? He looked upstream again. Maybe there was a glow that way too.

Well, he would follow fresh air and the promise of open fields, green grass, and sturdy branches. As he stepped out into the passageway, next to the trickle of water, he hoped with all his heart that the promise he followed was not false.

He moved along, as quickly as he dared. He was making good progress he thought, when a sudden rumbling came to his ears. He stopped to listen. The sound was chasing him, becoming louder and louder, filling the dark corridor he'd traveled! Then he could feel it, a horrible grinding and groaning that bore down on him at tremendous speed.

What now? What dread hunter raced toward him? The earth...it must be the earth...hating, in its own way, the hollow space the rushing water had created. The tunnel was collapsing on itself!

Where could he hide? How could he escape the heavy rocks and black dirt that must be tumbling into the cavern, squeezing breath from any flesh that dare stand in its way?

Frafan began to run. He strained his eyes. They might as well be closed. He kept stumbling in the dark.

"Ooh! Ouch!"

His forepaw banged against a large rock and he went sprawling, paw hurting terribly. He tried to get up. His leg gave out and he fell again. He was not gaining anyway. He rolled onto his belly, wrapped his tail around him, and placed his paws over his head. He put them down again. How silly! How laughable! Acting as though fragile paws and scrawny tail would provide any protection!

Frafan lay there, suddenly filled with a crazy mixture of despair, terror and disgust. His thoughts rushed along as fast as the rumbling earth raced toward him. Ha! he thought, small paws were no help. Never had been. Why hadn't they grown bigger? Like Ephran's and Phetra's? For that matter, why hadn't all of him grown bigger and stronger? Short legs made him a slow runner and poor jumper. No wonder he couldn't keep up with other squirrels. Why were his legs so spindly?

He remembered Redthorn pushing him around like a hazel nut...Wytail's referring to him as owlbait...Phetra's tears at leaving him behind after the big snowstorm...Ephran's need to rescue him from Blackie...Queesor's surprised expression when he learned that tiny, ineffectual Frafan might actually be brother to Ephran.

The earth's groaning passed over, almost ignored in the heat of Frafan's self-loathing. A few pebbles and a peppering of dirt rained down on his back. The rumble moved quickly down the tunnel and disappeared.

He lay on the cold earth. The stubbed paw throbbed hotly. Anger left him as suddenly as it had come. He was breathing, but he didn't really care one way or another. What difference did it make? He'd most likely never get out of here anyway. And of what value was a tiny, weak, hapless creature...to himself or anyone else?

He decided to sleep then. Right there, in the middle of the cold and damp path. Who cared what other creature might follow this trail? There was no way out, not for a puny little animal with no strength to move earth and rocks. If a hunter didn't get him, the cave and its shifting and grinding stones would. Frafan was totally drained, physically and emotionally. He fell asleep as soon as his eyes closed. And he slept for a long time.

He woke up to total silence. But there was a bit of light, he thought, at the far end of this tunnel. "The rising sun...," he thought. Maybe the sun, assuming a position in the sky different from when he'd come in here, was able to penetrate this terrible dark and dank place. Without spirit he trudged toward the brightness.

He could begin to see his own paws, one then the other, beneath him. Slowly, the rough walls of the cave became visible. Fresh air flowed more quickly across his nose.

As he turned around a sharp curve, a thin shaft of light almost blinded him. He stopped, blinked and moved his head to the side.

Yellow light poured through a small hole in the wall above, from among an intimidating pile of boulders, rocks and small stones. He decided it was worth a look. Frafan jumped carefully from one rock to another, slowly upward, paws slipping on the damp surface. When he reached the hole he poked his head through. A slender tunnel led a short distance, perhaps six or seven taillengths, to a larger cavern. The far end of that larger cavern was filled with light. It had to be the way out...to fields and forests. He told himself he didn't care. But he did. He wanted desperately to be out of this horrible place.

He squirmed into the hole, barely breathing, and pushed himself along with his hindlegs, belly and back scraping along the rough and irregular tunnel. He tried not to think what would happen if one of the boulders which surrounded him decided to shift, ever so slightly.

After what seemed like a very long time, his head popped clear. Then his chest and his belly. He was out! He was free! He could almost feel the bark of a solid branch beneath his paws!

He scrambled down the pile of rocks to the floor of the cavern and looked back. Coming from this direction no one would ever notice the tiny opening through which he'd just crawled. It was too small to be of consequence.

Too small to be of consequence? Like so many Wet Walnuts it was! That tiny crack, that miniscule gap in the earth, had saved him. And if he would have been any bigger...if he'd been a Wytail, even an Ephran, he would not have fit. He would still be trapped on the other side, with no place to go, with no hope for escape.

He turned and ran toward the steady stream of light. He was really hungry! His stomach grumbled. It would be good to dig in black earth, to look for last season's nuts. Maybe Ephran was out there already, waiting for him.

Frafan stepped into the shaft of light. It poured over him from above...too bright to keep his eyes open... Then something bumped against him. Something firm and furry. A claw brushed him. At last he met his nightmare, a monster from deep in the earth! With eyes closed against the brightness, Frafan raised his own claws and prepared to fight to his last breath.

Sometimes
it takes total darkness
to make the light
visible.

Mutterings of King Glenhope V
Chap. IX

CHAPTER XX

CAVERNS IN THE EARTH

ooff!" Ephran snorted as his back met the firm tunnel wall. He fell, less than a taillength, and bounced solidly on an overhang of rocky soil.

He struggled to get up, to call to Frafan down the black hole, but his breath had been taken from him. Neither legs or voice would work. The time for calling was gone anyway. It was too late to be of any sort of help. He lay back, gasping for air, while his eyes slowly became accustomed to the dim light.

The stump loomed over him, wedged into the sinkhole. Its bulk shut off the outside world, the world of sun and clouds and trees. Tiny spurts of water, getting ever larger, were slowly eating away the earth around the big stump. It occurred to Ephran that it was not safe here. The water would eventually wear away the sides of the narrow place and allow the stump to continue its journey — right down on top of him.

Air returned, gasp by gasp, to Ephran's chest. He struggled slowly to his paws. Checking himself, he found no wounds. No thick red water soaked his fur. Though wet and cold, his legs were steady. His luck had been the good kind again. But what of the others? What of Frafan and Kaahli? He bit his lip when he thought of his brother. What had the water done with him?

He had no idea, of course, where Kaahli might be. Except (and he smiled in the dark) she was not in this dreadful hole in the earth. She had found a tree. Frafan, on the other paw, was somewhere close by. Maybe. Hopefully, Frafan had been as lucky when he landed...if he had landed. There was no way of telling how far this terribly huge hole went down. Exactly how deep was the earth anyway? He'd never thought of it before. He'd never dreamed a treeclimber would have to consider such matters.

"Frafan!" he shouted, against the sound of the water, beginning to run faster and faster around him. The groan of wood, strained to the breaking point, was the only answer he got. He looked up in time to see the stump ease toward him a bit, roots sticking up like thick wet hairs...bending and breaking against the tunnel walls. The weight and force of water behind the stump must be immense.

The ledge he stood on continued at an angle downward, into the darkness. Above him the tunnel walls were steep and slick. There was really no choice about which way to go.

He crawled along, testing every step carefully before putting his full weight on it. The sound of water became fainter. His path leveled off. The ledge spread out, became wider and drier, went deeper and deeper. At times it was so steep he had to plant his claws to keep from

147

sliding. The path was now nearly solid rock. The muted roar of water rose again. He braced himself for its impact, but it rushed away under him. The stump must have come free.

He wished he could see, but his surroundings were like a moonless night in the forest. There were only shadows, dark gray to black, and vague outlines. Rocks, big and small. Humps and ridges...of what? Ridges of earth, of course, he told himself. There were no hunters crouching to leap at him down here. Or were there? What would a squirrel know of a huge place like this — a frightening and dark place beneath the surface of the earth?

Ephran shook himself vigorously and then lay down. He must get his bearing, decide on what should be done. Fortunately for a wet treeclimber, the air was warm in this cavern, at least as warm as it had been outside.

Should he try to go back the way he'd come? If, as he suspected, the water rushing into this sinkhole was so deep and wild because of the rainstorm, then the amount and force of the water would become less and less as time went on. If he waited a while, he might be able to climb out of here.

On the other paw, it would be a steep and slippery climb... even if the creek had returned to a trickle. He had crawled very deep into the earth. Such a climb would hardly be like running tried and true branches. What if he fell back, into the black hole? Not likely he'd be able to steer himself to his solid ledge a second time. He would most certainly end up wherever Frafan had. And where was that? The horror of losing his brother, of watching him fly helplessly by, brought warm tears to his eyes.

Ephran forced himself to think. If he went on, as he had been, he might discover what had become of his brother. But was it wise to look for Frafan down here? If Frafan wasn't badly hurt he'd have moved off, in who knew what direction, looking for his own way out. Or for Ephran.

Ephran put his head on his paws. What would Odalee say to him now? Which way would Jafthuh and Rennigan go? In his mind, he could see, with amazing clarity, his parents and his teacher.

"Let's try a new trail, sonny," Rennigan would say, "old one's a mite tricky."

"Anyway," Jafthuh would add with a laugh, "who wants to bounce around in the dark?"

"Don't avoid the hard path, but it's silly to follow it if there's a better one to the same destination," Odalee would say, nodding her head solemnly.

Ephran got to his paws again, mind made up. He would follow the ledge. It was a new path, and the only one that made any sense. He moved along, mostly by feeling his way. Darkness grew thicker and thicker until he could feel it pressing down against his eyes. An earthy smell, full of mold and must, filled his nose. A silence, like all the activity in the world had ended, left him straining his ears for any sound. His heart fluttered in his chest and he gritted his teeth. He fought panic, trying to think of clean breezes in green branches, white clouds against a bright blue sky, The Pond twinkling in afternoon sunlight, the sound of fluttering aspen leaves. Putting one paw in front of the other was as least as difficult as it had been the day he and Klestra had climbed Great Hill.

He moved patiently, trying to keep his mind busy. It looked a bit brighter ahead. He wanted so badly to see sunlight he thought he might be imagining it. He crept on. Yes, it was true, there was no doubt of it...it was getting lighter! Not a great deal lighter, but the blackness was less complete.

Then he realized the light was far above him. Ephran found himself in a huge, dome-shaped cavern. Stone formations, icicles the size of trees, rose from the floor of the cave. As his eyes adjusted he could see that they hung from the roof as well. That ceiling, from where came the light, seemed as far away as the sky on a starless night. The only source of sweet light that he wanted to think of would be that wonderful ball of brilliance, the sun.

Could he climb those slimy tree-icicles? He knew he could not. Straightening his legs and squinting against the darkness, trying to see a way up, Ephran took a few steps forward. Something swooped through the air above him. The fur on the back of his neck was ruffled by a breeze from silent wings. Bats! He had disturbed a group of bats!

Distracted by the bats, and awestuck by this astounding cavern, he took a step. Without a sound, without warning, his right front leg went out from under him. Gravel and small rocks slipped from the grasp of his other paw. He lurched forward. A cold breath of air brushed against his nose, coming from far below. He began to slide.

Ephran frantically dug his hindpaws into earth and rock. Just when he was sure there was no hope, that he could not help but fall, his sliding stopped. He lay there, balanced on the edge (of what?), listening to his own harsh breathing. Then he heard the rocks and sand he had dislodged. They splashed into water... somewhere a long way down.

Carefully, ever so carefully, he eased himself back, onto solid earth. He was afraid to stand up. He shivered, and then began to shake, violently. The shaking did not want to stop. He didn't even try to stop it.

He lay for a long while, listening, as the shaking weakened and became trembling. Silence, except for dripping water, was total. He hoped that the light would become brighter, but it didn't. His eyes burned from watching. He closed them. He was lost again. So were Kaahli and Frafan. More than being lost, he was in a cage. A much bigger cage than he'd been in before, but a cage in any case. And, as it turned out, a far more dangerous one than he'd found himself in at the Farm of Cages.

It would be an understatement to say it had been one difficult day. He needed rest. He needed rest very badly...

Ephran dreamt. He dreamt he was perched on the highest branches of a green ash tree. The sun was shining happily. It felt wonderful on his feathers. Feathers? Yes indeed, feathers! He stretched his forepaws, to find they weren't paws at all. They were the most beautiful big wings he'd ever seen! White and gray at the front, the back edge of these wondrous wings were long-feathered, a lovely teal green, all neatly placed, one overlapping the next. He should be surprised, but it all seemed quite reasonable, as though this was as it ought to be.

Ephran spread his grand wings and pushed off from the branch. For an instant he was falling, and his throat tightened and made a groaning sound. But then the air came under his feathers and lifted him, and he sailed away, high above everything. Clouds sailed around him, sometimes one with him. Smaller trees and bushes fled beneath and behind him. He followed a stream for a way, gracefully twisting and turning his way through a shallow swale. Sweet air blew in his face, butterflies fluttered below, and a glorious feeling filled his chest.

He swooped and turned and dived, wings cutting through the gentle air. A large hill loomed ahead. He could make out a hole in its side. He flew toward it, not really wanting to, not knowing why he did. He wanted to stay in the sky, not fly into the earth. But this was his path. Something below beckoned.

He flew into a dark cave, feeling more than seeing his way. He flew and flew. Around curves, down one steep passage and back up another. Over water and over rocks. Green moss grew everywhere. The air was moist and quiet. Its odor was deep and heavy, undisturbed from ages past. He flew down a cavern lined with heavy, smooth white boulders.

Then he found himself in a massive cavern filled with huge and elongated rock formations, light coming from somewhere above. He almost overlooked a treeclimber, looking very small and out of place, laying on a ledge below him. Ephran realized why he was here. He must find the light. He must find it for himself and for the treeclimber.

He flew up and up, toward the ceiling of vaulted rock, toward the light. It came from between two large, flat boulders. As he got closer he could see that there was an opening between them, a slit, a place through which light might squeeze. He hovered close, beating his wings rapidly. The slit was too small for his body.

He let himself float away. He must look for another place. He flew across the ceiling until he saw light poking through another opening. A wondrous shaft of brightness came through a small hole, this

"He flew up and up, toward the ceiling of vaulted rock."

time not in rock itself, but in sandy soil between the rocks. He could make it larger! He could use his claws to dig the earth away. Then he realized he had no claws. Badgers had claws to dig, foxes had claws to grasp, raccoons had claws to climb. Squirrels had claws too...and their claws could do many things. He looked down at his puny legs. They were thin and weak. Bird legs. He could not dig. He could not climb. All he could do was fly and cling to branches.

Again he turned away. Maybe there was one more opening. One more path to the light. He flew across the ceiling. Off in a corner he thought he saw a faint glimmer. As he sailed toward this promise, he realized his beautiful wings were tiring. The closer he got to where he thought the light originated, the fainter it became. Then, there was no light any more. Only some faintly shimmering slices of rock, solid as the blackness around them.

He had to get out of here. He had to fly out the way he'd come in. The treeclimber would have to fend for itself. There was nothing he could do for the hapless creature. He circled around the great stone dome. Around and around, back and forth. Where had he come in? Where was the tunnel he'd flown through? He could not find it. His wings grew heavier and heavier.

Finally he swooped away, looking for a place to rest, to fold his wings. But there were no branches, no high place of safety. He was no better off in this strange and unwelcome place than the treeclimber below him.

Then his wings gave out entirely and he settled down, almost out of control. He would land right next to, if not on top of, the treeclimber, who lay perfectly still on the wet rocks.

Ephran woke with a start, his dream shattered.

He lay in the darkness, wondering how long he'd slept, heart pounding. Paws, he told himself, not wings, were the important thing to have right now. Wings, by themselves, could not save him. One had to have other gifts to go along with wings. He would do the best he could with what he had.

Confused thoughts raced through his head, bumping into one another, careening away, making room for another. Jumbled and tangled they were. But he felt, somewhere underneath it all, he had come upon something. Something very important.

He moved away from the abyss. There had to be another way out. And, sure enough, a tunnel opened in front of him. But where did it lead? He sat down. He must not make any more mistakes. It had been a long time without food already. He could not afford to take the wrong path. Then he realized the walls of the tunnel were made up of big boulders...white boulders. He remembered his dream. This was the tunnel through which his dream wings had carried him. It had to be the way out!

Sure enough, in a short time the floor of the tunnel turned upward. Ephran's heart beat faster. He began to make out the vague outline of his paws, moving up and down. Then he realized the walls of his tunnel, glistening with wetness, were becoming easier and easier to see. A strong and steady light appeared ahead. Ephran ran toward it.

As he turned the corner, he closed his eyes against the brilliant whiteness that flooded over him. He was about to shout for joy when something bumped him on the side — something warm and furry.

With a squeal, Ephran swung at his attacker with his left forepaw. This threw him off balance. He rolled over, back up on his paws. He blinked desperately, trying to adjust his eyes to the bright light.

Ephran would not be denied. His breath would not be taken from him. Not when he was so close to freedom, so close to another chance to find Kaahli and Frafan, so close to being reunited with family and friends.

He sensed the enemy almost on top of him, and he attacked viciously. He struck out with his paws and felt for a place to bite — a soft place to bite deep and hard. The other joined the battle and they rolled over and over on the wet earth. He had to come out on top. He had to find the fatal place before the other did. He had to...

It occurred to Ephran that whatever he fought was a small animal, and not an underground scaly or slimy one like a lizard or a snake...smaller than a cat...certainly not a badger...

"Ephran!" a voice shouted in his ear.

Immediately a face flashed into his mind. A face that was surrounded by lacy curls of white smoke. He could almost smell it. But the voice he heard was not Maltrick's. And the face was not that of a fox.

"Frafan!" he managed, and pulled his head back to look in his brother's eyes.

They lay for a moment, tangled in each other's legs. Frafan gasped. Ephran shook his head. Then they began to laugh. A titter at first. Then harder. Until tears ran from their eyes.

Finally Ephran said, "So, my brother, the water carved different paths to the same destination, eh?"

"It seems that way," said Frafan.

"I was afraid I'd never see you again," said Ephran. "I was afraid your trip into the earth might never stop."

"I was I afraid too," said Frafan, "some for me and some for you."

Ephran shook his head. "I thought this time my separation from family and friends was forever."

"Ha!" cried Frafan. "I wasn't about to get separated again. I

153

went to one heap of trouble to find you in the first place. You're talking to a treeclimber who survived a terrible snowstorm as well as threats from a crazy rabbit. This small squirrel jumped into the back of a terrible blue van and now has come out of a deep cavern in the earth. From now on I'm sticking to you like a spiky cocklebur."

Ephran smiled and put his foreleg around Frafan's shoulder. "Be careful, brother. Rennigan would say you're braggin'. But I love you and your spirit." As he looked over Frafan's shoulder his expression changed. "I fear, however, that we haven't escaped the embrace of the earth yet. Do you realize we're at the bottom of one amazing hole?"

"What?" Frafan rolled over and looked up. "Wow! You certainly are right about that."

They had found their separate ways, along paths cut by rushing water deep under the ground, to the bottom of a very deep hole. Ephran squinted. Far above he could see fluffy clouds, sailing across the wonderfully blue sky. The hole stretched away, straight as an ash tree, right up to the light. Running water had not formed this perfectly round tunnel. Nor had any forest animal.

"Not your usual badger hole, is it?" said Ephran. "Too smooth. Too straight. And see the way rocks have been placed along the sides," said Ephran, pointing to the walls.

Frafan nodded slowly. The tunnel walls reminded him of the enclosure at Rocky Point. "I believe you're right, brother," he finally replied. Then he mumbled, "I think the two of us have found a hole we can't climb out of."

CHAPTER XXI

SNAKE CLIMBING

Ephran and Frafan peered up the rock-lined tunnel, to the bright blue sky far above. A swallow soared across the opening and, now and then, a filmy little cloud, twirling and twisting with the high winds, floated past. The thought of wings came to Ephran's mind. He put it aside. Feathers would never grow on these paws. Besides, wings would be only a temporary help. What the big world above held, once he reached it, would be far better faced with paws. His paws. Paws he knew how to use.

Ephran ran to the tunnel wall. He carefully placed his claws on the upper edge of the lowest rock. He barely managed to get one paw in front of the other before he slipped back down, small chunks of earth falling with him. The rocks were not particularly smooth, but they were damp and slick.

Frafan shook his head sadly. "Maybe we'll never escape."

"We'll get out." Ephran's voice was calm. "We have to. Kaahli is looking. Family and friends wait." He began to sniff and search along jagged holes and crevices among the rocks.

"It's no use looking into those holes, Ephran," said Frafan, "we don't want to go running off into another... Oh, Whiskers!"

"What's the matter, Frafan?" said Ephran, alarmed at the sudden change in his brother's voice.

"Up t..there...," stammered Frafan, pointing up the tunnel, cloaked in deep shade, "big...big s..snake."

Ephran backed up. His eyes followed his brother's pointed claw. Sure enough, along the darkest side of the wall hung a long, slender, cord-like shadow. Ephran stood stock-still.

"I don't think it means us any harm," said Ephran. "It does not move." He squinted. "One strange snake. Too thin to swallow anything of any size." Ephran took a step closer. "Wait a minute...that's no snake!"

"No snake?" squeaked Frafan.

"Some sort of vine," said Ephran, inspecting the end of the cord, dangling against the wall a taillength or so above his head. "Has a frayed end. And it goes on and on, up as far as I can see."

Frafan stood next to his brother and followed his gaze. "A root, do you suppose?"

"Possible," said Ephran, "but I've never seen a root like this. One that stays the same girth along its entire length, not wide at one end and slender at the other. Let's find out."

He backed up, took a run (as long a run as he could, considering how little room he had), and leaped at the "snake." He caught it between

155

his forepaws, clutched it with his rear claws, and scrambled up.

"Seems sturdy enough," he called back to Frafan.

"Any better idea of what it might be?"

"A vine," said Ephran. "But juiceless. There is no firmness here. Smells old and musty."

Ephran continued climbing. Frafan lost sight of him in the darkness. "Frafan," his voice echoed back, "this vine just keeps going. I think it may go all the way to the top. Can you reach it? And follow me?"

Ephran's words were followed by a deep rumbling, like the earth was belching.

"What was that?" Ephran called.

"The earth is complaining about open spaces. It did it when I was underground," said Frafan. "Didn't you hear it down there?"

"No, I didn't," said Ephran. "Sounds scary."

"Sounds scary but doesn't mean much. Lots of noise and little action," said Frafan with a bored snicker.

"You better get up here anyway," said Ephran.

"Okay," Frafan sighed. "Here we go." The earth rumbled again. He took his time, judging how much of a jump was needed, missed the vine anyway, and tumbled back to the floor. He lay for a moment, smiling and shaking his head. "Would still take longer legs if I could get them," he laughed to himself. The earth moved under him, like one layer was sliding over another. He got up quickly. Yes, the earth was definitely shivering. The smile left his lips.

His second jump was a bit more hurried but it was successful. He grasped the vine tightly and hugged it even harder as the earth shuddered again. Frafan looked down, gasped, and almost lost his grip.

The entire bottom of the shaft had dropped into blackness! Some of the big rocks in the sidewalls came loose and tumbled soundlessly away. The ground grumbled again, and then belched in satisfaction.

Paw after paw, Frafan struggled up the vine. Cold damp air, from deep in the earth, tickled his tail. What if the sides of the tunnel collapsed as the bottom had?

The climb was long and steep but the vine was thick, rough, and easy to grip. Would it continue all the way to the light? It had to. There was no turning back. If the vine did reach the top, he hoped there was not some yet invisible flaw, some spot frayed to near the breaking point, some defect that might show up any moment. And the vine's roots must grow deep and solid in the thick, silent earth.

These thoughts raced through Frafan's mind, and he hoped, with a hope that came from deep inside his heart, that the vine stayed firm and taut. For a treeclimber's worst fear was always that which had happened

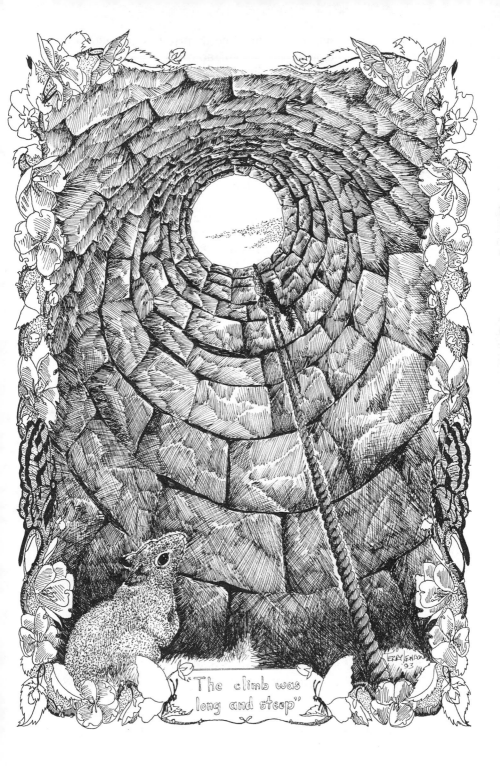

"The climb was long and steep"

to Kaahli...the feeling that they would find themselves gripping a thing which had no foundation, no inner strength, no roots.

Ephran crawled to the very lip of the tunnel. The vine continued up and over the edge. Sunlight poured down, into his eyes and his ears and his nose. With warmth and light came a feeling of intense gratitude. He could barely open his eyes. He would...he choked back the lump in his throat...he would be given the chance to find Kaahli after all.

He scrambled onto a ledge of rock, formed in a circle, up away from the earth. A wall, shaped around the hole in the earth. For what purpose? Who could tell? Frafan, wide-eyed, suddenly appeared beside him.

He quickly moved away from the vine, as though it might wrap itself around him and drag him back, into the darkness. He poked his nose over the edge. The earth at the bottom of the shaft, where he'd stood only a few minutes ago, was gone. He whistled under his breath. A cardinal seemed to answer him from a faroff tree.

"Oh, Ephran," sighed Frafan, "aren't the sun and the wind and the blue sky wonderful?"

They took in their surroundings. Not six leaps behind them, where they had not so much as looked after they rose from the tunnel in the earth, stood a many colored one den.

The den was not especially large, not compared to most they'd seen. It was pale green in color, white along the edges and around windows. The color was faded and peeling off in places, like an animal shedding its pelt. There were many windows, of various sizes, some reflecting light, most broken or cracked. Through one window Ephran could see streamers, their color faded as the den itself, hanging crooked. There was little else to see. The roof, made up of many small slices of wood, sagged in the middle.

After he sniffed the air, Ephran said, "This den is abandoned."

"When they come home," said Frafan, "if they do come home, they will find the hole they dug now goes down to the middle of the earth." He shivered, stretched, breathed deeply of the fresh air, and said, "Where to now, brother?"

"I'm not sure, Frafan. I know this much: that was not Rocky Creek on which we rode the stump. There were no stones or pebbles along its banks." He hesitated for a moment, then said, "I'm afraid we're nearer Lomarsh than we are The Pond."

Frafan's eyes grew wide. "Really?"

"I'm thinking that the big stump brought us in the same direction Rocky Creek would, but on a course nearer the nesting place of the warm winds."

Frafan shuddered. "I've heard of Lomarsh. I remember father speaking of it, but I didn't pay a whole lot of attention. I got the impression that Lomarsh is a long way from Corncrib Farm."

"Indeed it is," said Ephran, "but not so far from The Pond. When the leaves fall from the trees, one can nearly see Lomarsh from the highest ash tree atop Great Hill."

"Do you think if we hadn't plunged into that hole in the earth we might have been washed into Lomarsh?" asked Frafan.

Ephran answered, "Possibly. And though I fear Lomarsh less than most other forest creatures, that doesn't mean I think it's a lovely place of big trees loaded with walnuts and acorns."

"Doesn't sound like the best place for a treeclimber," said Frafan.

Ephran said, "Actually, I can't even be sure of which way Lomarsh is from here. I'm just guessing that we didn't travel so far toward where the sun rises that it isn't behind us. All I know for sure is that we've come a very long way from the park."

Frafan squinted at the sun and clouds. "Well, we'll just have to try to get our bearings. Clouds flying from the home of the cold wind, do you think?"

"Pretty much," agreed Ephran.

"Is that the way we run?"

"Not quite," said Ephran. He turned his nose at an angle to the path of the high-flying clouds. "That way, I think."

The trail through last warm season's tangled brown grass was a difficult and treacherous one. Short treeclimber legs were meant for running and jumping in branches. The weeds were so high and so thick Ephran and Frafan could not see any distance ahead. There were no trees. They found themselves scrambling up every little bush they came across.

There was something else strewn around the seemingly endless field they crossed: Rocks. Rocks the likes they had not seen before. These rocks made those along the banks of Rocky Creek look like pebbles. These were awesome boulders, scattered here and there on the soft and weedy earth, as though flung by a huge paw during some sort of game.

Ephran began to use the rocks, instead of bushes, for scouting the path ahead. If they found one with a gently sloped face, it was possible to scramble to the top with ease.

From rock to rock, they moved along at a snail's pace. It was terribly hard work. They stopped now and again at bushes, to nibble on fresh buds. The sun began to lower itself below the edge of the earth.

"Time to find a darktime shelter," said Ephran.

"Do you see a tree?" asked Frafan, glancing from side to side.

"No trees. I see a hole under a bush." He pointed. "Right over there."

"If you don't mind, I've had my fill of holes in the earth," said Frafan.

Ephran shrugged. "Okay. You can sleep here on the rock."

"Hold on there!" said Frafan, as he struggled to his paws.

"I should think you'd be getting used to the idea of sleeping on or under the earth," said Ephran. "Come on. We'll make a nest as cozy as the one you had in Great Woods Warren."

The hole had been used by a badger who had evidently slept in it over the cold season. The animal's musty scent was very faint. As the sky grew dark, Ephran and Frafan padded the hole among the roots of the bush with soft grass. There were two entrances. They blocked one with dry sticks and lay with their ears and noses close to the other.

By the time they lay down, tails curled tightly about them, they were both exhausted. Frafan was so sleepy he found he didn't even care if he was on the earth. Tired as he was, though, there was something he wanted to share with his brother.

"Not being bigger always bothered me, you know," he said. "But I didn't tell you that the tunnel that allowed my escape from the cave was a very small one. I mean, really small. If I was your size, I'd still be down there."

After a moment Ephran said, "I learned a lesson down there too. I think now that any place can be a cage. Or not a cage. The park, the barn, The Pond, Corncrib Farm... It all depends on how you think of where you are and how you use what you've been given. Like wings and paws. We have one and not the other, and that's the way it is." He chuckled softly in the dark. "Does this sound confused? Do you understand what I'm saying?"

"I think so," said Frafan. "Does this mean you've lost your interest in flying?"

"Not my interest, no. I would still love to fly. Maybe I'll get the chance again. But, if I don't, I don't. I can still climb and jump and run. Lots of animals can't do those things as well as I can."

"Sounds like some of Odalee's wisdom rubbed off on both of us. Just needed a little help from dark caves to take root." Frafan rolled over in the sweet-smelling grass. He was warm and comfortable. The hole near his nose was barely visible. He yawned and said, "So...what do you think tomorrow will bring?"

The darkness settled around them, like a big mourning dove closing her wings for sleep. For a few moments Frafan thought perhaps his brother had fallen asleep. Then, in a strong and steady voice Ephran said, "Tomorrow we find The Pond. And Kaahli."

CHAPTER XXII

THICK AIR AND BAD DECISIONS

espite being exhausted, Frafan slept fitfully. He woke often, heart pounding, straining to hear the crackle of dry stems breaking. But there was no sound. The underground nest was incredibly dark and terribly quiet. Frafan had to gently touch Ephran's fur to reassure himself that his brother was still there, laying next to him.

Ephran, on the other paw, slept so peacefully it was as though he didn't have to breathe anymore. Frafan could hardly believe the change in his brother. The memory of Ephran's disheveled appearance, that first day in the park, was still crystal clear in Frafan's memory. And his unreasonably hopeless attitude was even more unforgettable than his appearance. What had so totally changed his outlook? Queesor's starvation? His ability to face down a whole group of many colored ones? Kaahli's selfless sacrifice? His realization that the deep woods was the only hope for peace and happiness?

Whatever it was, Ephran was convinced he was going to find both home and mate. He was just as convinced that, when he did find them, they would be safe and unharmed.

After what seemed a nearly endless darktime, Frafan fell into a deep sleep. His breathing had hardly become soft and regular before a harsh and rasping racket caused him to bolt from his soft nest.

"RUUK...RUUK...RUUK!"

Frafan's sudden jump to his feet made him so dizzy he could barely stand. In the darkness, and with a sleep-thickened tongue, he whispered loudly, "Wake up, Ephran! Something is outside the hole!"

From the darkness Ephran's voice floated to him. "Yes, I hear it."

"What could it be?" asked Frafan, eyes desperately searching the walls of the den for the holes he knew were there. One of them, at least, had become barely visible. There was light outside. It must be morning.

"What do you think?" asked Ephran.

"Ephran! This is no time for guessing games..." Then it came to him. He recognized the sound. "Pheasant!" said Frafan.

"Sure sounds like one to me," said Ephran. "And you should recognize a pheasant's call better than I. You said you met one not long ago."

"I did. In the big red barn," said Frafan.

"Well, let's see if this bird is in a talkative mood," said Ephran. "Maybe we can find out how close we are to Lomarsh and The Pond."

Ephran pushed sticks and grass aside. The air was still, heavy and dense with cool water. It lay thickly on the grass and hung in tiny droplets from the bush.

"RUUK...RUUK...RUUK!"

161

The cry came from a clump of weeds only a few jumps from their bush.

"Hey, there! Friend pheasant!" Ephran called.

After a moment of silence, a high-pitched voice said, "May I ask who or what has the impertinence to address this splendid bird as 'friend'?"

There was no mistaking the voice. Or the style. Frafan's face broke into a wide grin.

"Ruckaru!" he cried.

Ephran turned to his brother with a puzzled expression. The head of a rooster pheasant poked through the grass with a matching look of bewilderment.

"Well, for all the corn in the country, if it isn't Frafan!" said the pheasant. "What, may I ask, is a treeclimber doing so very far from trees? Or need I ask that, since the last time I saw you was in a barn?"

Frafan laughed. "You're right, Ruckaru. I don't seem to find myself in the trees as much as I should. I'm so happy to see you. And to find you free in the fields."

"I will say the same to you," said Ruckaru. "The last time I perceived that scrawny tail disappearing into the van, I thought for certain it would be the last time I'd see it."

The rooster cocked his eye toward Ephran. "Who, may I inquire, might this be?"

"This, Ruckaru, is the brother I sought. Ephran, meet my friend, Ruckaru. He is the bird in the cage. The one I met at the Farm of Cages."

"A pleasure, Ruckaru," said Ephran.

Ruckaru beamed. "And for me. I am absolutely delighted Frafan's search was successful. More than delighted. I'm astounded." His smile faded. "But where is the mate? Kaahli, I believe is her name?"

"We became separated, Ruckaru," said Ephran. "I hope today finds us back together."

Frafan said, "Ruckaru, ever since I left the barn I've worried about Klestra and Janna. Do you know if they decided to stay at the Farm of Cages for the cold season?"

"Oh, my gracious," said Ruckaru, "there was no thought for that. They felt they had to find their branches. The wondrous pigeon sisters guided them back to a place called Rocky Point."

"Ah, they've returned to the deep woods then," sighed Frafan. "That is good news."

"Indeed it is," said Ephran. "And having someone with wings to talk to is good news too. I have some questions, Ruckaru."

"Happy to help."

"Ruckaru, might you know of a place called The Pond? Or another wet place — Lomarsh?" asked Ephran.

"Hmmm," said Ruckaru, "The Pond is totally unfamiliar. But Lomarsh...well, my bushy-tailed friends, we're practically awash in Lomarsh right now."

Frafan gasped. Ephran's eyes grew wide.

"What do you mean, 'practically awash in Lomarsh'?" Frafan managed.

"Just what I said. From this spot, about three good wingbeats would carry me to the very edge of Lomarsh."

Frafan turned to Ephran. "Green Gooseberries, brother, we built our one-night nest atop the place of evil!"

"Place of evil?" said Ruckaru. "What does that mean? Are you referring to Lomarsh?"

"Of course I am," said Frafan. "All the woodland creatures know that vicious and terrifying hunters roam Lomarsh. That no decent animal would dare nest there. That nobody who goes in ever comes out."

Ruckaru crowed, "HA! RUUK! Nonsense! Lomarsh is one of my very favorite nesting places. Wondrous spot to eat and rest. High and thick grass. Dark and fertile earth. Seeds and buds in abundance...thick as the hairs on a squirrel's tail. Beautiful little sweet-smelling flowers grow everywhere."

"How about owls and hawks? To say nothing of foxes?" countered Frafan.

"The sky above Lomarsh is no different from anywhere else. Same number of hawks — no more, no less. Since there are no trees to hide in, there are no owls to speak of. I don't even concern myself about foxes during the warm season. They don't like hunting with wet paws. And Lomarsh is always wet."

"Many colored ones then...," Frafan said in a weaker voice.

"That's the best part of all!" exulted Ruckaru. "Oh, a few many colored ones may be seen tromping around out there for a short time, just before the cold season really sets its teeth. Other times they ignore the place. What grows from the earth is left alone. The grass and bushes are not cut down. The earth is not gouged and scraped."

Frafan was silent.

Ephran sighed. "So it is as I suspected all along. No trees for treedwellers. No solid earth for earthdwellers. And because diggers and climbers cannot nest there, they decided Lomarsh must be a place of evil."

Ruckaru cocked his head. Frafan mumbled something. Then, from a long way off, another pheasant crowed.

"Ah yes, must be going," said Ruckaru. "So nice seeing both of you. Wonderful to meet you, Ephran. And congratulations to you on finding your brother, Frafan. I wish you all sorts of success in finding your pond."

With that, Ruckaru exploded from the weeds. He was out of sight before the squirrels could utter a word.

Too late Frafan shouted, "Wait! You can help us! We still need help in finding The Pond."

Ephran shook his head.

"What was his big hurry, anyway?" said Frafan.

"Unless I miss my guess, that call was a female pheasant," said Ephran. "It appears she has higher priority than us."

"As long as I'm with you, I'm not worried," said Frafan. "I'm sure you can find The Pond without Ruckaru's help."

"I hope so, Frafan. Since The Pond is unfamiliar territory to him, Ruckaru probably wouldn't have been of any help anyway."

They scrambled along a flattened path through the weeds to a small bush that had found a way to grow in the dense underbrush. Its stems were green, and laden with some of the sweetest and crispest buds they'd ever tasted. Huddled under its branches, the brothers made their plans for finding The Pond.

While they talked and ate, the air became thicker and thicker, wetter and wetter. Protected as they were beneath the branches, they did not realize what was happening until Ephran stuck out his nose.

"Frafan," he said, "we'd better find one of those big rocks and take a look around...while we still have time."

As he followed Ephran through the grass, Frafan realized the air had become very thick with water.

They scrambled up the long sloped face of a huge rock and found themselves in the densest fog either of them could have imagined. Frafan could barely make out a large bush that grew a bare taillength from the place he stood. Once in a great while the squawk of a blackbird might be heard. Otherwise, all was quiet.

"It looks as though we should have tried to keep Ruckaru's attention after all," said Ephran, "at least to direct us to the nearest trees."

"I know what you're thinking. Please don't ask me to go back into that hole while we wait for this fog to lift," said Frafan. "I spent all the time in earth-holes that I care to — for a long, long time."

"Well then, I guess we stay right here. Without wind, or sun, or landmarks, I am just as lost as I was under the earth," said Ephran. And he lay down on the rock.

Frafan lay down beside his brother. For a while he strained to see something, anything, through the thick haze. Every now and then he imagined he could see the outline of a branch, or a hill, or a bird. But the vision would be gone as quickly as it came, covered by rolling clouds of fog. Finally his eyes grew weary and he closed them and put his head on his paws. Ephran had done that a long while ago, and now seemed to be asleep.

But he wasn't. His eyes opened immediately when Frafan said, "I'm pretty sure I know from which direction the cold wind comes."

"I do too," said Ephran.

"You marked the place before we crawled into our hole last night, didn't you?"

"Just as you did," smiled Ephran.

"Why don't we set our noses in that direction, then? If your reckoning is true, we should bump into Rocky Creek before long."

"We should," answered Ephran, "and we might. But we might just as easily get turned around in this fog and find ourselves totally lost."

Frafan tried to lay still, to relax. But his paws itched to be moving. He knew his brother was becoming impatient too. They squeezed their bodies tightly to the rock when the sound of some creature moving through the undergrowth passed closeby. Time moved with painful slowness. This was an unnatural place for treeclimbers to be, on the exposed top of a rock. That hunters could see no better than squirrels in this thick air, and that their scent would not easily be carried to enemy noses, was important. But it did not make Ephran or Frafan more comfortable. The fog did not lift. And it became no thinner. Finally Ephran got to his paws.

"I'm not patient enough to wait for the fog to leave, my brother," he said. "Let's see if we can't find some way to keep our paws directed toward Rocky Creek."

Frafan jumped to his paws. "I'm ready. I think if we take our time, just go from one bush or rock to the next, we'll be okay."

But they weren't. They crawled down from the rock and set out through the weeds, Ephran in the lead, trying to keep to as straight a path as they could. It was impossible. There were simply too many obstacles. Sometimes a bush would rise out of the thick fog, and they would have to fight their way through or around it. Then a tangle of dense sawgrass would force them to double back on their original trail. Often a big rock blocked the way.

Eventually Ephran stopped and sighed deeply.

"Are you tired, Ephran?" asked Frafan.

"No, not tired, Frafan. But I've lost my heading entirely. Do you know which way to go?"

Frafan looked embarrassed. "I was confused some time ago. I was just thanking twinkling stars for having you in the lead, for you knowing where we were headed." They sat for a moment, listening for hunters...or for any sound. Then Frafan said, "Maybe we should return to the hole after all. Maybe Ruckaru will come back to talk again. Can you take us back there?"

Ephran shook his head. "The fault is mine. It was a poor decision to leave familiar territory. I have no idea how to find the way back, even though we probably aren't the length of a fullgrown ash tree from it."

"Well, I guess we'd better not sit here on the earth," Frafan muttered. "Let's find another rock. Or a big bush."

"Stay close," said Ephran.

They moved through the weeds slowly and carefully. The cold lost feeling filled their chests. When would this fog lift? Where could they stay until it did? What if a hunter happened upon them? What if they became separated again?

Rounding a corner, past a thicket of intertwined grass, Ephran ran nearly headlong into a large, round stick of wood, sprouting from the earth. Startled, he looked up.

Frafan, coming up beside him, exclaimed, "A tree! Oh, Ephran, you've found a tree! Not the biggest tree, perhaps, but certainly big enough to have branches."

Ephran's head was still tilted up. "I'm not so sure," he said, "I cannot see the top of it..."

"Who cares?" said Frafan. "Let's get up there."

Ephran held out his paw. "Slowly, Frafan. I ran up a tree just like this once. Slightly broader maybe. It had no neighbors. And all the while I ran, my tail was tickling the nose of your friend, Blackie."

CHAPTER XXIII

ALL PATHS LEAD TO...OR
AWAY FROM THE POND

The hawk had carried him a lot further than he'd thought, and it occurred to Klestra that Ephran's dream of flying had some merit; flying was a very speedy and efficient way to travel. No need for stretching to grab this or that branch. No need for long and difficult jumps, with the constant possibility of falling. No problem with leaves obscuring the path ahead.

"No sir," he said to himself, "traveling through trees and bushes is hard, even when there are no leaves. Especially when cold wind whips through the forest. And most especially when bruised muscles and deep scratches have not yet healed."

The red squirrel stopped to rest in the fork of a small basswood. He blew out a steamy cloud of breath. It would have been wise to stay in the chipmunk den a few more days, to allow his poor body to rest and his pelt to heal. He knew that. But the days and nights beneath the earth had stretched into an eternity. And the chipmunk's constant chattering and nagging were about to drive him up a tree. The deciding factor had been that some of his oldest and most stale food caches contained better food than what the chipmunk had to offer!

Anyway, just one more bend in Rocky Creek and he should be able to see The Pond. But it was not the thought of The Pond or his nest that made him move his aching legs before they were really rested. It was the sinking feeling that he'd had ever since the hawk gave up its struggle to dig him from the chipmunk hole.

That thought was of Janna. A long time ago the young female gray would have found his nest empty. She would have no idea where he'd gone. She would think he'd abandoned her.

Would she still be at The Pond? Or would she have wandered off, trying to find her way to Corncrib Farm and her parents' nest? He jumped to the next branch, a leap longer than he should have tried. It hurt something fierce.

Then he saw The Pond, and he imagined how Frafan and Janna must have felt when they saw it for the first time. And he thought how they must have seen it through watering eyes, just as he was seeing it now.

He was still a long way off when he began to shout.

"Janna!" he cried. "I'm back! Are you still here?"

He had run nearly up to his nest, ready to collapse, when he heard an answering chatter from across the water. He gathered a last bit of strength and ran some more. His legs felt like numb sticks. She was running through the trees toward him, chattering with happiness.

"Klestra! It is you! I'm so happy to see you. I was so worried," she shouted.

"You were worried?" he called back, unable to wait until she was close enough to speak in normal tones, "I was sick wondering what you might have thought, what you might have done! Wait until you hear my story. You won't believe how I left this place — and where I've spent these many days..."

He thought he was seeing double. Two squirrels running through the branches toward him. Weary and tear-filled eyes must be distorting what he was seeing, making him think there were two. Then she was in front of him and they hugged like they thought they'd never see one another again.

And there was...another squirrel...just behind Janna...but a red one...and a female...

"Oh, Klestra, I can't wait to hear your story. But there was no need for you to worry. I met a friend, and we've kept each other company, and she's wonderful. Klestra, meet Lylah."

"Lylah," he said.

He looked over Janna's shoulder, unable to take his eyes from the female's. His voice sounded strange when he said her name. But then, maybe he should expect that. He'd had a hard run. He'd be expected to sound breathless. Wouldn't he?

* * * * *

Jafthuh's thoughts were directed to the path ahead. He hoped he was going in the right direction. He knew, if he got turned, even the slightest bit, he might end up leading his mate and daughters in a big circle. It was an easy thing to do. He ran quietly and as swiftly as he could, trying to pick out a landmark ahead. The fog had thickened. But he had been in much worse. Nevertheless, when he reached one landmark, he immediately picked out another. Landmarks were getting closer and closer together.

The old gray squirrel wished silently for what Ephran had called "luck." His family depended upon him to lead them to the stream of stones. He hoped he would find it. And soon. He did not pretend to have either Ephran's or Frafan's ability to find his way around unfamiliar woods.

Jafthuh stopped running. Odalee jumped to his branch.

"Time to rest, my mate?" she asked.

"Perhaps," he said. "We've reached the first of our destinations. See there."

Through the fog could be seen the clear, cold water of Rocky

Creek.

"You are a fine guide, Jafthuh," said Odalee. "Once again you have led your family safely."

"Too early to rub my back. We're not where we want to be yet. And..." Jafthuh stopped speaking and turned his head.

"What is it, Father?" said Ilta, obviously alarmed.

"Listen...," he said. "Above the sound of running water."

Odalee lifted her ears. After a moment she murmured, "Something is coming this way."

"Young ones," Jafthuh whispered to his daughters, "flatten yourselves on your branch. Lay very still."

"And don't let your tail hang over," Odalee warned, as she crouched against sturdy wood.

In an instant the four treeclimbers had hidden themselves so well that any earth-creature, even those who might look up, would have seen nothing but thick and apparently deserted branches.

A most unusual group was moving through the haze on the far side of Rocky Creek. There was a gray squirrel, leaping from branch to branch. Nothing strange about that. But traveling along, fluttering from tree to tree, keeping pace with the treeclimber, were three pigeons! The squirrel was chattering intermittently, at first Odalee thought to the pigeons. Then she saw, pattering around the edge of a clump of bushes, the object of most of the squirrel's conversation. A dog! A muddied yellow hound was trotting along the earth, just beneath the squirrel. And they were chatting back and forth!

As they drew closer, Jafthuh got a good look. He stood up on his branch, shock and amazement written on his face.

"Aden!" he said loudly.

The other squirrel stopped as though he'd run into an oak stump. "Jafthuh!"

The dog and pigeons raised their heads. Tinga and Ilta stood on their hindlegs. Odalee was about to shout a greeting to Aden when another voice, behind her, nearly startled the old female into falling from her perch.

"Mother!"

Mianta, wide of eye and wider of smile, raced through the limbs toward Odalee. Behind Mianta was Laslum, and behind him were Phetra and Roselimb. Jafthuh's head spun around, from Aden to Mianta, as though being jerked from side to side.

"Jafthuh...Odalee," said Phetra, "how did you find us? How did you know we..?"

The dog began to bark. It leaped across a narrowing in Rocky Creek and raced up the shoreline, toward the trees from which Jafthuh and his family watched.

Aden shouted, "Fred, stop it!" to the dog.

A group of rabbits, one with a crooked ear, broke from cover and scattered in all directions. The dog had spied them hiding in tall grass near the stream, and galloped toward them. At Aden's shout, the dog slid to a stop and Jafthuh heard it mutter, "Oh, shucks! Fergot again."

Then, yet another voice, familiar to nearly every ear listening, could be heard through the trees. It came from the direction in which the crooked-eared cottontail had run.

"Mayberry, what are you doing here?"

It was Kaahli's voice.

The reunion was spectacular. Once Aden and Kaahli convinced everyone, especially the rabbits, that Fred was not a hunter to be feared, there was near-pandemonium. The collection of eleven squirrels, five rabbits, three birds and one dog attracted the attention of a flock of crows, who settled into the higher limbs of a big ash tree to watch the excitement through lifting fog.

Jafthuh and Odalee were speechless with delight. They greeted each member of their family with long looks and hugs. Aden and Kaahli hugged for a very long time. The young treeclimbers were very impressed when they met Rennigan and Fred.

Ilta asked Rennigan, "Are you the squirrel that taught Ephran everything he knows?"

"Hardly, young 'un," Rennigan answered. "That brother a yers learned more'n I ever 'magined."

The dog eyed the old fox squirrel suspiciously. "You makin' fun 'a the way I talk?" Fred asked Rennigan.

"Not likely, houn'dog," said Rennigan. "Almost sounds like we had the same teacher, though, don't it?"

Laslum laughed loudly when Fred looked up at him and said, "Not hidin' any nuts in yer paws, are ya? If ya do I hope yer takin' to eatin' 'em instead 'a throwin' 'em."

At first, after greetings, and hugs, and solemn "how-do-you-do's" and "I've heard a lot about you" and "Ephran told us all about you," everyone tried to speak at the same time. There was so very much to tell and such a great deal to share! They finally agreed to let Kaahli speak first. She obviously knew the most about what had caused so many animals and birds to be in this place, at this time.

Her story — from the day Ephran was struck by thundersticks, their rescue on Cloudchaser's back, through the long cold season in the park, to the wild ride down the stream with a rat — was met with ooh's and aah's and whistles of near-disbelief. Aden and Laslum were flabbergasted by the news that The Farm of Cages was actually a good place, a place where birds and animals were cared for. Mayberry added what he knew of Frafan and Janna's search and their stay in Great Woods

Warren. Phetra, Roselimb, Mianta and Laslum shouted with joy at hearing that Janna and Frafan had survived the great snowstorm. Phetra made a special point of thanking Mayberry for what he and the cottontails had done for the squirrel family.

The pigeons told of bringing Frafan, Janna and Klestra back from the Farm of Cages, to almost this very spot along Rocky Creek. Fred told of what he'd overheard in the warren of many colored ones and Rennigan confirmed the town squirrels' evil intent. Kaahli explained how those misunderstanding treeclimbers' dastardly plan for Ephran, herself, and Frafan had been unsuccessful.

Although many mysteries had been solved, loose ends abounded. Where were Frafan and Ephran now? Might they still be searching for Kaahli? Or would they be on their way here? Would they be able to find Rocky Creek? The consensus was that, if they couldn't, no animal could. And where were Janna and Klestra? Had they remained at The Pond all cold season? Janna would certainly have wanted to go home, to share what she knew with her family. Might she and Klestra have started their trek to Corncrib Farm?

"Our search is not over," said Odalee. "Let us finish. The Pond is not far."

"Yes," agreed Aden, "let's find out who, exactly, is nesting near Great Hill."

"Sure thing. You folks up there lead on. I'll just trot along with these here cottontails," said Fred.

Fastrip eyed the dog, obviously ready to bound off if Fred made a move in his direction.

Fred saw the mistrust in Fastrip's eyes. He smiled widely and said to the small rabbit, "Meybe you and me kin have a little race, huh?"

Mayberry laughed and said, "You're talking to one old trickster, Fred. He'd lead you right into a patch of brambles."

They set out then, pigeons and squirrels in low branches, dog and rabbits on the earth.

One of the crows (Fred recognized Mulken) called down to them, "Eeyah! No neet gop 'ond. Deycum fine you."

Aden cocked his head. "Are they saying that somebody is coming to find us?"

Sure enough, as three squirrels, one gray and two red came bouncing through the trees from the direction of The Pond, two ducks sailed overhead, quacking loudly.

Jafthuh's voice cracked. "Janna. It's Janna."

"And two red squirrels," added Odalee.

"A welcomin' party!" exclaimed Fred.

"Cloudchaser! Marshflower!" Kaahli shouted. "And Klestra. Dear Klestra..."

The mallards settled on the earth. Kaahli ran to them, hugged them both, eyes full of happy water, unable to speak. Then she hugged Klestra and Janna. Phetra and Roselimb, certain that Janna had probably joined last warm season's leaves under a melting snowdrift, nearly smothered her.

Fred looked up at Klestra and said, "Been hopin' I'd run into you again, Klester. Had some interestin' times in thet old barn, didn't we?"

Klestra said, "Yes, we did. Never seen the likes of that search...or of you. I hate to admit it, but I was looking forward to seeing you again too."

Again, there were introductions all around. Some of the creatures knew one another, of course, but none had met Klestra's pretty new mate, Lylah.

"This is wonderful!" said Odalee. "Everyone is safe and well. The only ones missing are Ephran and Frafan."

"And when they show up we can all go to The Pond," said Kaahli. "I can't wait to see our nest."

Klestra had been unusually quiet. Now he said, "Actually, we did not come this way to greet you. We didn't even know you were all here."

"You didn't come to greet us?" said a puzzled Kaahli.

"No," said Janna, "we were running away."

"Running away from The Pond?" asked Phetra.

"Yes," said Klestra sadly. "The many colored ones have returned."

In the end, knowledge is what
makes the difference.

Thomas of the Dark Blue Hair

CHAPTER XXIV

SO MUCH FOR
WHO KNOWS WHAT

Frafan scrambled up the wooden post. He quickly found there was not much to climb. Ephran, still on the earth below, was barely visible through the fog.

"I've run out of tree, Ephran," he said.

"I was afraid of that. Can you see anything from up there?"

"Not much. This must be a broken treetrunk. But a strange one at that. It has a very smooth top. And two vines attached, running in opposite directions..."

"Then it's not a treetrunk," said Ephran, as he joined his brother, clinging to the rough wooden surface.

"If it's not a broken tree, what is it?" asked Frafan.

"I've seen this sort of thing before...," said Ephran, poking his nose up to Frafan's level, and looking down the vine, to where it disappeared in the haze. "A long time ago. When Father and I went exploring. We watched two many colored ones, pounding posts like this into the earth."

Frafan reached down and ran his paw along the black vine.

"The vine is cold," he said, "and hard as stone."

"Like the mesh of cages," said Ephran.

"Of course! Now I remember," said Frafan excitedly. "This sort of vine is strung from tree to tree near the Farm of Cages. It encloses a grassy place for cows." He squinted. "I can almost make out the next stick. The vine is attached to that one too. Ephran, do you think we might follow the vine?"

"We could. I'm not sure that would do us any good. We have no idea where the vine leads. We might end up going away from The Pond instead of toward it. No, I'm afraid we're stuck here until the fog goes away."

"I don't like this situation one bit," said Frafan. "We're too close to the earth...and without cover. Even if we could see, there's no place to run. We've been lucky not to find our noses up against that of a hunter before this."

"I know, Frafan, I know. Once I thought I could make my own luck. I've learned differently."

"We have to do something." There was a ragged squeak in Frafan's voice.

Before Ephran could answer, there was the unmistakable sound of something large moving toward them though the fog... something already very close. Whatever it was must have been hiding nearby the whole time.

"Ephran!" Frafan whispered, nostrils flaring, legs stiff.

Ephran held up his paw. "It's inside the vine, Frafan. We're outside. Besides, it moves slowly, not like a hunter."

Like a massive apparition, a large female cow appeared out of the gloom, eyes focusing on the squirrels. She stopped a few steps away, gazed at them with big brown eyes, then bent her head and began to munch at the damp grass.

Frafan sighed. "Whew! I was sure that was a hunter. I'm glad it wasn't but, on the other paw, I wish it had been someone who could help."

"I'm afraid we're just going to have to sit here and wait until we can see where we're going," said Ephran. "There's no way we can find our way to The Pond when we can barely make out the whiskers on our noses."

The cow's head came up.

"Ooommm," she said, the noise rising from the deepest part of her very large belly.

Ephran glanced at her. Big brown eyes locked with his. The cow tossed her head. Ephran sighed and looked away, down the vine, hoping the next post would be easier to see than it was a moment before. Frafan was getting very restless. Almost any kind of action would help...

"Ooommm," the cow repeated.

Ephran's eyes shifted back to her. Then, disgusted, he told himself to stop wasting his time on this poor ignorant animal. He was letting his mind wander. He told himself the reason he was so easily distracted was that it was so quiet. And he seemed unable to come up with ideas to get Frafan and him out of this exposed and dangerous situation.

The cow tossed her head once more. She took a few steps, down the path of the vine. Just as she began to disappear into the fog, she swung smartly around and came back toward Ephran, never taking her eyes from his.

As she moved close, he found himself almost hypnotized, his whole being seeming to fall into those huge liquid eyes. It occurred to him that there was something there, behind the eyes. A sparkling? A warm glow? Was it possible? Was there more here than he'd suspected? Was he, once again, in the presence of another unlikely teacher?

"Ooomm?" Ephran said, and it sounded so funny, coming from him, he would have sworn that the cow smiled.

"Ephran!" said Frafan sharply, eyes straining at the fog, not looking at his brother, "this is no time for silly games. What's the matter with you? Don't you understand how much trouble we're in, right out here in the open? I can almost feel a fox breathing down my neck."

Ephran did not answer. The cow nodded again, twice, directing his attention along the path of the vine.

Ephran nodded back to the cow and he said to Frafan, "I've decided your idea of following the vine is a good one. I can see the next post now. Let's run to it."

"Wait a minute. I thought you said that was foolish...that you have no idea where the vine leads," Frafan said in surprise.

"I don't. But I think someone else does."

"What?"

"Come, Frafan," Ephran said. He jumped to the earth.

The cow cantered slowly ahead, down the path of the vine. Ephran scrambled through the deep and wet weeds after her, to the next thick post. She looked back, nodding her head up and down, then moved on.

Before Ephran's tail disappeared in the mist, Frafan followed. He was not going to be left behind. What had gotten into Ephran? Imitating cow sounds! Wanting to follow the vine after he'd said it was a bad idea. Had his mind gone soft? Maybe his recovery in the park had not been so complete as Frafan had hoped. Maybe he had lost touch. Maybe he was so anxious to find Kaahli that his thinking was confused, that he could not keep his thoughts straight.

Straight, in any case, is how they ran. Straight under the vine, through the dew-soaked grass, from one post to the next. The cow moved along ahead of them, looking back now and then, as though making sure they were still behind her.

Then the vine made a sharp turn. Before Frafan could utter a word, the cow had stopped. So had Ephran. At this corner of the cow-cage the vine was attached to — Ripe and Ready Walnuts! — the trunk of a big gnarled oak tree. And through the mist could be seen the tips of other branches. Trees! All kinds of trees!

Frafan grabbed the rough bark and scooted up, wishing to get his short legs all the way around the trunk, wanting to hug the tree. At the first thick branch he stopped and looked back.

Ephran had come up the trunk only as far as the cow's head. She stood there, so close to Ephran that his tail brushed her shoulder.

"Thank you," he said softly, into her ear. "Once again, I find luck in a most unexpected place."

"Ooommm," said the cow. She put her head to the earth, and moved slowly away, taking great mouthfuls of wet grass as she went.

Ephran climbed to where his brother lay. Frafan wore a distressed look. "The cow showed us the way to the trees, didn't she?" he said, watching the big animal fade into the mist.

"Yes."

"The cow cantered slowly ahead."

"Back there, in the fog. When we were talking. She could understand everything we said, couldn't she?"

"I don't know that for a fact. But I think she could."

Frafan put his paw to his nose. "I insulted cows, you know. In the barn. At the Farm of Cages. Klestra was trying to get information from one of them. About you and Kaahli. I thought they couldn't understand. Blackie told me they couldn't. She must not have known either. And even the horses, who nest with cows, said that cows and pigs were in their own world."

"Their own world, perhaps. From what we've seen, it appears there are many worlds besides the small deep woods one we know. In any case, you and Blackie and the horses weren't alone. I had no idea about cows. Not until today. What did Klestra ask the cow in the barn?"

"Now that I think about it, he never really got around to asking anything," said Frafan. "Just made a lot of remarks that intended flattery and sounded foolish."

"Well," said Ephran. "I guess not understanding is one thing. Deciding you are superior because you can't understand is another."

They moved into the high branches and found a comfortable place to lay down and wait for the fog to lift. There were buds on the ends of the younger limbs, good for nibbling. The near-silence of the shrouded woods and the knowledge that they were at last safe led to heavy eyelids. In no time at all both of them were sound asleep.

When Ephran woke the air was clear. A breeze had risen, wafting from where the sun would set. A fresh and clean odor came to his nose. He stood on the branch.

"Spruce trees!" he thought. His brow wrinkled. He pivoted to face the opposite direction. "Frafan, time to wake up."

Frafan wiggled and stretched. He opened his eyes to find a strange and faraway look on his brother's face.

"Ephran! What is it?"

Ephran pointed. "See the spruce trees?"

"Yes, I see them," Frafan answered.

"That's Spruce Hill. And over there." Ephran swung around and pointed the other way, to a place of dense weeds, scattered bushes, and no trees.

"Yes."

"That's Lomarsh."

Frafan rubbed his nose with his paw. "So...we have Spruce Hill on one side, trees in the middle, and Lomarsh on the other. What of it? Ephran, are you sure you're feeling all right?"

"I'm fine, Frafan. Best of all, I know exactly where we are. Through the trees just ahead lies Rocky Creek. I've been here before..." He rose to his hindlegs and smiled widely.

"We are nearly home."

179

CHAPTER XXV
MOVERS AND SHAKERS

loudchaser had flown into the branches of a small ironwood tree. He said to the animals on the earth, "Ephran was right after all. The Pond is theirs."

"They are building something," said Klestra, his voice filled with sadness.

"You mean, like nests?" asked Laslum.

"I don't know what they build, Laslum," said Klestra.

"They are using very big, round sticks," said Lylah.

"Are they building in the trees or on the earth?" asked Mayberry.

"On the earth," said Janna.

"How many of them?" asked Aden.

"Only two," said Klestra.

"That doesn't seem like many to build anything of consequence," said Odalee, thinking of the two old and bent ones at Corncrib Farm.

"It doesn't take many of them to make a lot of mischief," said Jafthuh soberly.

"I wish Sorghum was here," Fastrip whispered to Mayberry. "I think these poor creatures need some distraction."

While the others talked, movement caught Cloudchaser's eye. He turned to see two gray squirrels, coming toward him through the trees. An immense unhappiness had clouded his mind and his first thought was, "Now who could this be? One would think that every gray squirrel in this part of the forest must already be gathered here." Then, as they drew closer, Cloudchaser recognized the larger of the squirrels. He tried to speak...and found he could not.

Aden was saying, "Try not to feel badly. The Spring is a fine place to nest. All of you are welcome there."

"That's very nice of you, Aden. But The Spring is not The Pond," Klestra said quietly.

"How 'bout High Hill?" said Rennigan. "Kin see a long ways from up there. Plenty'a oak and butternut."

"No place for ducks around High Hill," observed Marshflower.

"Wonderful view. But awfully tiring to get to and from," said Phetra.

"There's lots of room around Corncrib Farm," said Jafthuh. "No reason you couldn't all come over there. Even if the corncrib's almost empty, I'm sure there's plenty of food for everyone."

"Yes," said Odalee, "and a nice stream nearby for ducks."

"Pretty small stream, actually," said Janna.

"I guess we'll never find an ideal place to nest. It's just that The

Pond was the closest thing to it," said Klestra.

"What about Smagtu and Fetzgar?" asked Phetra. "They can't be abandoned at The Pond, left at the mercy of the many colored ones."

Everyone was quiet for a moment.

"What we need just now is Ephran's courage and Frafan's knowledge of many colored ones and their ways," said Odalee.

"QUACK!" Cloudchaser finally managed.

The sound, loud and raspy, brought terrible memories of a wounded friend to Klestra's mind. All the animals and birds looked up as one. Their eyes followed the drake's.

"Ephran! Frafan!" Odalee gasped.

The celebration that followed had to be the biggest, happiest, loudest, and most unusual the forest had ever seen...and, most assuredly, would ever see again. Fear, caution, and timidity were thrown aside. No hunter would dare interrupt this gathering. Especially with a dog smack in the middle of things. Indeed, hidden back in the woods, watching the festivities, were a family of red foxes and a large white owl.

A group of seven whitetailed deer had heard the racket and now stood at the edge of the celebrators, smiling and laughing, but also casting an occasional nervous glance in Fred's direction. Practically every crow in the forest perched in the branches, cawing back and forth. This time they offered no insults, no disparaging remarks. A family of raccoons had appeared along the far bank of Rocky Creek. Jafthuh didn't even blink when Frafan ran down his tree, up to the smallest raccoon, and shouted, "Farnsworth! I can't believe it's you!"

There were more backslaps and pawshakes. Those who did not know one another were introduced. Odalee was nearly overwhelmed with happiness. The squirrel family could not get enough of one another. When Frafan was given Blackie's message, and was told that his friend now slept in the cold earth, he left the rejoicing animals for a time, and sat in the highest limbs of a nearby cottonwood, gazing at the horizon.

Everyone got to meet the pigeons and Lylah. Though most had heard of the hunter-who-was-not-hunter, the squirrels and rabbits were fascinated by Fred, and eventually clustered around him, listening to modest admissions of amazing tracking feats as he searched for his friends.

Jafthuh's only comment was, "Well, there goes one more old, comfortable, twisted notion." He shook his head. "Cats and dogs. What next?" He looked over at Klestra, whom he'd just met, and smiled widely. "I guess what's next is red squirrels who have become family."

Klestra's and the mallards' reunion with Kaahli and Ephran was nearly silent, and so filled with emotion that some of the gathered creatures had to look away for fear of showing their own tears.

"Thank you, dear Klestra, for not giving up," said Kaahli, as she held him close.

Klestra smiled and nodded at Frafan. "It seems all I had to do was to point this one's curious snout in the right direction."

"This day would not be possible without you," Ephran said to Cloudchaser.

"Not true, my friend," said the drake. "Long ago, when you jumped from the branch of a frail willow onto a hawk's back, you made this possible."

Marshflower said, "This warm season, Ephran, it will be you who tells the bizarre and exciting stories, and me who listens."

Kaahli could not get her fill of looking at Ephran. The feeling was mutual.

Phetra held Frafan for a long time, nose buried in the fur of his younger brother's back. Frafan whispered in his ear, "Told you we'd meet again before the next batch of hickory nuts ripened."

At last Ephran said, "Well, what are we all doing perched here along Rocky Creek? Let's get to The Pond. I've waited so long to see it again...Fetzgar and Smagtu as well."

Silence fell over the entire group. Frafan looked from face to sad face. Then he said quietly, "Don't tell us...not bad news. Not again."

"I'm afraid so, Frafan," said Klestra. And he angrily knocked a chunk of loose bark from the tree branch. "Why is it that both times I've come to welcome Ephran and Kaahli home, it has to be with sadness?"

"What is it this time, Klestra?" asked Ephran.

"Same problem as last time, sort of. Many colored ones. Only this time they haven't hurt anyone. Not yet."

Ephran sighed deeply. "Tell us about it."

"I sure hate getting stuck bearing the bad news every time," Klestra protested again, looking around. No one made a sound. "Anyway, two many colored ones are building something near The Pond."

"What do you mean, 'building something'?" asked Frafan.

"They're pounding sticks into the ground. With other sticks."

"Anything else? Are they stringing a vine between the sticks?"

"Not that I saw."

Janna and Lylah nodded their agreement.

"How about big, flat pieces of wood?" asked Ephran. "Were they laying wood like that between the sticks? Fastening the sticks and wood together?"

"No."

Frafan leaned closer to Klestra and asked, "How far apart are they placing these sticks?"

"Oh, very far apart. We watched them for some time. There are sticks at the base of Great Hill and at the far side of The Pond. There are sticks along Bubbling Brook, right up to The Meadow."

"Are the many colored ones still there?" asked Ephran.

"I don't know," said Janna. "They were very busy. Too busy to notice us as we ran away."

Ephran nodded at Frafan. "I think," he said, "that Frafan and I will sneak a look at these many colored ones and the sticks they pound into the earth."

"No, Ephran!" protested Kaahli. "Don't go."

"Don't fret, Kaahli," he said. "We will keep ourselves well concealed. I must see this thing for myself. Between Frafan and I, maybe we can gain some understanding about what the many colored ones plan to do at our Pond."

"Good for you, Ephran!" said Klestra, flexing his foreleg as though throwing a punch, "I like the way you talk. It is indeed 'our Pond.'"

Fred chimed in, "I'm goin' with. In the back a that blue van I told Frafan we wuz gonna work together again. Looks like now's the time."

"Old friend, we don't want to endanger you," said Frafan.

"Lissen, if these got thundersticks, I kin be of help. I know how ta distract 'em. And they won't go blastin' at no dog."

"Oh, Fred, thank you. I'd feel so much better knowing you were with them," said Kaahli.

"Okay, Fred," said Ephran. "Come along then. But let's all try to stay unnoticed if we can."

The forest dwellers watched silently as the dog and the squirrel brothers set out through the trees along the banks of Rocky Creek. It was an old, familiar trail to Ephran. And Frafan had followed this path enough times to recognize a number of landmarks. Both the squirrels were amazed at how Fred slipped like a shadow through the underbrush.

They came within sight of The Pond just as the two many colored ones Klestra spoke of were picking up the leavings of their work. A large bag lay between them, and they were stuffing it with all the things they held in their paws while they worked. Finally it was full, and the many colored ones closed the bag. The larger slung it over his back. They both stood for a moment, gazing at their handiwork. They spoke quietly for a moment. Then they turned and walked off toward Bubbling Brook, where Ephran knew of a path that must lead, eventually, to their dens.

"Let's move closer," Frafan said, "and see if we can figure out what they were up to. And if they might plan to come back." When he looked over, Frafan was taken aback to see a wide-eyed look on Ephran's face.

"Ephran, is something the matter?"

Ephran took a deep breath, shut his eyes for a moment and said, "I will be fine, brother. And I hope nothing is the matter. We'll discuss it later. As you said, right now we have to see what they've built."

One of the solid posts the many colored ones had erected stood, as Klestra had said, near a basswood on the side of The Pond away from Ephran and Kaahli's nest.

Ephran and Frafan ran through the branches until they were in a tree overlooking the post. Fred was directly beneath, sniffing around in the trampled grass. The brothers sat, close together, gazing down at the shiny white and red slab attached to the top of the post.

"Why, it's just like the post they use in their warren...to warn cars and trucks not to enter the one-way path!" said Frafan.

"A lot like those, but not exactly," said Ephran.

"It has the same red slashs across it."

"I know. It has the crossed sticks and the circle too. But the other had the likeness of a car under the red slash."

"Yes," agreed Frafan, "which meant that cars were not allowed to enter from the direction this faced."

"This does not bear the likeness of a car," said Ephran. "Do you know what they are trying to show here?"

Frafan looked closely. "I think so. Though I've never seen one, I've heard enough about them. Is it a..."

"Dingbust, I know whut them is," said Fred, squinting up at the post. "Thunderstick!"

Frafan stood straight up on his hindlegs.

"Are you saying...? Is it possible...?"

"That they are telling one another that thundersticks are not allowed around The Pond?" said Ephran. "Though it's hard to believe, it appears that way. Let's look at another. I see one over there."

Frafan followed Ephran to another post, facing away from The Pond. It bore a design identical to the first.

"Are they all the same?" asked Frafan.

"We can check them out later," said Ephran, "one at a time. I think we will find they are all alike."

Frafan thought for a moment. "This is absolutely wonderful! No doubt posts of wood with slashes and black lines can't keep the fox or the hawk from your nest, but what a relief to know that they forbid themselves to hunt here. But who?" he muttered. "And why?"

Frafan scratched his ear. Ephran did not answer. His eyes were fixed on Great Hill, as though in a trance.

Frafan cleared his throat and said, "Those who erected these posts, they must have been those gentle creatures from the Farm of Cages."

"Nope," said Fred, shaking his head vigorously. "Weren't them. I know those folks."

"Who then?"

"I know who they are," said Ephran quietly.

"You do?" said Frafan.

Ephran nodded slowly. "I would not forget these." He looked into Frafan's eyes. "They are the ones who pointed thundersticks at me."

Fred's ears stood straight up. Frafan gasped, "The hunters?"

Ephran nodded. "Those who knocked me from the tree."

After a moment Frafan said, "But why would those who carry thundersticks forbid their use?"

"Unless you find a way to ask them, Frafan, I think your question will remain unanswered."

They listened and watched the woods around The Pond. With a lump in his throat, Ephran recognized Janey wren's twitter on the other side of water. Robins and mourning doves were singing too, somewhere near his and Kaahli's nest. Fetzgar had surfaced atop one of his dens.

"Well, brother," Ephran finally said, "why don't we go get the others. They'll be wondering what's happening here. Then we'll introduce you to Fetzgar and Smagtu. You too, Fred, after we prepare them for the introduction. Otherwise, Smagtu might present all of us with a new odor. After that, I think there will be time for a very long and very merry party."

EPILOGUE

Ephran, Kaahli, Klestra and Lylah curled contentedly in the shade atop Fetzgar's old den. Rennigan had draped himself over a branch in the little willow, which had grown considerably larger than the day Ephran had used it as a springboard to the hawk's back. A stray breeze, confused in its flight across The Pond, playfully ruffled the fur on Ephran's tail.

Cloudchaser and Marshflower dunked their heads beneath the clear water, pulling up wonderfully crisp and tasty white tubers. Klestra nibbled on one, as did Fetzgar. The old muskrat was seated on a nearby den, one he'd built just to be near the ducks. He'd never admit that he built it there for that reason, of course. And, when told of all the events and adventures that supposedly took place after he went into hibernation last cold season, he refused to believe any of it.

Smagtu the skunk rolled about in thick green grass nearby, kicking his short legs in the air, and wrestling with his tail. "Git out here, ya striped rascal!" Fetzgar would shout at him. "Spend a little time in the water and you'd smell better."

Smagtu shook his head, smiled, and shouted back, "Fetzgar have chance at not-so-ugly if stay dry."

The sun shone down with a glory and intensity saved for the finest warm season days. Blackbirds squawked back and forth among thick cattails. Cool water teemed with creatures of all sizes and shapes. Trees around The Pond were full and robust, ripening acorns and hickory nuts as big and firm as anyone could remember. Four young squirrels played a game of tag at the edge of the water with six ducklings, under the watchful eye of their parents.

Kaahli stretched and said to Ephran, "I hope your family is having a wonderful warm season at Corncrib Farm."

"I'm sure they are. According to Mulken and Kartag, they took their time getting back to their nest after leaving us."

"With Roselimb and Janna poking their noses into every bush and tree, they couldn't expect a fast journey," said Kaahli.

"Especially since they were going to stop at Great Woods Warren with Mayberry," said Klestra. "He invited me to visit him sometime. That would be something, wouldn't it? To sleep in a rabbit warren."

"I'm sure you'd enjoy it, if you could find Great Woods Warren. Frafan said the warren is well hidden. Speaking of trouble finding things, I'm glad the pigeons were around to lead Fred back to the Farm of Cages," said Kaahli.

Klestra giggled. "Good old Fred. I hope he never tries to pay a visit to The Pond on his own."

"Frafan and Aden were with him for part of the trip to his new

188

den," said Ephran. "Some day Kaahli and I must do what Frafan is doing. I, too, would like to spend some time with Aden at this wondrous place they call The Spring."

"I've flown over it many times. It is beautiful," said Marshflower.

"But not as beautiful as The Pond," said Cloudchaser, standing on the water and flapping his big wings.

"Now that the warm season is here in all its strength, how do you like The Pond, Lylah?" asked Kaahli.

"What can I say? I love it. It's even more enchanting and peaceful than I dreamed. There are so many different kinds of birds and animals here. And they are all so friendly, and helpful, and...and..."

"Caring?" finished Rennigan.

"Exactly," agreed Lylah. "And it's such fun to be with the young ones — ducks and squirrels."

"When ya gonna have some 'a them young 'uns yerself, Lylah?" asked Rennigan with a smile.

Lylah blushed.

"Pretty soon, you old rascal," said Klestra, "pretty soon."

"Good t'hear," said Rennigan, rising on his branch. "Can't see a young branchjumper without seein' Ephran when he was wet ahind the whiskers. Forest needs the young 'uns. Oldtimers kin go and find a nice quiet place to rest, knowin' there's somebody ta carry on."

"Since when did you want a quiet place to rest, my friend?" asked Ephran.

"'Bout time, Ephran. Time ta pick one nest. Watch the sun rise a few times. Watch it set."

"Please stay here with us," said Kaahli. "I enjoy our chats so very much."

"Git a kick outa 'em, m'self, Kaahli," Rennigan said. Then he closed one eye and nodded to Ephran. "How about us stretchin' our legs, m'young friend," he said quietly.

A shadow seemed to cross Ephran's eyes. The expression on his old teacher's face, as well as the whispered request, frightened him. He rose from the woven reeds of Fetzgar's den and said to Kaahli, "I'll be right back. Rennigan and I are going for a bit of a run."

He crossed the water on the old fallen branch, to the willow. He and Rennigan climbed into the high limbs of a cottonwood, The Pond sparkling behind them. They had not gone far when Rennigan lay down. He seemed exhausted.

Now Ephran was really concerned. "Rennigan, is something the matter?" he asked.

"Not t'speak of, Ephran," the fox squirrel answered. "Nothin', anaway, that subtractin' a few seasons off this ol' hide wouldn't cure."

And he laughed.

"I don't care for this sort of talk," Ephran said, trying to look stern while the lump in his throat grew.

"Son, we all gotta go along with the change 'a seasons. There's a time fer leaves ta sprout. And a time fer 'em to go back ta the earth. There's a time fer sunny days like this one. And a time fer the snow. No use fightin' it. All part 'a the same game. Don't bother me none. Shouldn't you either. Had it good. Coulda been better in some ways, I s'pose. Coulda been a lot worse too."

Tears sprang to Ephran's eyes. Rennigan saw them.

"Ephran!" Rennigan said sharply. "Don't git slobbery. Ya got responsibilities now. Ta them young 'uns. Teach 'em what yer mammy and pappy taught ya. What I taught ya. And the more important stuff ya added onta that."

Ephran choked and nodded.

"I think ya learned that makin' luck is lots easier if ya let others help. And if you help them. Didn't ya?"

"Yes," Ephran managed.

"By the way, whippersnapper, ya still think it's a big deal ta fly?"

Ephran shook his head.

"Ain't give it up entire, though, have ya?"

"No."

"Good. Good idea ta dream. But bad idea ta spend too much time wishin' fer what ain't possible." He tipped his head. "Still think them many colored folk are in charge 'a everythin' in this bright-eyed old world?"

Ephran shook his head again.

"Better yet. Ya seen a lot more a this world than I have," he said. "Ya know lots more 'bout it. Ya must understand, better'n me, that something...somebody...else done all this..."

Rennigan lifted his face to the bright blue sky and the clouds skittering along, so high above. He looked at the big woods that rolled away from them in all directions. He sniffed the aroma of leaves and flowers and earth.

Ephran managed, "I know what you mean, Rennigan. Somebody who makes both sunshine and luck."

"Ya got it right, son." He opened both eyes, smiled widely, and said again, "Got it right."

Ephran sat perfectly still as the old fox squirrel moved slowly through the trees, jumping from one to the next. He watched until Rennigan disappeared in thick green leaves. And then he turned to The Pond, eyes finally dry, to where Kaahli and the young ones waited.

* * * * *

The search is ended . . . Or is it?

Contents of the author's nest . . .

. . . and the illustrator's.